# Rock Chick Rematch

# Also From Kristen Ashley

**Rock Chick Series:**
Rock Chick
Rock Chick Rescue
Rock Chick Redemption
Rock Chick Renegade
Rock Chick Revenge
Rock Chick Reckoning
Rock Chick Regret
Rock Chick Revolution
Rock Chick Reawakening
Rock Chick Reborn
Rock Chick Rematch

**The 'Burg Series:**
For You
At Peace
Golden Trail
Games of the Heart
The Promise
Hold On

**The Chaos Series:**
Own the Wind
Fire Inside
Ride Steady
Walk Through Fire
A Christmas to Remember
Rough Ride
Wild Like the Wind
Free
Wild Fire
Wild Wind

**The Colorado Mountain Series:**
The Gamble
Sweet Dreams

Lady Luck
Breathe
Jagged
Kaleidoscope
Bounty

**Dream Man Series:**
Mystery Man
Wild Man
Law Man
Motorcycle Man
Quiet Man

**Dream Team Series:**
Dream Maker
Dream Chaser
Dream Spinner
Dream Keeper
Dream Bites Cookbook

**The Fantasyland Series:**
Wildest Dreams
The Golden Dynasty
Fantastical
Broken Dove
Midnight Soul
Gossamer in the Darkness

**The Honey Series:**
The Deep End
The Farthest Edge
The Greatest Risk

**The Magdalene Series:**
The Will
Soaring
The Time in Between

**Moonlight and Motor Oil Series:**
The Hookup

The Slow Burn

**River Rain Series:**
After the Climb
Chasing Serenity
Taking the Leap
Making the Match
Fighting the Pull

**The Three Series:**
Until the Sun Falls from the Sky
With Everything I Am
Wild and Free

**The Unfinished Hero Series:**
Knight
Creed
Raid
Deacon
Sebring

**Ghosts and Reincarnation Series:**
Sommersgate House
Lacybourne Manor
Penmort Castle
Fairytale Come Alive
Lucky Stars

**The Rising Series:**
The Beginning of Everything
The Plan Commences
The Dawn of the End
The Rising

**Wild West MC Series:**
Still Standing
Smoke and Steel

**Misted Pines Series:**
The Girl in the Mist

The Girl in the Woods

**The Mathilda Series:**
Mathilda SuperWitch
Mathilda SuperWitch, The Rise of the Dark Lord

**Other Titles by Kristen Ashley:**
Heaven and Hell
Play It Safe
Three Wishes
Complicated
Loose Ends
Fast Lane
Perfect Together
Too Good to Be True

# Rock Chick Rematch

A Rock Chick Novella

## By Kristen Ashley

1001 DARK NIGHTS

PRESS

Rock Chick Rematch
A Rock Chick Novella
By Kristen Ashley

1001 Dark Nights

Published by 1001 Dark Nights Press, an imprint of Evil Eye Concepts, Incorporated

# Acknowledgments from the Author

Darius's book was never meant to be. He was too precious to me, our relationship too personal. He wanted me to keep his secrets, and I was so protective of him, I agreed.

The thing is, Malia did not want the same thing.

Rightfully so, she was proud of the man she loved, and she wanted his story told.

Darius gives the ones he loves everything they desire, so he set me on this sentimental journey.

It was one I was honored to share with these two amazing people, their fantastic son, families and friends, guiding me back into the Rock Chick world, a place I never thought I'd be again.

But Malia was right. In that world, there was one more story to tell.

And here it is.

First, I'd like to thank Donna and Liz for being my cheerleaders. Emotionally, this was a lot, to be with Darius and Malia through their love story, and I was delighted to have two die-hard Rock Chick fans at my side while I wrote it.

Second, I want to reiterate my thanks to Malia Anderson, a friend who started as a reader of my books. I hope with all my heart I got Malia and Darius's story right, especially for my friend Malia, who has her namesake in this novel.

And last, as ever, my love and gratitude to Liz Berry, Jillian Stein, MJ Rose, Stacey Tardiff, Asha Hossein, Kim Guidroz and all of the team at 1,001 Dark Nights for all they do for me and the romance community.

Rock on!

Love, Kristen

# One Thousand and One Dark Nights

*Once upon a time, in the future…*

*I was a student fascinated with stories and learning.
I studied philosophy, poetry, history, the occult, and
the art and science of love and magic. I had a vast
library at my father's home and collected thousands
of volumes of fantastic tales.*

*I learned all about ancient races and bygone
times. About myths and legends and dreams of all
people through the millennium. And the more I read
the stronger my imagination grew until I discovered
that I was able to travel into the stories… to actually
become part of them.*

*I wish I could say that I listened to my teacher
and respected my gift, as I ought to have. If I had, I
would not be telling you this tale now.
But I was foolhardy and confused, showing off
with bravery.*

*One afternoon, curious about the myth of the
Arabian Nights, I traveled back to ancient Persia to
see for myself if it was true that every day Shahryar
(Persian: شهريار, "king") married a new virgin, and then
sent yesterday's wife to be beheaded. It was written
and I had read that by the time he met Scheherazade,
the vizier's daughter, he'd killed one thousand
women.*

*Something went wrong with my efforts. I arrived in the midst of the story and somehow exchanged places with Scheherazade — a phenomena that had never occurred before and that still to this day, I cannot explain.*

*Now I am trapped in that ancient past. I have taken on Scheherazade's life and the only way I can protect myself and stay alive is to do what she did to protect herself and stay alive.*

*Every night the King calls for me and listens as I spin tales. And when the evening ends and dawn breaks, I stop at a point that leaves him breathless and yearning for more. And so the King spares my life for one more day, so that he might hear the rest of my dark tale.*

*As soon as I finish a story... I begin a new one... like the one that you, dear reader, have before you now.*

# Prologue

*His Father*

"Don't make me check that backpack," I shouted to my son.

"Mom!"

I'd had sixteen years to navigate the wide spectrum of my son's different varieties of *Mom!* and get a lock on each version.

This one said, *I don't need my mother to check my backpack. I haven't since I was twelve. I'm all grown up. Stop already.*

And yet, the boy was always forgetting something.

I was in the kitchen, dealing with the pork in the slow cooker.

I was doing this against my will.

Not against my will when it came to cooking. I was a damn good cook, and I did say so myself. Also, I liked doing it.

No, it was because it was summer. Summer wasn't about slow-cooker meals. That was winter. Winter was stews and chili and enchiladas. Summer was meat on the grill and some kind of salad (preferably one with potatoes or macaroni in it, let the good Lord bless the woman—and it had to be a woman—who deemed those "salads").

It almost hurt to put that pork shoulder in the crockpot that morning.

But I was a single mom. I worked. My kid was busy with end-of-school-year stuff (though, Liam loved to cook, just right now, with finals and friends and parties and making plans for the summer, he had less time than me).

And, I told myself, I was making barbeque pulled pork (the vinegary North Carolina style, and don't give me any guff about that goodness, I was a barbeque aficionado, and I could appreciate all the different styles, but if you were pulling pork, you went NC).

Pulled pork sandwiches were a summer thing.

Though, I wished I had a smoker. That said summer to me.

Also winter. A smoker didn't discriminate.

These were the thoughts on my mind so I didn't think of other things.

Like the weird stuff going on at work that was giving me a very bad vibe.

Or more importantly, like the chat I'd had with Lee and Eddie yesterday. About the decision I'd made. About the conversation I'd had with my son that morning. About the decision he'd made.

And about how his father was going to handle it.

(My take: he wasn't going to handle it very well.)

(My next take: my first take was an understatement.)

Liam walked into the kitchen, all tall, gangly teen.

As I watched him, I took the hit I always took once the boy started to fade out of him and he began to look like the man he'd become.

In other words, he began to look just like his father.

"You do my head in sometimes," he grumbled.

Liam was a master grumbler. There was some backtalk, and he made an art of being a moody teen, but that was as far as it went. I'd never had any real trouble with my son. Not a day of it.

Wait, no. I referred to his terrible twos as my torrential twos. I'd never seen a more fearless, curious, intelligent child in my life. He found ways to get into everything. It was ingenious and exhausting.

(Like his father.)

Nor had I met a sweeter, more thoughtful and compassionate kid in my life.

(Also, like his father. Gah!)

"I don't need a phone call at work tomorrow, asking me to bring something into school," I replied.

He leveled his warm, brown eyes on me. Though warm, they had a tinge of a spark.

"When's the last time I asked you to bring something to school that I forgot?"

"Last week."

Those eyes rolled.

"You did," I asserted.

And he did. I'd learned part of the teenage hormonal growth cycle included not only selective hearing, but significant short-term memory issues.

"Tomorrow is the last day. I don't have anything I need to take to school," he reminded me.

"How about this? Next year, you do you," I suggested. "If you pull this absent-minded professor stuff, once you're in school, you deal."

"If I had a car, I could come home myself and get it."

Here we go.

It wasn't like I didn't have the money to buy my kid a car. I made good money. And I got an envelope every month that more than made things comfortable for us, *way* more.

(Again, his father, even though his father didn't know I knew it was from *his father*.)

I could buy my kid a car.

And it'd help. Liam used mine, which was inconvenient.

And if he had his own car, after school, I could send him to Sonic to get me a diet cherry limeade so he could drop it by the office to help get me through the afternoon and buy a bag of Sonic ice for us to use at home because that ice was the shizzlesticks.

I just didn't think giving a sixteen-year-old something as huge as a car just because I could was a good idea.

If this was a different world, I could talk to his father about it.

Since it was this world, I was going to talk to his father about it, I just had to wait until the man got his head out of his behind (again).

And…well, wait until we all got beyond what Liam had decided that morning, which, considering how things had been the last few years, I wasn't sure his father was going to embrace.

"Let me think about it," I mumbled, shifting my attention back to using the forks to pull the pork apart.

"That's what you said the last time I mentioned it," Liam told me. "And the time before. And the time before that. And the time—"

I looked up at him, and that *up* was far. He was tall.

Like his father.

"I'm not done thinking about it."

Another eye roll and that did it. I was making a calendar. Countdown to the end of the teenage eye rolls.

Liam was used to my calendars. We had a countdown to the end of his comebacks of a snappy "*So?*", which was a habit he got into when he was eleven and testing the boundaries of my authority. We had a countdown to the end of him dribbling his damned basketball in the house when he was thirteen. We had a countdown to the end of his annoyed "But why?" when he wanted to update his room from Transformers to Tupac when he was fourteen (no shade on Tupac, and I got it my kid going into high school didn't want to have little boy stuff around him—it was just that he had to learn, you don't get stuff just because you want it—though, full disclosure: his room went from Transformers to Tupac, but even though Liam didn't know it, that was his father).

But I loved my boy, so he was getting a warning.

"I'm making a calendar about that eye roll," I shared.

Another eye roll.

I nearly started laughing.

I didn't only because he teased, "Absent-minded professor? You're such a goof."

"What?" I asked. "You're going to be a professor."

He leaned against the island in a casual way that had one effect on high school girls, that effect something I refused to think about, and another effect on his mother. This effect pushing me to think about those high school girls and how I once was one and I caught the eye of a certain handsome, popular boy who had command of his body at a young age, a kind smile, a great sense of humor, and an amazing streak of loyalty, which ended up with me being Liam's momma.

"I'm going to be a lawyer, then a senator," Liam stated.

I tried not to quell my son's ambitions. In fact, the opposite.

But I was a paralegal. Before that, I was a court reporter. I had a lot of experience with the legal system. And I didn't keep a database or anything, but off the cuff, I felt I could say with a good deal of authority that five-sixths of attorneys were pure a-holes.

I didn't want my son to become an a-hole.

I opened my mouth to share (again) he could *teach* law, this being a prelude to rehashing our conversation from that morning to make sure the decision he'd made was one he wanted to move forward on, when the doorbell rang.

"I'll get it," Liam said, moving that way.

I tamped down my fear of my son opening the front door. He was tall and athletic. He was sixteen, not six. It wasn't like our doorbell rang fifty times a day, but this also was far from the first time he'd answered it. And we lived in a nice neighborhood.

Even so, he would always be a little boy to me. It was my lot as a mother, the worry, the drive to protect, even though now, my son thought that last part was his job.

And this was the problem. Liam was a little boy to me, but he was something else in reality, and he needed me to trust him to find his way with that.

Ugh.

I needed to buy him a car.

I put the forks on a spoon rest and was about to put the top back on the slow cooker so the meat could cook in its juices and barbeque sauce for a while when I heard Liam's tentative, "Mom."

I looked up.

And I saw the man standing with him. Bushy gray beard, long gray hair pulled back in a braid, rolled bandana around his forehead, black leather vest over a long-sleeved Harley tee and jeans.

Duke.

I hadn't seen Duke in…

"Honey." His gravelly voice rolled my way, that one word making fear grab hold of the entire length of my spine. "It's Darius."

The tone of his voice, the look on his face, the earth fell from under my feet.

Because Darius was my son's father.

And he was the love of my life.

But my boy had never met him.

# Chapter One

*The Boxer*

## Rock Chick Rewind

*Some time ago…*

"I cannot *believe* we scored tickets to *Prince*," Ally shrieked.

"That lick, the one that starts off 'When Doves Cry,' *man*," Indy was fanning herself.

I was trying not to freak out.

We were hanging in the front of Ellen, Indy's grandma's bookstore, Fortnum's. There were some beat-up leather couches (that were super comfortable) and armchairs so people could chill out after they bought their books and read.

And off to the side, there were some tables and chairs, where right then, two old guys were playing chess. A checkers board was set up at another. And in pure Ellen style, because Indy's grandma went her own way, Battleship was set up on the last.

"Lee! Will you take us?" Indy shouted to where Lee Nightingale, Indy's huge crush, was sitting with Eddie Chavez and Darius Tucker in some armchairs not close, but not far.

Lee, acting like he didn't know Indy was there (when, let's face it, he was at Fortnum's because Indy was—I wasn't sure what was keeping those two apart (yes, I was, it was Lee being a stupid *boy*), but it had to end or they'd both spontaneously combust), turned his head her way.

Darius didn't have to turn his head our way. He'd been staring at me for a while.

The reason I was failing at not freaking *out*.

"No fucking way," Lee replied to Indy. "I still haven't gotten over your bullshit when I was your ride to Def Leppard."

Lee had a foul mouth. Sadly, it was attractive, but only because he was top to toe *hot*.

Not as hot as Darius, and I wasn't into white guys, but still.

Also, I'd heard about that Def Leppard thing with Indy and Ally and how Lee, Eddie and Darius got dragged in (like they often did because Indy couldn't get enough of Lee, Lee couldn't get enough of Indy, Eddie also couldn't get enough of Indy, a tangled web, so unsurprisingly, shizzle happened). The whole high school had heard about it.

The story was hilarious.

I still hoped nothing like that happened at the Prince concert. I really liked Indy and Ally. They were fun and sweet and nice, but I wasn't a shenanigans type of girl.

Indy and Ally were synonymous with shenanigans.

"A master at his craft." Ellen flitted through wearing some weird, filmy muumuu and a terry-cloth braided headband around her forehead, her wispy white hair a cloudy wonder of flips and curls haloing her entire skull, though, the part of it at the crown was tamped down by the headband. "That meaning the Purple One," she explained.

She smiled and winked at me.

I smiled back.

You really never knew what you'd get with Ellen. Fortnum's was a cool place to hang (though, they needed a coffee counter or a soda fountain or something), and Ellen was the reason it was. She was a bit weird, but in a good way, and she welcomed everybody. I'd even seen her ask a homeless person in, sending Duke off to go buy the guy a sandwich.

Today it was that muumuu. Last week it was a fringed vest and jeans and high-heeled sandals with sparkles that would go better with an outfit you'd wear to the Oscars.

Though, her terry-cloth headband was ever present. As far as I could tell, she had one in every color, just as long as that color was pastel.

She loved it that Indy and her friends and half the high school hung at her store, even if none of them bought books (that being *them*, I bought books all the time).

"I'll drop you girls at the concert," Ellen offered.

Indy looked upset because Lee blew her off, even if she replied, "Thanks, Gram."

Yeesh.

Lee was acting like a jerk. And if he didn't get himself together, he was going to lose that girl.

I mean, she was younger than him, she was also younger than me, but not *that* much younger.

I saw movement in the stacks and looked that way.

Duke was there, his dark hair graying, his beard getting out of control.

I got up, because he was my dealer, he had something to pimp, and I could never resist what he was pimping.

I didn't look at Darius as I passed where he was sitting because I might trip or something, which would be so embarrassing, I wouldn't be able to deal. I wasn't sure Mom would accept the excuse of, "I can't go to school for the next two years because I tripped in front of a hottie."

Though, she'd get it, she just wouldn't accept it.

Dad definitely wouldn't (and he wouldn't get it either).

As I made it his way, Duke turned and sauntered deeper into the bookshelves.

I followed him, thinking I loved the smell of Fortnum's. Must and dust, the portal to a million different worlds, a cornucopia of knowledge.

I'd just started hanging with Indy and Ally, mostly because I'd started hanging at Fortnum's, seeing as that's where the kids hung.

And the first time I went there, I fell in love with it.

Now it was my favorite place on Earth.

Duke moved into a row.

P-Q-R-S, fiction.

I followed him.

When I stopped in front of him, he lifted his hand and offered me a book. *Fahrenheit 451.*

I took it even though I said, "We read this in school last September."

"Read it again when you don't have to write a term paper on it."

I smiled at him. "Is there a difference?"

"There's reading something because you want to get a good grade, and there's reading something because every person on Earth needs to read it and *get it.*"

Well, I thought I got the book when I read it, but right then, I got him. We shared a love of words. We had a different language than other people.

Since he knew I understood him, he nodded and took off, as usual (Duke was a man of few words, the spoken kind, the other kind, he had gazillions to offer).

As was becoming our way, I didn't follow.

I leaned against the shelves and opened up the book, knowing what I'd get.

This time, it was "The Boxer" by Simon and Garfunkel.

Duke always put a sheet of handwritten song lyrics in front of the books he gave me. He said there was poetry everywhere, you just had to look for it.

To prove his point, in one of the books he gave me, he once put a snapshot he took of a fawn and its mother in the forest around his cabin up in Evergreen. It wasn't the greatest picture of all time. But it was pure poetry.

I read the words of the song.

And at the bottom, I read Duke's note:

*They'll cut you 'til you cry out.*

*Be the boxer.*

*Remain.*

"Hey."

I jumped, fumbled the book, the note fell out and fluttered to the floor, but I didn't go for it, because Darius Tucker was standing right there.

*Right there.*

"Uh…uh…"

Oh my God!

I was strangling. Why was I strangling?

I couldn't breathe!

His lips curled up at the ends before he crouched and picked up the paper, straightened and held it out to me.

"You dropped this," he said.

My hand was trembling when I took it and forced out, "Yeah."

He looked down, and it was only then I realized he wasn't letting go of the paper.

This meant he had his fingers on the paper, and I had my fingers on the paper, which was only two steps away from us, like, *holding hands*!

"What is it?" he asked.

"What?"

He dipped his head to the paper, and I lost track of what was happening, considering all I could think about was how smooth his skin seemed, how warm and soulful his brown eyes were, how long and curly his eyelashes looked, how beautiful his lips were formed.

He gently tugged on the paper. "This."

"What?"

He smiled, wide and white, it made his expressive eyes taper, his cheekbones pop out.

Okay…um…

What was going on with my legs? I was having trouble standing.

"Malia?"

"Hunh?"

"You okay?"

"Uh…uh…"

Oh Lord! I was strangling again!

He pulled the paper from my fingers and looked at it.

"I know this song," he said.

I said nothing because I had to focus all my attention on not passing out.

"Why's Duke giving you song lyrics?" he asked.

I didn't answer because I couldn't.

And…okay, this was stupid.

I had to get myself together.

Indy wouldn't stand here like a moron, uhing and fighting for breath.

Ally would have probably kissed him by now just so he'd be under no illusions she was into him.

I jerked my head from side to side to shake myself out of it and replied, "It's poetry. He gives me stuff to make me think, you know, like, to *decipher* it. Figure out what it's about."

Even though I'd made the mammoth effort to string some words together, I wasn't sure he was listening to me.

I knew he wasn't when I saw the expression on his face when he looked at me again.

"Who's cutting you 'til you cry out?" he growled.

Oh my.

I'd never heard a boy *growl*.

Hearing it, something was happening in other regions of my body, not just my legs and my ability to provide it with oxygen. That something felt very good, at the same time it was utterly terrifying.

"No one. It's just…life. Life will…I haven't had a good look at it, and I'm not sure I know that song, but from what I could tell, it's about life. You know, standing strong like a boxer when life hits you. Um…I think."

He handed me the paper again, this time letting it go when I took it.

"No one's gonna cut you," he said, staring straight in my eyes.

"Life is life, Darius," I whispered, then for good measure, shrugged.

Did I look like a dork shrugging?

I looked like a dork shrugging.

I shouldn't have shrugged.

Someone kill me!

"You'll never have to be the boxer, Malia."

It was said soft, but strong, and that did funny things to my heart.

All I could think to say was, "Okay."

"Wanna go out?" he asked.

There was only one thing to say to that.

"Okay," I repeated.

Darius again smiled.

I again almost swooned (now I was getting all that romance novel nonsense, which apparently wasn't nonsense at all, *shoo*!)

I didn't swoon.

I kept it together.

And smiled back.

\* \* \* \*

We neared the crest, and as I continued to pretend the hike wasn't killing me, Darius, who was a few paces ahead of me (and not breathing hard at all!), stopped and looked to me with a brilliant smile on his face.

"Here it is," he said, then turned his head to look back over the crest.

I stopped beside him and didn't, at first, look where he was looking.

I was watching him.

It was our first date. He'd taken me up to the mountains. And if the big backpack and small cooler he was carrying was any indication, we were going to have a picnic.

At least, I hoped we were going to have a picnic. That hike was long, and most of it was uphill.

I was a cheerleader. It wasn't like I wasn't in shape.

But…*dang*.

Seriously, altitude was no joke.

Now I was hungry, thrilled we were finally there, even more thrilled the way back was all downhill, all of this while being thrilled I was with Darius at the same time hoping the massive effort I'd put into getting ready that morning hadn't been in vain.

In one of our five (yes *five*, in less than that many days!) phone conversations since he asked me out at Fortnum's, Darius had warned me I needed to wear comfortable clothes for our date. He told me we were going into the mountains, the hike was a little over a mile, and it'd take some effort.

Although on the face of it that sounded romantic, it was harder than heck to figure out what to wear during a date like that.

So hard, my sister Lena and best friend Toni had spent two hours rejecting outfits I tried on until I found the right one.

We'd decided jean shorts and a cute little top that was orange and had a gold design in it. It was gathered at the high neckline and held up by a spaghetti strap that ran through the front and back of the material.

I wore my hair straightened, and I'd twisted it up in a messy topknot. But I was worried that the wisps of hair around my face that I'd laid down so carefully had now peeled away and gone curly and made it all look just plain messy.

Since Darius didn't stop looking at whatever "here" was, I turned my head that way.

And caught my breath.

In front of me, a wide basin lay, flanked by mountain peaks and filled with wildflowers.

"Oh my God," I whispered reverently.

"Hank found it," Darius told me.

Hank being Lee Nightingale's older brother, a guy everyone knew even if he'd already graduated because he was a) a talented athlete, b) super sweet and c) gorgeous, so he was also d) very popular.

Hank was also the antithesis of Lee's bad boy. Perfect grades. Perfect boyfriend (reportedly). The boy next door. The good guy.

"We hike up here all the time," Darius went on.

"It's amazing," I told him.

He took my hand, and I looked to him.

"C'mon," he said softly, his eyes on me in a way I suddenly didn't care if the wisps around my face got too wispy.

Actually, the way he was gazing at me, I felt the kind of beautiful you just always knew you were, no matter what your hair looked like or your outfit or whatever.

You could be in the throes of delirium from a bad flu, sweaty and nasally, raw-nosed and croaky, having a wracking cough, and Darius would look at you like that.

No.

Look at *me* like that.

Oh my.

He guided me to a place among some aspen trees, the wind sifting through the silver-dollar-sized leaves, making a kind of soft music that was the perfect soundtrack to this adventure.

There I found, after he shrugged off his backpack and put down the cooler, I'd been right. He pulled out a blanket and spread it on the ground then gestured for me to sit.

He sat with me, and out of the cooler came some sodas and bottles of water, sandwiches, then from the backpack came a big bag of chips and some homemade cookies.

He'd even remembered to bring napkins.

"Mom made the cookies for us," he told me as he set them on the blanket.

Okay, so maybe his mom reminded him to bring napkins.

But when he shared this, I felt something strange. Strange and beautiful.

Because he said that not like it was simply a fact, or with any nuance he was embarrassed about his mom making him cookies to take on his date, but like he was proud of it.

It was then it hit me. One of the reasons I liked him (outside of him being so cute, and tall, and his lashes so perfect).

He just knew who he was.

I had no idea who I was. I didn't know anyone our age that knew who they were.

But Darius did.

He knew the perfect place to take a first date and he loved his mom and didn't care who knew it.

Having these thoughts, something was happening. Something fierce and frightening and wonderful, all at once, and I wasn't feeling it because I was out with the cutest, most popular boy in school.

"That's sweet," I replied, but my voice was husky with the thoughts I was thinking and the things I was feeling.

He smiled at me then unwrapped his sandwich.

He took a bite, chewed, swallowed, then looked again to me while I was chewing my own bite. "I want you to know that it's only ever been Lee, Eddie, Hank and me that have come up here."

In other words, this wasn't his normal date spot, where he took girls to impress them with his romantic sensibilities and picnic-packing capabilities in an effort to get into their pants.

It was a spot for him and his buddies.

And me.

Lord.

There they were, more things I was feeling. Lots more. *Oodles* more.

And they were all *awesome*.

"Oh," was all I could think to say.

"Yeah," he replied, that smile still in place, a tease in his voice. "Oh."

"It's beautiful," I told him.

"I know," he said, not taking his gaze from me.

I pressed my lips together because he wasn't talking about the meadow, and knowing I was correct earlier, that Darius thought I was beautiful, pushed its way to the top of my feelings, and that feeling felt *amazing.*

"Eat," he encouraged, "So we can get into the fun stuff."

I wasn't sure what he considered "the fun stuff."

I just knew, with a sense that was fierce and frightening and wonderful, whatever it was, I wanted to do it with Darius.

* * * *

"The fun stuff," it would turn out, was lying on our backs and watching the clouds drift by.

You might not think this was fun…as such.

But lying on my back beside Darius, our fingers linked and resting where he'd pulled them, on his flat belly, our arms pressed together, both our knees bent (and every once in a while, he'd move his leg and bump it against mine, which was adorable and electrifying, both at the same time), talking and watching the clouds drift by was the best time I'd ever had *in my life.*

"Do you ever try to see things in the clouds?" I asked. "Like dragons or elephants?"

"Do you see something like that?"

I lifted my free hand (because, straight up, I wasn't letting go of his, no way, no how) and pointed. "Well, that one kinda looks like a T-Rex."

"Which one?"

I looped my finger. "That one."

"I don't see it."

I turned my head on the blanket and looked at his profile. "Maybe squint?"

He squinted. It was adorable too.

I started giggling.

He turned his head to look at me, his lips moving like he was fighting a smile, before he asked, "Are you messing with me?"

"No," I lied. "I totally see a dinosaur."

Something changed in his eyes, and suddenly, he let my hand go as he turned to his side and got up on a forearm.

For the second time on that mountain, my breath caught, this time because of the expression on his face.

"You ever been kissed, Malia?" he asked, his voice soft.

I liked the tone of his voice, but…

Uh…

I was so sure!

"You're not the first date I've ever had, Darius Tucker," I returned.

I mean, really.

Did he not think I lived a life until he walked down that row at Fortnum's to me?

"No, I mean properly kissed," he replied.

Oh, now I *really* knew what he meant.

I turned and got up on my forearm too.

"You're hot and all, but that is not where this is going," I told him. Because, *gah*! This was our first date! Feeling something crushing my chest in a manner that caused actual physical pain, I suggested, "Maybe we should head back down the mountain."

"You're misunderstanding me," he said.

"I am?" I asked but didn't wait for his answer. I ordered, "So clear things up."

He shook his head, looked away, then back at me, "I guess I'm asking if it's okay if I can kiss you."

Not expecting that, I stared at him.

"If you're not ready, then I can wait for when you're ready," he hurried on. "But I'd really like to—"

He didn't finish because I leaned forward and kissed him.

It was chaste, no tongue.

Then it was not chaste, I was again on my back on the blanket, Darius's chest pressed to mine, and there was lots of tongue and even more happening to my body.

It was a warm day, but I wasn't warm.

I was hot.

Burning up as the wind whispered through the aspens and Darius's tongue played in my mouth.

It felt *perfect*.

Because it *was* perfect.

But Darius didn't even try for second base. He cut off the kiss by putting his hand to my face, lifting his head away and sweeping his thumb across my lips.

This gesture was as sweet as him asking for a kiss.

"We should probably stop now," he whispered.

I was having trouble breathing.

So he was right.

"Do you wanna head back?" he offered. "Or watch the clouds more?"

I wanted to kiss more, but he didn't offer that option.

So I took the one I wanted most, in that moment, in all the world.

"Clouds."

He grinned.

"Anyway, we haven't eaten your mom's cookies yet," I pointed out.

"You're right, we haven't," he agreed. "You wanna walk around, get a different view?"

I didn't want to leave that spot for the rest of my life.

I shook my head.

He settled back down, filtered his fingers through mine and put our hands to his belly again.

"Then we'll stay right here," he murmured.

That was the first time Darius Tucker gave me what I wanted, no discussion, no hassle.

It would be far from the last.

\* \* \* \*

Darius took hold of my wrists and pulled my hands from his behind to between us.

This was a feat, considering he was flat-out on top of me on the couch in his parents' rec room (which used to be their garage).

"Baby," he said after he tore his mouth from mine, sounding like he was choking on something, at the same time sounding like he was trying not to laugh.

"Why'd you stop me?" I asked, sounding annoyed, *which I was*.

Whenever we started to get to the good part, he kept doing that!

He touched his lips to mine, lifted his head and stated. "Malia, I'm not gonna have our first time being on an old, grungy couch in my parents' garage."

This was his constant refrain, ever since I told him I was a virgin (and this happened on our first date, under the clouds, hours after our first kiss, when we'd talked about everything, well…under the clouds, and that was *months ago*).

"Argh," I grumbled, arching my neck and looking at the arm of the couch.

"How 'bout this?" he murmured, now just sounding like he was trying not to laugh.

But I wasn't paying attention to what he sounded like.

I was paying attention to what his hand was doing, that being going down my stomach, toward the waistband of my jeans, also toward my...

"Darius," I whispered.

He touched his lips to mine again, but didn't go far away when he told me, "We're gonna go back to the meadow."

His hand went inside my jeans.

"And I'm gonna bring some fancy shit for us to eat," he went on, his fingers curling in.

My neck arched for a different reason this time.

He kissed my throat, and his fingers...

*His fingers...*

They worked *magic.*

His lips were now at my ear. "And we're gonna watch the clouds go by again. And while we do, like the last time, we're gonna talk about everything there is to talk about..."

I squirmed under him, feeling it, the muscles down there rippling, my breasts seemed heavy, my nipples were tingling, and he wasn't even touching them.

I was getting close. I'd heard about them—orgasms—but I'd never had one, and the way his fingers moved, the pressure he was putting on, it wasn't just right.

It was *everything.*

"Then I'm gonna tell you I love you, and after that, I'm gonna make love to you," he whispered in my ear just as it happened.

I came for the first time...for Darius.

I started to cry out, but he kissed me so all I was feeling, all he'd given me was swallowed by his mouth, coaxed deeper by his tongue.

It was *phenomenal.*

His hand was gone when it was over, but it was like he sensed it had washed through me, because, with perfect timing, he rolled us so I was cocooned between the back of the couch and Darius.

I'd been here before (we did a lot of making out, we also did a lot of cuddling), and it was my second favorite place to be (my first favorite was where I was ten seconds ago, and my new first favorite place for Darius's hand to be was where it was thirty seconds ago).

But even if I'd had my first orgasm, given to me by Darius Tucker, my boyfriend, the best boyfriend in history, the sweetest, most thoughtful, loving, teasing, awesome boyfriend of all time…

I was stuck on what he'd said when he'd given it to me.

"You love me?" I asked.

"I love your big, chocolaty eyes. And I love your pointy chin."

Ugh.

"I don't have a pointy chin. My face is oval."

"It's a beautiful chin," he muttered before he kissed it. "It's still pointy."

"Whatever," I mumbled.

"And I love how short you are," he carried on.

For heaven's sake.

"I'm not short, I'm average," I told him, though, in all honesty, maybe I was a tad bit on the low side of that. "It's just that you're tall."

"So…short to me. Still short," he teased.

I pushed at his shoulders (however, it must be noted, I did this half-heartedly). "Darius, be serious."

When he looked me in the eyes again, my heart stuttered to a halt.

Because he *was* being serious.

Deadly serious.

"I love your perfect nose and your thick lower lip and the shape of your eyebrows," he continued.

I wouldn't say my lower lip was "thick," more like "full" (though, even I liked the arch of my brows, it rocked). But I wasn't going to interrupt him.

No way.

Thus, he kept going.

"And your gorgeous skin and your huge smile and the fact you use words like 'alcove' and 'omnipotent' that no one else knows what the fuck they mean."

I started giggling even though I kind of wanted to start crying.

Darius wasn't done talking.

"And I love how you get on with my sisters, even though they're pains in the asses, and when you're over, you always help Mom with dinner, and you sit and listen to Dad going on about the Rockies or the Nuggets or whatever, like you give a shit, when you don't."

One must say, I wasn't a sports person.

But I loved Darius's dad, and he was, so there you go.

"Darius," I whispered.

"But I'm not gonna tell you until we're under the clouds, or the stars, or whenever we stop talking, even though something else I love about you is that we always have something to talk about."

Okay, it was safe to say, I was feeling this.

Feeling everything.

I knew what my dad would say about what I was feeling. He would say it's too soon, being sixteen and finding the guy of your dreams that you know you want to spend the rest of your life with.

My mom would say that too.

(Lena wouldn't, she adored Darius and already told me she wanted him as her brother.)

But I knew it.

I knew it now and ten minutes ago and when he tickled me so much last week, disaster nearly struck because I was *this close* to peeing my pants.

And when he helped my dad, who had no sons, but had started treating Darius like one, put in our new kitchen cupboards.

And when Darius took me out to a fancy dinner on our one-month anniversary.

And again on our two-month one (you get the picture).

And on our first date in the wildflowers.

And all the times in between.

I knew it.

I might not know everything about myself, who I was or who I was going to be.

I just knew, whoever that was, I'd be her with Darius.

"So, yeah, it's gonna be special," he concluded. "When I say that and when we do that."

"Okay." My reply was soft.

His answering smile was tender.

I touched my fingers to it in wonder, even if I'd seen it before. It was just that wonderful.

I lifted my eyes to his. "But can I say it now?"

His arms around me got tighter and he shook his head.

But he said, "You don't have to say it, baby. You show it all the time."

Okay, the tears were coming.

So when I said, "I try," it sounded croaky.

"You succeed," he assured.

I was glad. So, so glad he knew I loved him. He deserved that. And more.

Everything I could give him, everything, it was his.

To communicate that, I kissed him.

He kissed me back then ended it before it got too much for the both of us (See? Annoying!).

And then we cuddled on the couch and watched a movie.

I didn't pay a lot of attention to the movie.

I was reveling in the fact that this would be my life. Me and Darius and talking and kissing and TV and nights out and family and friends and knowing Darius had been right back in the stacks of Fortnum's when he told me nothing would ever cut me.

I'd found him, and I'd done it early.

So I knew down to my soul, nothing ever would.

No, that wasn't right.

We'd found each other so we had it all.

And I knew, lying in his arms, feeling his long, strong body behind mine, smelling him all around me, we always would.

* * * *

*Not long later…*

"Malia, honey, come on down. We've got to go," my mom called.

I didn't want to go.

I really, really didn't want to go.

But I had to go.

However, I had to do something else first.

I sat at my desk, the paper Duke gave me at Fortnum's what seemed like forever ago on top, my notebook open next to it, and I was copying the words of the song.

And just like Duke did, I wrote at the bottom:

*They'll cut you 'til you cry out.*

*Be the boxer.*

*Remain.*

But I finished mine with:

*I'm here for you, forever.*

*Love you always, Malia*

I tore the page out of my notebook, folded it so it was little and tucked it into my purse.

Then I walked down the stairs to go with my parents to Darius's dad's funeral.

* * * *

*One week later…*

I knew Ally didn't want to, but she did.

She passed the note to me in the hallway at school that day, the look on her face saying it all.

I didn't need the look. I felt the look. We all did.

Darius's dad, Morris had been murdered.

It was unthinkable. Unconscionable.

And, no surprise, those two were exactly alike, super close, Darius being the apple who proudly stuck close to Morris's tree, it had torn Darius apart.

I knew the writing on the outside, the slants and drifts that spelled my name, so I knew I couldn't open it, until now.

I was home from school, up in my room.

He was gone from me, which was bad, considering I was pregnant with our child.

Yes, we'd been back to the meadow…and then some.

Mom didn't know about the pregnancy…yet.

Dad didn't either…yet.

Darius didn't know about it either…yet.

So obviously none of them knew I was going to find a way. I was going to figure it out. I was keeping our baby. The baby we made together amidst his sweetness and kisses that made me melt and tender teasing and the love in his eyes when he looked at me like there was no other girl in the whole world and he was going to be my shelter from every storm until I died…

At least they didn't know…yet.

But I talked to Mom about Darius and how he had shut down, gone somewhere dark, somewhere scary.

"Grief, sweetheart, it's nasty business," Mom had shared. "I know you're grieving Mister Morris too. He was a good man. But you have to seek patience. Darius will find his way."

I wasn't sure. Since that day in the shelves at Fortnum's, we'd spent as much time together as we could, and if we couldn't be together, we were on the phone talking to each other about people we knew, dreams we had, plans we needed to make to realize them, and how we felt about each other.

I knew him pretty well.

And this wasn't him. This flatness. The blankness. The seething anger barely contained under the surface.

And then there was the fact I was sixteen and pregnant.

Yeah, I had some worries and patience wasn't going to work.

I couldn't tell my uterus, "You know, you need to hang tight for a month or two or eleven while your daddy figures stuff out. You can carry on gestating after that."

I mean, I could try, but I wasn't sure he or she would listen.

Now, I had that note from him and I didn't know what was inside.

It could be him pouring out his heart to me, doing it on paper, because boys were weird about showing emotion.

And Lord, he loved his dad. I loved my dad too, like, a lot, but I could see it was a different thing with boys. It was almost worship. And I understood that. Mister Morris was that kind of man, that kind of father. He'd deserved it.

It could be something else.

I didn't have time to wait. I had enough to figure out, so there was no time to wait.

I unfolded the note.

What I read made my insides go hollow.

I didn't want to, but I forced myself to read it all again.

Lyrics.

To a song.

Nine Inch Nails' "Hurt."

With a note at the end that said, *We're done. If you know what's good for you, stay away from me. -D*

I knew exactly what was good for me, which was why I grabbed the phone on my bedside table and dialed his home number.

No one answered.

And later, one of the times Miss Dorothea or one of Darius's sisters answered the phone, they were sweet, they sounded sad, but every single time, Darius refused to take my calls.

* * * *

Fast Forward – Hit Play

*Now…*

We stood in the hospital waiting room with Duke and the gang was all there.

*All* of the gang was there.

The place was crowded, standing room only.

But I didn't have it in me to take them in, to look for familiar faces.

All I could think about was Darius.

And Ally, who was in front of us, her gaze on my son.

"That's your father's," she announced.

I moved close to my boy as Liam's eyes got huge and they were fixed to Ally's bloody hand.

I heard a gasp.

Dorothea.

Damn.

She didn't know about Liam…

Yet.

Well, now she knew.

"Don't, Ally," Eddie bit out.

"Lay down the truth, darlin'." Duke's rough voice encouraged. Ally looked to him. So did I. He nodded to Ally. "Now's the time."

"It's not the fuckin' time," Lee bit out.

Ally's attention returned to my son.

"A bad guy was touching me," she declared. "Your father had already been shot in both legs and slammed in the head with a tire iron, but he still got him off me. He barely got a hand on me, and your father dragged himself to me and pulled him off. I was drugged. I couldn't defend myself or help him. But he kept him off me even when that asshole stabbed him. He kept him off me until help came. Blood pouring out of him, and he kept him *off me*."

"Ally—" I whispered, my voice pained, because I was pained.

I got her need to do this, I hated what had happened to her, but *my* need was finding out if the love of my life was going to survive all of that.

Ally spoke over me.

"Look around you," Ally ordered Liam. "All these people, *this*," she jerked her bloody hand in the air, "*that's* your father." She turned to me. "I don't know what went down with Eddie and Lee. What I know is if Darius makes it through this, he's gonna stay away. From you. From his son." She swung an arm out behind her. "From everybody."

She took a step toward us. Liam put an arm around my waist and pulled me back just as Lee put an arm around Ally to stop her.

"Don't let him, *please*," she pleaded in a whisper.

"Zano, a little help," Lee said about two seconds before he released

Ally.

He did this because a dark-haired, fine-looking man clamped down on her with both arms.

His lips at her ear, he said, "All right, baby, that's out. Now come sit with me."

"Don't let him," she repeated to me.

Okay, she was flipping out.

I had other things on my mind, but this was something I could sort pretty easily.

So, before she could turn away (or be pulled away by her fine-looking man, trust Ally to score that long drink of hot water), I moved forward and caught her hands.

"I talked with Liam this morning and he wants to meet his dad," I whispered.

Ally looked uncomfortable.

Yeah, her big speech was effective, but unnecessary.

"Well, uh…that's good," she muttered.

I tipped my head to the side, and even though I still had other, more pressing things to think about, I felt a small smile play at my mouth, because this was pure Ally, and boy…

I'd missed her.

I squeezed her hands. "I see you haven't changed."

"Nope," she agreed, and her gaze strayed to Liam. "Though I'm not usually this crazy."

My kid was smart. In this instance, his intelligence showed in the fact that he looked like he didn't believe her.

"Yes, she is," Eddie said.

Ally glared at Eddie.

Then her man pulled her away, but she squeezed my hands back before she let me go.

I looked to Dorothea.

She was staring at Liam with a face full of wonder mingled with nuances of hurt.

I'd have to tackle that later.

But for now, I turned to Eddie.

"News?" I asked.

He shook his head, his expression grim.

My heart slid back up into my throat, a place it had taken residence in since Duke told us what was happening in my kitchen.

And my son pulled me closer.

# Chapter Two

*Thick and Thin*

**Rock Chick Rewind**

*Some time ago…*

"I wanna go on record as saying this is *not* a good idea," my friend Toni proclaimed.

"Yeah, you told me on the phone when I asked you to come with me tonight," I replied, navigating Colfax in my car on our way to the bar. "And again when I picked you up. And when we turned onto Colfax. And just now."

"The last one was official," Toni sniffed.

I glanced her way, thinking I really should have reconnected with Ally and/or Indy for this operation. First, because they wouldn't go on the record telling me something I already knew: this was a fool idea. They'd be all for it. Second, they'd probably be able to form a better plan as to how to go about doing what I intended to do, considering they had a lot of experience with implementing fool ideas.

But I couldn't reconnect with Ally and Indy.

It had been years, for one.

I'd taken off without a word of explanation, for another.

The explanation I had I couldn't tell them, not yet, since the person who most should know still didn't (yet), for another.

Too much was at stake, for the last.

I turned into the parking lot of the bar, and even not having entered it, I could see this place was somewhere I didn't want to be.

Nope.

Somewhere I *shouldn't* be.

One could stretch this further and say I should never have moved us from living in the apartment over the stables at my aunt and uncle's place in Fort Collins back to Denver.

Sure, on occasion, you could smell horse manure.

But it was quiet, a lot bigger than my current apartment, safe, and it had a funky vibe I liked.

That said, it wasn't home.

It wasn't Denver.

I was a young mother. I'd gotten my training to be a court reporter and scored a job. I was taking courses to become a paralegal, which was a step down from what my plans had been before I'd gotten pregnant and my baby's father's dad had been murdered, sending him so far off the rails, I didn't recognize him anymore. But it didn't matter I didn't, he'd cut me out of his life.

I'd wanted to be a lawyer.

But life was tough with a curious two-year-old, even if my mom and dad and sister and all the aunties and uncles and cousins pitched in to help me out.

I needed to keep my nose clean.

And I needed to stay away from Darius Tucker.

Everyone told me he'd turned to the dark side.

However, I thought it was time. It was time he shook himself out of this garbage.

It was time he learned he had a child and had to step up.

It was time three years ago, but I'd been young and scared and hurt, so I'd made an emotional decision and my parents had stepped in to support and protect me.

Off I went to Fort Collins.

Now I was back.

So, yeah.

It was time.

While I was thinking these things, Toni was doing something else. I knew this when I turned to her and saw her tying the silk scarf under her chin. It covered her hair and the sides of her face. She complemented this by sliding on a massive pair of black-framed glasses.

"What are you doing?" I asked.

She turned to me, more than likely unable to see me through her opaque lenses.

"Donning my disguise."

"It's night."

"Yeah."

"We're going into a bar, not traveling through time back to the fifties to take a ride in a convertible."

"I don't want anyone seeing me here."

"That much is clear," I muttered.

"You shouldn't want anyone to see you either, including someone in particular," she pointed out.

I let my gaze drift through the busy parking lot before I returned it to her. "It's obviously going to be crowded. I'm going to blend in."

She lifted a hand to the arm of her sunglasses, dipped them low on her nose and looked over them at me.

"Girl, this place is trashy. You are not trash. No way you're gonna blend in." She slid her glasses back and crossed her arms on her chest before she demanded, "Tell me again why we're here."

"I just want to see him."

"I told you the scuttlebutt about him."

"I still want to see him."

She shook her head, and I couldn't be certain, because it was dark and so much of her face was covered, but I could swear I saw her expression get soft with worry.

"The him you knew is long gone, sis," she informed me gently.

"I want to see for myself."

My eyes clashed with her shades for a long time before she blew out a breath, murmured, "Let's just do this," and turned to her door to push out.

I got out too, and after I'd closed my door and locked the car, I realized my hands were trembling.

I put my keys in my purse, then shook my hands to get the trembles out.

Really, I should have reconnected with Ally or Indy. They'd know what to do and they'd give me the strength to do it.

"It's now or never, Malia," Toni called over the roof.

"Right. Do this. Okay," I mumbled to myself and rounded the car.

We went in and I was relieved I was correct. The place was packed. If you wanted to see someone, you had to be looking.

I was, however, concerned that Toni was also correct.

This place was rough.

I scanned the crowd as Toni latched onto my elbow and pulled me through bodies to the bar.

I doubted it was gentlemanly manners that had the two men skedaddling from their stools as Toni barreled us their way so we could assume them, and more that Toni looked mildly insane in her getup, and they might be tough customers, but they wanted nothing to do with her.

She deposited me on my stool, sat on hers, and after a nanosecond of glaring at the bartender, she wrapped her knuckles impatiently on the bar.

He turned his attention to her, did a double take, then wandered down to us.

"Well, you were there. Was it a lone gunman?" he asked Toni.

It was part my nerves, part the guy was funny, which was why I burst out laughing.

Toni ignored his comment and ordered, "Two vodka martinis."

The guy's eyes narrowed on her, and he asked, "Got ID?"

"Sure," she said, opened her purse and fished out her fake ID.

"Both of you," he said to me even as he held his hand out for Toni's.

The nerves came back.

In preparation for this operation, Toni had procured the same for me. She'd had hers for years. Considering I was nurturing, then birthing, then again nurturing a baby, partying wasn't my top priority (or any priority), and as such, I had no need to score a fake ID.

We were both only a year away from legal, but that year was still a year.

I pulled mine out and gave it to him.

He studied them, then handed them back, saying, "Those are good. So good, we get busted, it'll be on your asses, not mine."

He then grabbed two low-alcohol-content wine coolers from a refrigerator, snapped off the caps, put them in front of us and moved away.

"Huh," Toni said as she picked up the bottle and stared at the label with so much distaste, I could see it from around her disguise.

"We didn't come here to imbibe," I reminded her.

She turned her dark shades to me. "Oh, so you intend to blend in at a bar by wandering around, not drinking, and being obvious about looking for somebody? Being obvious about doing that in a bar where not one of these people wants to be found? That sounds like a good plan. Wish I'd thought of that. Let's go do that."

Totally should have brought Ally or Indy. They wouldn't point out I was an idiot.

They might think it, but they wouldn't point it out.

She threw back a sip, made a face, then put the bottle to the bar, and very clearly pretending not to be obvious, which made it totally obvious, she scanned the bar.

"Can you see anything through those glasses?" I asked under my breath.

"I can see the pull of the bad boy," she replied. "Look at that man. He is *fine*."

I peered over my shoulder in the direction her shades were aimed.

A man with close-cropped hair, handsome face and beautiful dark skin wearing a loose-fitting button down up top, and criminally well-fitting faded jeans on the bottom was staring our way.

He tipped his beer at us when I caught his eyes.

I turned back.

"We're not on the make," I told Toni and took a sip of my cooler.

I also made a face.

Yikes. Who drank this stuff? It was awful.

"You might not be, but I just changed my objective for the night," she replied.

"You might want to lose the glasses and scarf, then," I suggested.

"Ladies."

I looked over my shoulder again.

Not wasting time, the man had made his approach, now he was eyeing me, but when Toni made a move, he turned his attention to her.

"Incognito?" he asked like he saw women in Toni's getup in that bar every night.

And who knew? Maybe he did.

"Damn straight," she replied, throwing back more wine cooler.

"Cheating boyfriend?" he asked.

She tipped her bottle my way. "Baby daddy."

I closed my eyes and sighed as his attention shifted again to me, but he'd shut down.

Men had no interest in women with children. They could go around making them and moving on and not many women would blink in taking them on.

But a guy found out you had a kid, he was out.

It shouldn't be surprising. If they didn't take care of their own children, they wouldn't be in to take care of yours.

Not that I'd gone out and looked, just that I was a young mother, but I still had a life, and I wasn't hard to look at, so I'd learned. I'd decided it was good. It kept them at bay so I could focus on Liam…

And pining for my high school boyfriend.

"Maybe I can help," he offered. "Got a name?"

"Not one I'll share with just anyone," I said quickly so Toni wouldn't pipe up.

"Just trying to help," he murmured, visibly looking for his out.

Toni really should have taken off the scarf and sunglasses. She was way prettier than me with her round cheeks and button nose and almond eyes.

"You can help by buying a girl a martini. The bartender got our order wrong," Toni put in.

He and I both looked at her, and incognito was a memory. Gone was the disguise and she was blasting out her Hollywood good looks, because she had the base elements in spades, but even in high school, Toni didn't leave the house without a full face of makeup and perfect hair, and she hadn't changed.

This was what he got a load of right then.

So this was why he turned his wide shoulder to me and gave her his full attention.

Her smile got big and her come hither blasted out farther than her Hollywood looks.

Right, I'd lost Toni.

I did my own scan, some people shifting, giving me a direct shot to the back of the bar, and I froze.

The people shifted back, hiding me from her, but I'd seen her.

And she'd seen me.

Darius's Aunt Shirleen.

Okay, *now* it was official.

This was a bad idea.

"We've got to go," I told Toni.

Her head jerked. "What?"

I pulled some money out of my wallet, threw it on the bar for our drinks and slid off the stool, all the while repeating, "We've got to go."

"I'll take you home," the guy said hurriedly to Toni.

I straightened my spine and tapped his arm to get his attention.

He twisted my way.

"No, you won't," I told him. "Like a gentleman, you'll ask for her number. You'll then call her, not in three days, so she'll have to wonder for those three days if you're into her. You'll call her tomorrow. You'll talk and see if you vibe. If you vibe, you'll ask her out to dinner and take her someplace nice so she can dress up. Bonus for you, you'll want to see her dressed up. And then you both will take it from there."

I thought he'd get upset about me being so bossy, but he grinned, returned his attention to Toni and said in a soft voice, "Can I have your number, baby?"

In my opinion, he could have lost the "baby," but I could see from Toni's face it worked on her.

She fished a receipt out of her purse, and at her request, I fished a pen out of mine. She gave him her number, and they did a lot of checking each other out, Toni doing it twisted to look behind her as I pulled her out of the bar.

I would have advised against the finger wave she sent his way right as we walked out the door, but it happened before I could stop it.

"Something else is official," she announced when we were in the car. "You are now my official wingwoman. You rock that shit."

Well…

Duh.

What were friends for?

"Wanna tell me what our swift exit was about?" she asked after I'd started up the car and headed through the parking lot toward Colfax.

"Darius's Aunt Shirleen saw me."

"Okay, I might be slow right now. I got a little dazzled by the attention of a good-lookin' man, but weren't we there looking for him?"

"*Looking* for him, yes."

"Not sure I understand the emphasis," she noted. "But just to say, she's his aunt. Wouldn't she know where he is?"

"*Looking* for him, Toni. Not *finding* him. I didn't want him to know I was looking, remember?"

"You were just at a bar, Malia. You're allowed to be at a bar."

"Not legally."

"Hmm," she didn't quite agree, even if she agreed.

"And it's a bar everyone knows he hangs at."

"Because his aunt and uncle own it," Toni stated. "Which would stand to reason, since she owns it, she'd be there."

Something else was official.

"Okay, I get it. I'm an idiot," I told the street.

Toni reached out and patted my leg, saying, "Hon, you aren't an idiot. You love the guy. You miss him. Shit went down, and I can see that time has passed, so now you think it's time he sorted himself out and stood up for you and Liam. There's nothing idiotic about that."

I should have known my girl would come through for me in the end.

"Thanks, Toni," I whispered.

"Just call him," she whispered back. "Finding his phone number'll probably be a lot easier than tracking him down on the mean streets of

Denver."

Darius lived on the mean streets.

I didn't usually take those.

"I'll think about it," I told her.

"I hope you do, because, don't forget, I was around during the great love affair of Malia Clark and Darius Tucker. I know it was high school, but some things transcend high school, and you two were one of those things. Everyone knew you were the real deal. Everyone knew you two were going to make it. Thick and thin. Life smacked you both in the face way before it ever should have. You're in thin. I know that boy and the man he'll become. He's Mister Morris through and through. He'll do right by you."

Even though I knew she was right, I still hoped she wasn't wrong.

\* \* \* \*

I laid my sleeping son in his crib, marveling at how beautiful he was, reveling in how peaceful he slept, pleased he hadn't woken up when I picked him up from Mom and Dad's house after I dropped Toni, and thinking I was crazy for missing him being awake and driving me crazy by learning his way around the child-protection latches Dad installed on the cabinets.

I touched his chubby cheek, his little nose, then bent over to kiss him before I pulled up the side of the crib and locked it into place.

It was a moot action. He'd learned how to climb out, which was why I had stacks of pillows around the crib just in case.

If he woke before me (and he always woke before me), they'd come in handy.

Before I left him in there with his blue elephant night-light glowing, I made sure the pillows were where they needed to be, and only then did I head out.

We had a two-bedroom apartment, even though the second bedroom was just bigger than a closet. Since Liam didn't need tons of room yet, it worked. But I needed to get my degree and get a job that paid better, because soon he'd need his own space, and more of it. Liam was at the top of the scales height wise. He was going to be tall, like his daddy. And it was time to get him out of the crib and into a bed.

These were my thoughts when I went out of his room, headed for our tiny kitchen to get myself a glass of water before I got ready for bed.

I stopped dead and squeaked when I saw the man standing in my living room.

After the surprise wore off, I *saw the man.*

He had his arms crossed on his chest. He'd had his hair done into twists. He'd lost weight, looking lean…

And mean.

But no less beautiful.

Darius.

Shirleen had told him I'd been out looking for him.

"Who's the kid?" he asked.

Oh God.

He'd seen me with Liam.

This wasn't how I'd wanted this to go.

"Darius—"

"Who's the fuckin' kid, Malia?"

"How did you—?"

He leaned toward me, not uncrossing his arms, and gritted, "Who's the *fucking kid?*"

I'd turned the light on in our tiny entryway to guide my way through the apartment, so even though no other lights were on, I could see him.

He was still handsome. Fit. Broad shoulders and trim hips and long legs that made his simple T-shirt and jeans look like a fashion statement.

But his expression was all wrong.

His eyes were cold, his face hard.

"Malia—"

I cut him off this time by blurting, "Liam Edward Clark."

He leaned back with a jerk and the air in the room got oppressive.

This was it. It wasn't how I wanted it to go, but I had no choice. I had to work with it.

"I had to guess, but I named him what I thought you'd want to name him," I shared.

And I had. Liam, his best friend Lee's name. And Edward, for his other best friend, Eddie.

"You've gotta be fuckin' shitting me."

"No."

"You had my kid, and you didn't fuckin' tell me?"

His voice was quiet, nevertheless, his rage was glaringly evident.

The man he was now, I was certain most people quaked in their boots at his mood.

But…wait.

Hang on.

I was pretty even-tempered. I had great parents. I was close with my sister Lena, who was my other best friend, along with Toni. I had a tight-knit family. I had friends like Toni who thought I was an idiot, and she still packed her scarf and sunglasses to go on some moronic quest with me. Growing up, we weren't rolling in money, but we were never hurting. I was a teenage mom and not a single member of my family or that first friend did anything but support me and help me through my pregnancy and beyond.

I didn't have much to get shitty about.

But with what Darius just said, I was feeling the need to get shitty.

"Well, you know," I started sarcastically, "I did call…*eighty thousand times*. You refused to speak to me."

"You got my baby in your belly, you figure out a way to fuckin' *tell me*," he shot back.

"I'm sorry." Yep. Still sarcasm. "How was that supposed to go? 'Oh, hey, Miss Dorothea, I know you have a few things on your mind, but I really need to speak with Darius, since he got me pregnant.'"

"Don't take that tone with me, Malia," he said in that quiet, scary voice. "You don't got the high ground here."

Oh yeah.

I felt the need to get shitty.

"I don't? Wait, was it *you* who found out you were pregnant at sixteen? And was it *you* who called and called and posted letters and begged to speak to *me*, only to be shut out time and time and *time again*? And was it *you* who carried a child, pushed that child out, breastfed that child, changed his diapers, chased after him when he started crawling, chased after him more when he started walking, struggled to put clothes on him when he went through that phase where he decided the only suit he wanted to wear was his birthday suit? And was it *you* who took classes even though all this was going on, leaning on your family to help out, so you could eventually make decent money to put a roof over his head and food in his belly? Sorry, I thought that all was *me*."

"I could have given you money," he bit out.

"I don't want your money, Darius," I retorted. "I wanted you to be Liam's father. Which was why I was at the bar for Shirleen to see me tonight. It's time for you to be his father."

"I'll get you money, how much do you need?"

"Darius—"

He threw a hand my way. "You got this, obviously. You don't need me."

All I could do was stare.

"There were ways, woman," he went on. "You made your choice, don't put that shit on me."

"You can't be serious," I whispered.

"*I* didn't disappear for three fuckin' years."

It felt like he'd punched me in the throat, the pain so bad, I couldn't speak.

And the look that came into his eyes, the look of disgust…no, revulsion, nearly brought me to my knees.

He was also whispering when he said his last.

"Fuck, the one person in my life I didn't think would carve a piece out of me cut off the biggest piece of all."

And with that, he walked right past me and out the door.

\* \* \* \*

*Three days later…*

The envelope was on my kitchen counter when Liam and I got home that evening.

It had my name on it, written, and I didn't recognize the handwriting.

Inside, in fives, tens, twenties, a few fifties and two hundreds, was three thousand dollars.

I could buy a toddler bed with that money.

I could feed both of us for three months with that money.

I was still furious at Darius. How our conversation went three nights ago was not okay. This wasn't about him. It wasn't even about me. It was about Liam.

I was so furious, I wanted to take that money to that bar, hand it to Shirleen and tell her to tell Darius from me he could go jump in a lake.

The thing was, this wasn't about me.

It was about Liam.

He needed a toddler bed, and he was going to need a room that it would fit in.

So I took the cash, stuffed it in my underwear drawer and went about my evening, making dinner and being certain my kid didn't figure out how to pull the childproof plug from an outlet and electrocute himself.

# Chapter Three

*Playground*

## Rock Chick Rewind

*Still some time ago, but not as much…*

"Do I need to make my feelings about where we're standing right now official?" Toni asked.

I didn't move from my position of leaning against the trunk of my car next to Toni where it was parked at Shirleen's bar on Colfax.

I also didn't answer.

"Okay, don't get mad…" she started, but didn't finish.

However, her words made me take my laser beam stare off the front door of the bar and turn it to her.

"What?" I pushed when she still didn't speak.

"I kinda talked to Tony about…you know."

As fate would have it, the guy we met the last time we were here was named Anthony and went by Tony.

It was cute, Tony and Toni.

It was also good, since Tony might hang out at rough bars, but he was a good guy and way into Toni, so they'd been seeing each other for the last four months.

Though, it was bad because now Tony knew Toni was only twenty, which meant he was not down with her going to this bar for two reasons. One, it was illegal, and two, he was protective and didn't want her anywhere near the joint.

What was also not good was that I knew what "you know" meant.

This was why my voice was pitched two octaves higher when I asked, "You talked to Tony about Darius and Liam?"

She shook her head.

"No. Not Liam. I just asked him about Darius. I was real casual, I promise," she didn't quite assure me. "I said I was friends with him back in high school, since, you know, *I was*, and wondering after what went down how he was doing."

Okay, maybe this wasn't so bad.

And now I was interested.

"What did he say?"

It appeared she didn't want to say what she was going to say next, but she said it.

"He said steer clear. He didn't know him back then, but now, he's one serious bad dude."

I turned my attention back to the front door because I already knew that. The "bad dude" leaked all his bad dudeness all over my living room four months ago.

I'd also come home to an envelope sitting on my counter like clockwork the first day of every month. The first two were three grand, the last two were four.

All cash.

"So, you know," Toni went on, "he made it clear he was in for child support, which is good, right?"

I didn't answer, because I'd told her all about Darius's visit, and the envelopes I kept getting, and it didn't need to be said that fourteen thousand dollars in cash was good when you made a salary that was semi-kinda okay for one but didn't really stretch to two.

She kept going.

"But he's out for the rest. So why are we standing here again?"

This was a good question because Darius's feelings on the matter did, indeed, not leave a lot to interpretation, so I didn't really know.

However, things had definitely been left unsaid, and for some stupid reason, I had the overwhelming urge to say them.

Before I could answer her, a truck pulled into the parking lot.

But it didn't park.

It drove right up to us and stopped.

The window went down, and I saw Eddie Chavez behind the wheel.

Dang.

Darius knew I was here, or Shirleen did, but it was Darius who was making the statement that he didn't want to see me.

Eddie vocalized it.

"Go home, Malia."

"Well, Eddie Chavez," Toni drawled. "Look at you. You grew up good."

His black eyes shifted to her, he murmured, "Toni," then he looked at me, "This is no place for you. Either of you."

"Tell him I want to speak to him," I ordered.

Eddie said nothing.

"Tell him, Eddie," I demanded.

"Go home, Malia," he repeated, the window went up, and he rolled through the parking lot.

But I noted, when he turned around, he sat idling, his lights still on, waiting for us to load up and head out.

Yeesh.

Those boys.

Always having each other's backs.

I thought it was cool back in the day.

It was annoying as all get out now.

"I don't think Darius is gonna show," Captain Toni of the Obvious pointed out.

I huffed out a breath and got in the car. Toni got in beside me.

Eddie followed us out of the parking lot.

"You know, he's a cop now," Toni remarked.

"What? Who?"

"Eddie Chavez."

I couldn't help it. I was frustrated and ticked, but that made me laugh out loud.

"No, seriously, he is," Toni said through my laughter.

"The only reason Eddie Chavez wasn't a bonafide juvenile delinquent was because…"

I didn't finish.

It was because Darius tempered that trio.

Lee Nightingale and Eddie Chavez were two young men who weren't challenged enough by school or sports, so they sought out other challenges, and when you were a teenaged boy, those challenges often were nefarious.

Darius had been their moral compass.

I would have thought…

"Do you know what Lee Nightingale is doing?" I asked Toni.

"He's in the Army. I think he's stationed in North Carolina or somewhere."

Well, there it was. I was no psychologist, but the only reason those two didn't go off the rails was because Darius kept them on track.

Then he went off the rails and they found them, probably to lead by example, remind their bud who he really was, show the way or be in the position to look out for him as best they could.

Those three had been inseparable, and I should have known they'd find a way to continue to be, even if life took them in very different directions.

"So Lee and Indy never got together," I said, feeling sad about this, for Indy, and for Lee.

They were always so into each other, I figured he was just waiting for her to grow up.

I guessed I figured wrong.

"Nope, but she isn't taken, so there's still hope."

I wasn't so sure. I was running low on hope these days.

I dropped Toni at her place, and the minute I pulled into the parking spot in front of her apartment, Tony opened the door and leaned against the jamb.

Damn, he *was* fine.

"Can't deny," I remarked, gaze aimed at her man, "something good came out of going to that bar."

"No, can't deny it," Toni replied. Then her voice got softer, sweeter. "Just saying, he's got friends, and they're good dudes."

I looked to her and gave her a smile I didn't really feel even though I felt the words I said, "I've got a friend too, and she's the best dudette ever."

She pulled a face. "Oh my God, do not *ever* call me a dudette again."

The smile I had then, I felt.

Toni was awesome at taking your back and guarding your heart, but she wasn't really good with talking about feelings.

"Go to your guy," I urged. "Next time Mom and Dad take Liam for the night, we'll do something fun."

"Promises, promises," she muttered as she exited the car.

I waited until she got to Tony, but I didn't watch him greet my friend.

I remembered love in first bloom like it was yesterday.

And I missed it.

Instead, I drove to an empty home (and incidentally, Eddie hadn't yet peeled off, which told me exactly what Darius had ordered him to do, and that was make sure Toni and I got home okay), wishing I hadn't caved when Mom begged me to let Liam spend the night.

She and Dad doted on my kid.

Though I knew she had an ulterior motive, thinking I was young, I needed to go out and be young with a girlfriend and forget I had a huge responsibility at home that limited my ability to go out and be young.

The thing was, I doted on my kid too, and I wouldn't mind heading out to see a concert or movie once in a while, but I loved spending time with my son. Even when I was saving him from electrocuting himself.

I parked at my apartment complex, grabbed my purse, got out, secured the car, then let myself into my apartment, glancing back before I closed the door and seeing Eddie finally driving away.

As usual, I flipped the light on in the entryway, and again squeaked when I saw the man standing in my living room.

I put one hand on my heart, walked into the room and threw my bag on the couch.

Only then did I order, "Stop breaking in."

"You haven't moved," he stated bizarrely.

"What?"

"His room is tiny. This isn't a good neighborhood. And you haven't moved."

I didn't know what to say. My mind was darting from one thing to the other, including but definitely not limited to the facts he was here again, he'd broken in again, but he'd also obviously had a look around, something that was totally invasive, or, more invasive than him just breaking in, and he was saying words I didn't understand.

"You got the money…*move*," he pressed.

"You're giving me that money?"

"I'm not giving you that money," he lied, since he knew about it, and exactly three people knew about it: me, Toni and the person giving it to me.

Why would he lie?

"Darius—"

"There's a complex close to Colorado Boulevard. Cleaner. Bigger cribs. Green space. A playground. A pool. A security gate. There's a waiting list. I know a guy. You're bumped to the top and they got a two-bedroom townhouse open. He'll call you with the details."

"Darius—" I tried again.

"Know another guy, he's got a moving company. He'll see to that shit."

"I still have six months on this lease."

"I'll make a call."

He'd make a call and now he was making a move…to leave.

He went to pass by me, but I caught his biceps and snapped, "Darius!"

He stopped, looked down at my hand, then to my face, and his preference that I take my hand from him was perfectly clear without a word escaping his lips.

I didn't take my hand from him.

"We have things to talk about," I told him.

"Yeah, you gettin' out of this pit and putting my son in a decent pad. We talked about that. I'm gone."

I held on tighter. "I have other things to say."

"See I gotta make myself clear I don't wanna hear them, so this is me makin' it clear. I don't wanna hear them."

I pulled at his arm at the same time I moved in front of him to block his path. "Well, I want to say them."

"Malia, no."

"I can't afford a bigger place."

"Not gonna be your problem, since the rent's gonna be paid by me."

My eyes got big.

Then I got mad.

"So, what? Is this guilt?" I asked. "Because I don't need your guilt, Darius Tucker."

"It's not guilt."

"Then what is it?"

"Move outta my way, woman."

"Tell me. What is it?" I demanded.

"Outta my way," he clipped.

I didn't get out of his way.

I got up on my toes and got in his face.

"Tell me!" I snapped. "If it's not guilt, *what is it?*"

"You wanna know what it is?" he whispered, the tone sinister.

I shivered at the tone, but still found it in me to nod my head. "Yeah. I wanna know."

He was still whispering when he replied, "This is what it is."

And then his arms were around me and his mouth was on mine.

For a second, I was stunned. I hadn't been touched by a man since...well, *him*.

And then his tongue touched my lips, I opened them, and it swept inside, and it wasn't like I'd used up ten years of hormones making my kid.

It was like I was fifteen again and the cutest boy at school was kissing me.

But I wasn't fifteen, and Darius wasn't sixteen.

This was different.

This was better.

*Much* better.

He had one arm so tight around my back, it was like he wanted my body to fuse with his.

His other hand was at the base of my neck, fingers up in my hair, holding me steady for the onslaught of his kiss, when there was no way I was going to do anything but go for the gusto and kiss him back.

Something I did.

When his hand strayed down to my behind, how much better this kiss was hit me, and how it could get so much better hit me too.

Fury washed through me. Fury and jealousy and misery, a lethal mix of poison permeating my every cell, and I tore from his arms.

He was breathing heavily, and I was breathing heavily, and we were staring at each other.

His stare was wary.

Mine was enraged.

"Seems you got plenty of opportunity to get really good at that," I jibed. "Guess you weren't pining for me, hunh?"

The wariness went out of his features, the blankness setting back in.

But he didn't answer, not until he walked by me, and I pivoted to watch him move to the door.

He stopped at it and turned back to me.

"You move, last day of the month."

"I don't need—"

"I don't give a fuck what you need. My son needs a safe place to live with a playground close. And that's what he's gonna get."

He opened the door but again turned back.

Then he delivered his final blow.

"And I got good at it 'cause I got an imagination. If I'd let myself have a woman, there's only one woman I'd let myself have. But she doesn't need my shit. Her kid doesn't need my shit. No one needs my shit. So I'm gonna let her have her life and raise our boy and keep them clear of the shit that is me."

With that, leaving me eviscerated, he was gone.

\* \* \* \*

FYI:

A man with a moving truck showed at my door on the morning of the last of the month.

I hadn't packed.

The man with the truck and his boys packed for me.

I threatened to call the police, but he was undeterred.

I didn't call the police.

Darius had said there was a playground at this new complex.

And a pool.

We moved.

The next day, there was an envelope on the new, gorgeous, granite counters of my roomy new kitchen.

In it was five thousand dollars.

# Chapter Four

*This Is Meant to Be*

## Rock Chick Rewind

*Still some time ago, but now even less...*

"Okay, does doing crazy, stupid shit run in you all's family?" Toni asked.

"*Shh!*" my sister Lena shushed her.

She was looking through a pair of binoculars.

Toni was in the middle of the back seat of my car. I was in the driver's seat. Lena on the passenger side.

And Lena was spying on her boyfriend, who she was certain was cheating on her.

We were parked across the street from his place, so the binoculars were overkill.

She put them down, turned to me and announced, "I'm going in for a closer look. Cover me."

I opened my mouth to stop her, but she was out the door before I could.

"Cover her?" Toni asked.

I smiled, trying not to laugh because this wasn't funny, not really.

And it wasn't because I was pretty certain my sister was right. Michael was cheating on her. The dude was shifty as all heck.

But still.

We watched as Lena tiptoed across the street, looking every which way, her long braids swinging along her back (causing me to wonder if I should make an appointment at the salon, those braids looked good on her), making it so obvious she was somewhere she shouldn't be doing something she shouldn't be doing, in broad daylight no less, I no longer felt like laughing.

Instead, I groaned.

"She's terrible at this," I stated the obvious.

"One of us should stop her," Toni noted.

She was right.

"And that someone isn't gonna be me," Toni went on.

Ugh.

I started to open the door to go fetch my sister but stilled when Toni muttered, "Holy crap."

Holy crap was right.

This was because, out of nowhere, Eddie Chavez and Lee Nightingale were there.

Lee was heading to my car.

Eddie was heading off Lena.

"Oh boy, that man grew up f-i-n-e, *fine*," Toni declared, eyes glued through my windshield. "Both of them are *fine*. But seeing as I've already taken in the grown-up fineness of Eddie's fine, and I'm just now witnessing the same from Lee, I can tell you the two of them together is too much fine. I might not be able to handle this. And I got experience with fine, since Tony is right now at home, waiting to get the call to bail me out of jail. He said I better make this a misdemeanor, since he isn't pawning our new flat screen for your foolishness."

Lee rapped on my window with his knuckles, and when I hit the switch to roll it down, he bent over to look in at me.

And, um…*yeah*.

He was a good-looking kid.

But now he was *fine*.

"Hey, Lee," I greeted. "Long time. Are you home on leave?"

"Yeah," he grunted.

"Hey, Lee. Lookin' good," Toni greeted, pushing in between the seats to peer around me at Lee.

"Toni," he returned, his lips twitching in a ghost of that famous Liam Nightingale smile. Then, with no further ado, he got serious and said, "Eddie's gonna put Lena in the car and you three are gonna get the fuck out of here."

I noted his mouth had not cleaned up since back in the day.

And it was still hot.

"Sure, sure, good," I babbled.

"She thinks her man is cheating on her," Toni told Lee.

I lost his face when he looked over the roof of my car.

He came back into the window when I heard the door open beside me and the car bobbed when Lena's bottom hit the passenger seat.

The door closed again.

Lee pinned me with his eyes.

"Go home," he ordered.

I nodded, because he said two words, but other words were unspoken. How I knew that, I couldn't tell you. I just knew.

He disappeared from the window. I heard his knuckles rap on the roof, his macho-man reminder to get the eff out of there. I hit the button for the window, started up the car and we rolled out.

It was a miracle I didn't plow into some cars considering my eyes were fixed to my rearview mirror, watching Eddie walk through my now vacant parking space to join Lee on the curb, both of them watching us leave.

Toni was right.

That was too much fine.

"Did you see that?" Lena's voice was breathy.

"Oh, I saw it all right," Toni answered.

"Eddie was a cutie in high school," Lena started, and I snorted, because "cutie" was not how I'd ever describe Eddie Chavez.

A baby shark was cute, it was still a shark.

"But...*whoa*." Lena finished.

"You got *that* right, sister," Toni agreed.

"He was so *whoa*, and Lee was so *oh man*, I forgot what I was doing," Lena said.

I could totally see that.

"And now I don't know if Michael has a girl in there with him or not," she concluded.

"Let me put my ear to the ground," I said.

"What ground?" Lena asked.

My eyes found Toni's in the rearview.

She knew.

But I hadn't told my sister.

If Lena knew I was holding out on her, she'd be ticked, but more hurt.

It was just...I couldn't tell her. I couldn't tell anyone, but Toni.

And I wasn't even sure I should tell Toni, but I had to tell somebody, and I trusted her not to do anything I wouldn't want, like tell my parents, or Lena, or get up in someone's face who wouldn't appreciate it.

This being the fact that three years had passed since Liam and I had moved back from Fort Collins, and in that time, it wasn't a habit, but it wasn't infrequent, and the fact Eddie and Lee showed up when I was doing something stupid with my sister wasn't a surprise.

Because, first, Darius Tucker kept an eye on me.

And second, Darius Tucker found reasons to visit me.

It was always at night, when Liam was asleep, and it was always when we needed him.

Like when someone plowed into my car in the grocery store parking lot and didn't leave a note. Thus, in order that I wouldn't have to claim it on my insurance, Darius showed with a loner car that very night, had my car taken away and brought back, not only fixed, but detailed.

And when Toni and Tony moved in together, and were in the market for a new couch, and I'd gone with her to look, and oohed and aahed over the furniture. Darius was at my place late that night, telling me I was going to get a delivery in three days, and someone needed to be at my townhouse between noon and four to accept it.

That "it" being entirely new living room furniture, all the pieces I most oohed and aahed over.

So out went the ratty, secondhand furniture I'd scrounged from relatives and friends, and in went classy, expensive stuff I probably would be able to afford only after Liam finished college.

A week later, he was back, sharing someone had to be around for another delivery, and that one was our flat screen TV.

Of course, there were three Christmases and Liam's three birthdays, when Darius brought wrapped gifts for his son, but all the cards said they were from Santa...or me.

How he knew Liam's birthday, I didn't know, because he didn't ask me.

He also didn't give me the opportunity to ask him.

In all that time, with all those visits, he never clapped eyes on his son (that I knew). He never asked to see him, not so much as to walk upstairs and watch him sleeping.

And he never hung around enough for us to have a conversation.

He told me what he was going to do to take care of me, of us, and then he vanished.

Okay, not vanished, he wasn't a superhero. He walked out. But he made no bones about it and took great pains not to be waylaid, those pains being *my* pains, since he gave me a wide berth and exited, pronto.

I was confused by all of this.

Toni was confused by all of it.

But the only person who could explain it was in my life, in my son's life, in very real ways.

Except he wasn't.

And the way he was, he gave no explanation.

It had occurred to me I could probably track down Eddie and ask him, but something stopped me.

Not something, I knew what it was.

I loved Darius.

This was all he felt he could give.

And since I loved him, I was letting him give what he could how he could give it and not push for more.

I suspected Toni knew I was doing this, but in that scenario, she loved me. So she didn't push it either.

By the way, that five thousand dollars was still on my kitchen counter the first of every month, and my rent was paid, and never by me.

In fact, I had enough (actually, more than enough) to make a down payment on a house, and I was considering it because Liam was going to be in school next year—real, big-boy school, first grade. And I needed to settle into a school district that was good for him in a home he could count on.

"What ground?" Lena pushed, cutting into my thoughts.

"I'll just…ask around," I said lamely.

"Me too. And Tony too. He knows everybody. He'll get the skinny," Toni added.

This mollified Lena because I had no ground to put my ear to. My life was my job, my kid, and every once in a while, going out with Toni and/or Lena, but always getting home before nine so Mom or Dad or one of the aunties or cousins could go home after babysitting Liam.

But Toni did not lie. Her man knew everybody.

"Okay, now that I'm over that one-two punch of Eddie and Lee, um…does anyone but me think it's weird they showed up?" Lena asked.

Again, I glanced at Toni in the rearview.

"Maybe Eddie lives around here," Toni said, giving me guilt eyes in the mirror, since she was lying for me.

"Lee said he was home on leave," I added.

"I kinda hope Michael's cheating now because I sure had cheatin' thoughts when I clapped eyes on Eddie when he grabbed me," Lena muttered.

She was lying too. She'd fallen for Michael.

I saw in him what I saw in a lot of the attorneys who tried their cases in the courtroom I worked in.

Narcissism.

So I hoped he was cheating on her too, because I'd rather my little sister be in a bit of hurt after scraping off a cheating boyfriend, than live her whole life with a man who thought the most important person in the world was him, and everyone should agree.

"I'm hungry," Lena declared. "Brother's for a sandwich and a beer?"

"I could do a ticky turkey," Toni said.

I could always do a ticky turkey.

I pointed the car toward My Brother's Bar.

* * * *

I knew he'd come. I just didn't know he'd come that soon.

The evening after our run-in with Lee and Eddie, I was in the sapphire blue velvet sectional Darius had bought us, on the lounge section, with a glass of wine and a book, when the door opened.

Something else I didn't know, and had never asked, was if he had a key from the guy he knew who got me this pad, or if he picked the locks.

I was dying to know.

I was also dying to know, if he picked the locks, when he learned how to do that.

I was further dying to know how his mom was, his sisters, and if they knew about Liam.

They should know.

But if he wasn't taking that step, I knew he wouldn't want me to.

Something else I wished I could talk to him about, because Miss Dorothea was a lovely woman, she'd be a great grandma, and although my boy already had one, it never hurt to have two.

In fact, it was impossible to enumerate all the things I was dying to know about Darius Tucker.

But I was getting really good at burying how much I needed to know them, and ignoring how not knowing them, or being able to ask, was slowly killing me.

He showed in the living room, and he looked as good, and as scary, as ever.

This time, he was holding a large manila envelope.

Yes. I knew he'd come.

Because I needed him.

In this instance, Lena needed him, but to him, it was the same thing.

He took me in where I was stretched out on the lounge section, his body held in a weird, still way that I understood, because I was holding mine in the same way.

It'd been three years.

Three years since that kiss.

It felt like yesterday.

This happened every time he showed, both of us bracing, both of us fighting it.

Fighting the need to jump each other like crazed fuck bunnies and have at it until we couldn't breathe.

He broke the stillness first by tossing the envelope on the lounge at my bare feet.

I put my wineglass aside, the bookmark in my book, and set it on the couch, pushed up and retrieved the envelope.

"She needs to dump him," he said.

I pressed the metal tabs back and pulled out the pictures.

On viewing the top one, my face scrunched.

"Ew! You could have warned me," I said, shoving the photos back in, now having seen more of Michael, not to mention his side piece, than I'd ever wanted to see.

"We made sure she didn't have any questions."

"You did that all right," I muttered.

"You need to date."

My stillness came back at his words. That was, it did after my head snapped back to look at him.

"Why aren't you dating?" he asked, his words gruff, forced.

I could hear the emotion. I could even feel it.

And it ticked me off.

"Oh, are we chatting now?" I asked back. "Are we buds? You show with the means to save my sister a lot of heartache." I waved the envelope in the air then tossed it to the side. "We share about our lives, then you vanish for a couple of months. Where are my manners? Would you like a glass of wine?"

"Stop it," he grunted.

I was lamenting sitting on the lounge section, because even if it was comfy, it was a pain in the behind to get out of gracefully.

Even so, I was so mad, I scrambled out, took my feet and put my hands on my hips, ignoring how Darius's beautiful brown eyes watching me do that made me feel, and asked, "Are *you* dating?"

He dropped his head but lifted a hand, palm out my way, and said to his boots, "Fucked up. Apologize. Not my business."

"It's not?" I demanded. "How's the couch look, Darius? It's nice, isn't it? Liam is into plants. He makes me let him water them. I have to follow him around—"

He lifted his head and dropped his hand.

"Stop it," he bit off.

I didn't stop it.

"And he begs me to take him to the nursery so we can buy more, which I can afford, seeing as my baby daddy gives me three times more than I make in a —"

I didn't finish that time, because one second, he was four feet away.

And the next, he was towering over me and right in my face.

"Don't ever fuckin' call me that."

He was trying to intimidate me.

I was so done with this dance, I wasn't about to be intimidated.

"Why not? That's what you are, aren't you? You don't even ask to see him."

"I don't exist for him."

"You're standing right here."

"I don't exist for you either."

"My couch and car and bank account says different."

"You're not gonna want, and neither is he."

"Well, rest assured, you aren't falling down on that job. It's just other jobs you aren't up for."

I saw the anger flare in his eyes. It was intense, burning.

But that didn't intimidate me either.

"What jobs you want me to see to, Malia?"

"How long you got?" I asked. "Because I have a list and you might want to take notes."

His voice got warm, sexy…*lewd.* "Like you said, baby, I'm right here. What you need?"

And now he was trying to be an a-hole.

I wasn't buying that either.

But he wanted to play with fire, we'd see who'd get burned.

"I haven't had a man touch me since I was sixteen, you could take care of that."

Another flare in his eyes, surprise.

And something else.

Something deep.

Possessive.

Hungry.

Okay, dang.

It was me about to be burned.

It would turn out I was right. I just had no idea how much I would love dancing in that fire.

His arms closed around me, and his mouth slammed down on mine, and I should have stopped it. If he was going to hang around, we had so much more to talk about.

I didn't stop it.

He kissed me, and more fool me, I kissed him back.

Three years since we kissed.

Even longer since we took it further, but he was in my life, in my business, in *my heart*, I couldn't stop it.

This time, I wasn't going to tear myself away.

I *needed* it.

No.

I needed Darius.

I tried to pull him down on the couch.

He resisted, and fear took hold of my soul, because one thing I'd learned these last few years, when Darius was done, he was gone.

But he said, "No, baby, not on the couch. Not this time, not our first since…will he wake up?"

"He's a sound sleeper."

That was all I said, all he needed.

He let me go but took my hand and we were up the stairs before I could blink.

We were in my dark bedroom before I could get my head straight.

And then he was kissing me again, so I wasn't thinking about anything but that.

He might be hungry, but I was starving.

Starving for his warm skin and the touch of his hands.

Starving for his mouth on mine, his tongue in my mouth, dancing with mine. His lips on my neck. The crush of his arms around me.

Then my shirt was off. His shirt was off. He went after my jeans. I went after his.

Both of us only in underwear, he leaned into me, and I fell to my back on my bed, Darius on top of me.

Oh man, he felt good.

Even so, I rolled him to get more of him.

He rolled me to get more of me.

I squirmed under him to push down my panties.

He took over and *whoosh!* they were gone.

*Nice.*

I pushed at his boxers. "Now you."

"Slow down, sweetheart," he murmured, hand at my breast, thumb and finger teasing my nipple, the sensations he created firing their way all over my skin, his mouth was in my neck.

"Slow isn't an option, Darius," I told him.

His fingers stilled, his head came up, and he looked down at me through the dark.

"You sure?" he asked, and I closed my eyes.

There he was.

That tender sweetness.

There was my Darius.

I knew it.

I *knew* he was in there.

I opened my eyes and put my hand to his cheek. "I'm sure, honey."

"I don't have any condoms."

I nearly started weeping.

*I got an imagination.*

A man who was getting some somewhere else, or open to it should it happen, would carry condoms.

It was me for him.

And it was him for me.

I knew then, just like me, there was no one else.

"I love him with everything I am, and I'd never make another choice, but I got pregnant at sixteen, baby," I whispered, smiling so there'd be no sting. "I'm on the pill even if I'm not active."

He started to detach, murmuring, "This is a mistake."

I grabbed on with everything at my disposal and held tight.

"This is meant to be," I informed him of something I knew he had to know. "I'm not stupid."

"I didn't say you were."

"Let me finish."

He shut his mouth.

I smiled again. "You don't buy a couch for a baby momma."

"Sure you do," he muttered.

"No, you didn't hear me correctly. *You* don't buy a couch for a baby momma."

Another eye flare, but after it happened, he said, "You're gonna regret this."

"I can assure you, I...am...not."

He hesitated a beat.

But he was Darius.

And I was me.

He didn't leave.

He kissed me.

I pushed down his boxers.

Darius took over.

In everything.

Then he proved how vivid his imagination was.

And I was right.

I didn't regret a damned thing.

\* \* \* \*

I lay with my head on his chest.

Darius was on his back. He had his arm around me, his fingers drawing random patterns on the small of my back.

We'd been silent after.

But now, when his fingers stopped and his muscles bunched, I knew what he was doing.

"If you leave me, there are going to be problems," I warned the delightful bulge of his pec.

"Malia—"

I lifted my head and looked down at him. "Don't leave."

"Fuck," he murmured, put his hand to my face, slid it back, curled it around my head and pulled my forehead to his before he bit out, *"Fuck."*

I wanted to jump off the bed and do a victory dance.

Because this meant he not only didn't want to leave, he wasn't leaving.

We were so...totally...*meant to be.*

And seriously, he'd given me orgasms back in the day, but usually with his mouth or fingers.

But the sync we just got into made the slow burn we'd endured totally worth it.

And yeah, I knew what I was saying.

Six years' wait.

Totally...

*Worth it!*

He relaxed his hand so I could pull back an inch, but just an inch. He put enough pressure on I couldn't get too far away.

"I don't want him seeing me."

And there was the splash of cold water at the end of my victory lap.

"Why?" I whispered, not able to hide the hurt weighing down that word.

He rolled us so I was on my back, he was pressed down my side, but our faces were still close.

"It's not safe," he said.

I opened my mouth, but his finger rested on my lips.

"Hush," he whispered. "Hear me out. Please."

I closed my mouth.

"It's...I can't..." He drew in a deep breath. "I can't explain how hard it is to be this close to him and not—"

I framed his face in my hands and whispered, "Honey."

"The shit that I've made of my life—"

"We can—"

"Baby, let me get this out."

I shut up again.

"If anybody knew about him. About you. They could hurt me. Through you. And I don't give a fuck about hurting, except they'd hurt you."

"Whatever you're into, we'll get you out," I said.

I mean, he was this "bad dude," but you could just stop being a bad dude. Other people had turned their lives around. I couldn't imagine it was easy, but it wasn't like he wouldn't have support. He'd have me. My family. His family. Eddie and Lee.

"I'm in now—" he began.

"Okay, so—"

"And I can't get out while she's still in."

She?

Who was *she*?

"She?"

"Aunt Shirleen."

"Miss Shirleen?" I asked, shocked.

I couldn't say I knew his aunt as well as I did his mom, but she'd been around. She was funny. She gave good hugs. Though, she seemed...*removed*. Like she was isolated, even when she was with people who loved her.

And I'd never quite understood, with how loving and sweet his family was, why she always seemed so sad.

"It's him. He got me into it. He got her into it. And he isn't...*nice* to her."

My muscles got tight. "He isn't *nice*? Who's he?"

"Leon."

"Your Uncle Leon?"

Leon was Shirleen's husband. I'd met him, once.

He was all expansive smiles and grand gestures. He gave me the creeps.

Darius nodded. "It happens less because I'm around now. But it still happens. If I get out, it'll happen like it used to. All the time."

"Then both of you get out."

"She can't."

"Why not?"

"Fuck," he whispered. "I love it that you can ask that question and it's a genuine question, because you don't know how deep this shit is, how it sucks you in until you're under and you can't breathe anymore."

My heart was beating so hard, he had to feel it. "Darius, you're scaring me."

"Good, you'll get it then when I say, I'm giving you tonight. Tonight, we pretend. And after that, like I've been doin', I'll do what I can to look out for you. But this can't happen again. Leon doesn't know about you, and he can't know. No one can know. The more people know, the more dangerous it is because he's the kind of guy who puts his thumbs to something you care about to make you squirm. He did that with me to keep Shirleen in line. He'll do it to you and Liam without blinking."

It was the first time he'd spoken our son's name out loud.

"If Liam meets you, it's not like he can tell this guy," I pointed out.

"Baby," he said softly, "can't you see? Think about it. You don't have him, but you know he exists, but you can't be a real part of his life. If I get one look, I know I'm done. I won't be able to walk away. But what I do, what I got myself into, you don't get out. You don't get out without paying in one way or another. And the fee for that is steep. I won't let Shirleen pay. You pay. Our boy pay. And I can't make it so I can't give you two what you need. I got no choice. I gotta stay in."

"Forever?"

"I don't know. And tonight, we're pretending. We're not talking about that now."

"Darius—"

This time, he put his whole hand to my mouth and said, "You derailed your life to give our son to this world. That's the sacrifice you made. I fucked up. This is the sacrifice I gotta make. And you have to trust me, Malia. I sense you know, if I could, I wouldn't be anywhere but here. But I can't. You have to trust that there are reasons why. Because it is *killing* me, and if you add pressure, baby, I'm gonna cave. And I know what that could mean, and I can barely live with being apart from you two, don't make me live with that."

I wrapped my fingers around his hand, pulled it away, and said, "Okay."

His relief was so great, he instantly buried his face in my neck and let out a heavy breath.

I turned into him and wrapped him up in my arms.

Because I might have agreed.

And he might think we were pretending.

But I knew the truth of it, my mom had told me that truth six years ago.

I just had to grow up and learn the way of it.

Not pressure.

Patience.

In other words the bottom line was…

I had to take care of my man.

\* \* \* \*

I woke when the bed depressed at my side.

I opened my eyes to see Darius, fully clothed, sitting beside me.

It was early dawn.

"You're leaving," I mumbled, not bothering to hide I wasn't happy about it.

He ran his knuckles down my cheekbone. "Yeah, but not before we talk about something we should have talked about last night."

Last night's convo hadn't been fun.

Luckily, after I came to terms with what I had to do, I distracted him by kissing him, which lead to a fresh round of orgasms for both of us. But we were in a lot less of a hurry that time, so it took longer, and we'd broken the seal, so in the end, our climaxes were less intense, but that didn't mean they didn't reach soul deep.

Or, at least, mine did. But the way Darius had looked at me after he'd recovered from his, it was a guess, but I was thinking he felt the same way.

I got up on a forearm and held the covers over my breasts with the other hand.

"Do I need my teeth brushed and coffee before this talk?" I asked.

"No, since I'm gonna tell you not to do stupid shit with your sister again, and you're going to nod your head and say, 'Yes, Darius. That was a one-time thing, baby. You don't have to worry about me doing stupid shit with Lena or Toni anymore.'"

Oh boy.

I could see the challenge ahead of me since it hadn't even been twelve hours and my patience with my man was waning.

"I think you were wrong. I need coffee. Or at least an empty mug in hand I can throw at you."

He grinned, wide and white, and my breath left me.

God, I forgot how drop-dead beautiful he was when he smiled.

He then leaned in and touched his mouth to mine.

When he lifted away, he wasn't smiling anymore.

"Michael is a low-level player. He's also ambitious. I'll take care of him. You can show her the pictures, but don't do anything stupid anymore. If Lena had looked in his windows, she might have seen him cutting coke. And he wouldn't have liked that. Get me?"

"Yikes," I breathed.

"Yeah," he agreed. "So, you get me?"

I nodded.

"You need anything?" he asked.

I thought about orgasm three, but asked back, "Like what?"

"Clothes, shoes, for you? The same or toys for the boy? Tuition for your last year of college?"

It was my turn to smile. "I think we're covered."

"Mm…" he murmured, and I had a feeling I knew what that meant.

"We're fine, Darius."

"Great, baby. Gotta go before he gets up."

I really, really, *really* wanted to encourage him to just stick his head in and watch Liam sleep for at least a beat. He was adorable when he was asleep. Though, it must be said, he was pretty adorable when he wasn't asleep too.

But I got it. If I took one look at our boy, I wouldn't have been able to stay away either.

Patience.

"Okay."

"Later," he said.

Oh yes, there'd be a later.

I smiled.

*Love you*, I thought but did not say.

He saw it anyway. I knew when he dipped in to touch his mouth to mine again.

But he was way stronger than me.

He left it at that.

And then he left me.

* * * *

By the way, I was right in my earlier thoughts.

My envelope at the first of the month didn't have five thousand in it.

It had seven.

# Chapter Five

## *In It to Win It*

### Rock Chick Rewind

*Still some time ago, but now even less...*

I pulled into the church on a screech of tires, driving like a lunatic because Toni had forgotten her shoes at home, she only trusted me to go get them, and she was due to walk down the aisle to Tony in T-minus five minutes and counting.

I swung into a parking spot that was way too far away from the sanctuary, lamenting the fact I hadn't changed out of my strappy heels before I went on this mission. I had to run if I was going to get there on time, and I had maid of honor duties to attend to, I didn't fancy doing them with a sprained ankle and skinned knees.

However, I froze in place after I caught movement in my rearview.

Movement that was Toni, sprinting toward me in her wedding gown, the ruffle at her hip flapping, her veil flying out behind her.

She was even carrying her bouquet.

Quickly, I hit the locks to open the doors as she hit the passenger side.

She threw it open then tossed the bouquet at me.

I caught it.

She folded in, slammed the door, turned to me and screeched, "*Drive, bitch, drive!*"

"Okay, slow down, take a breath and tell me what's going on."

She sucked in air through her nose, let it out like a bull, and said, "Okay, like, this is forever, like...yeah?"

"Yes," I said calmly. "Ideally, marriage is forever."

"What if he's a secret perv?" she asked.

I smiled encouragingly. "You've been living with him for four years, Tone. He's not a secret perv."

"What if he's, like, you know, that Arnold Schwarzenegger character in that movie." She snapped her fingers repeatedly. "What's that movie?"

"*Terminator?*"

"No."

"*Predator?*"

"No."

"*Conan?*"

"No!" she shouted. "The one Jamie Lee Curtis was in, wearing that hot LBD."

"*True Lies?*"

She snapped again, but only once, ending it pointing at me. "That one. What if he's that?"

"A secret agent?"

She nodded. "One that gets me dangling from a helicopter. Girl, you know I'm scared of heights."

"No, you're scared of how happy you are right now and that it's going to end. Sorry to say, honey, it's going to end."

She blinked at me.

"Then it's going to come back. Then it's going to end. Things are going to get hard. Then they're going to smooth out. And before you know it, you and Tony are going to be watching your grandchildren open their Christmas presents, knowing you don't have to cook that big dinner anymore, but you are going to be critical of your daughter-in-law's ability to do it right, and then you're off on one of your many retirement cruises for New Years'."

She turned to face forward, folded double and dropped her head in her hands.

I reached out and rubbed her back.

"What if I fuck it up?" she asked her lap.

I caught sight of Toni's mom, Vanessa, leaning to peer into the passenger window, backed by Lena, who was wearing the same strapless aubergine number as me, skintight, with a filmy bunch of material in the same color at the left side of our waists that drifted down the center of the skirt in a flirty ruffle.

Toni wasn't playing with the bridesmaid dresses. They were very pretty and demurely sexy.

Her gown, an ivory, off-the-shoulder column, with more structured ruching to the more nuanced ruffle at her hip, was understated and sophisticated.

And her most important quality when she'd been searching for the perfect dress, she could dance in it.

I shook my head at Miss Vanessa so she wouldn't spook Toni by opening the door.

She nodded hers, but still looked freaked and didn't move from the window.

"You're not going to fuck it up," I said to Toni, considering the circumstances, dropping the F-bomb when I did my very best not to curse, since my son had superpowered hearing, and he picked up everything anybody laid down, and I didn't need my kid F-bombing his way through elementary school.

"He loves me so much," she whispered.

I smiled because he did.

So much.

"Yeah, he does."

She lifted her head and looked at me.

Her hair was smoothed severely back into a big, intricate bun in the back, the veil now attached to it.

The perfect move, letting her beautiful face do all the work.

"You look gorgeous," I said quietly. "He's going to lose it when he sees you."

"Yeah? He likes my hair full. Should I—?"

I set the bouquet on the parking brake and reached for her hands, holding tight.

"You're perfect. Every inch, perfect."

She stared into my eyes.

I bounced our hands, "Let's do this, okay?"

"You're a good friend, Malia Clark," she declared.

"I'm not your friend, honey. I'm your sister."

Tears filled her eyes.

"No!" I shouted, she jumped, so I calmed myself down. "It's waterproof, but let's not take any chances with your makeup."

"Right, right," she mumbled.

I nodded to Miss Vanessa.

She pulled open the door.

I grabbed the bouquet, got out, stopped to open the back door, nabbed Toni's shoes, and after Lena gave me a *that bitch is crazy* bug-eyed look, which I returned with a *just wait until you get married* smug-eyed look (yes, we were sisters, we could communicate like this), we all headed into the church.

\* \* \* \*

My heart was awash with love.

Because it was an amazing day where my best friend was marrying a good, decent, hard-working, loving man.

And because my boy was her ring bearer.

He looked adorable in his little tux with his back straight and his shoulders squared, taking his duty of holding that frilly pillow as serious as if he was delivering a promise of forever bliss from a merciful God to the altar.

He was such a cutie.

I was standing in my maid of honor spot, preening (I was a proud momma, I had no regrets) and smiling at him, when I felt something funny tickle the hairs on the back of my neck.

I tore my gaze from Liam, who was staring with hyper alertness at the spot he was supposed to walk to, ignoring the flower girl beside him making a show with her ivory petals (I'd noticed during rehearsals she was very extra), and looked to the last pew at the back of the church.

It was then, my heart stopped beating.

Darius stood there, looking a thousand ways of fine in a dark suit, his gaze riveted to his son.

Oh God.

Oh shizzle.

Oh *shizzlesticks* times a *hundred*.

I'd been right, he hadn't been able to stay away from me. He showed at my house, always when Liam was spending the night with his grandparents or Auntie Lena, so he could spend the night with me.

And I'd been right again, he couldn't hack it.

He had to see his boy.

I'd told him Toni was getting married and she'd asked Liam to play his part. He'd agreed, because he loved his Aunt Toni, he loved his Uncle Tony, and "I'm gonna look awesome in a tux" (his words).

And Darius hadn't been able to stay away.

Helpless, I stood at the front, watching the emotions wash over my man's face. Pride. Love. Desolation. Pain.

My hand tightened on my bouquet as my throat constricted.

His gaze shifted to me, and I forced a swallow.

Because all that was left was the pain.

I ripped my gaze from his to watch our son walk to where he was supposed to stand, in front of Tony's best man.

I held a hand out to the flower girl, and she took it and stood in front of me.

Then my eyes went back to Darius, to see he was gone. I moved them to the doors of the sanctuary just in time to see him disappear.

But I had no chance to do anything.

Because Toni was next.

And I'd told no lies.

Her very soon-to-be husband lost it when he clapped eyes on the beauty that was his bride.

It was everything.

\* \* \* \*

When I got home that night, I knew he was there, and not just because Mom and Dad had left the reception early, taking Liam with them to spend the night at theirs, so I could party with my friend on her big day.

So, after I locked the door behind me, I dropped my clutch on the table in the front hall and headed up the stairs without taking off my shoes, even if my feet were killing me.

The light in my room was on.

And when I hit the door, I saw Darius, still in his suit trousers, but his jacket and tie were gone. He was sitting at the side of the bed.

I went right to him.

He opened his legs, and I stopped between them.

He put his hands to my hips and stared at my stomach.

Then he face planted there.

I put my hands on his head.

"Baby," I whispered.

"Fucked up." His voice was muffled by material. "Again."

"I wouldn't have been able to stay away either," I said.

He tipped his head back, and my breath stopped at the expression on his face.

"You did so good," he said softly. "I'm so proud of you. You did so good, baby. He's perfect. *Perfect.*"

I gave him a soft smile. "You had a hand in that."

He shook his head.

I caught it in my hands. "Stop it. You did."

"I need to get out of your life."

No.

Nonononono.

I tried to push him back so I could climb on.

He resisted, and this time he meant it, I knew, because he didn't budge.

"This was a mistake. You're better off without me," he declared.

"Let me be the judge of that."

"You don't get it."

"Then tell me."

"I'm not a good guy."

"I think I should be the judge of that too."

"I'm no father."

"How do you know? You haven't tried. But just to say, we want for nothing. You don't forget birthdays. You don't—"

"That's all bullshit," he clipped. "He took that seriously today."

I was confused.

"What?"

"Liam. It was important, what he did today. You know why?"

"Because he's a smart kid, and he soaks things up, and because of that, he understood how important today was to his Aunt Toni."

"No. Because the only man in his life is his Uncle Tony and he wanted to stand up for him."

Oh boy.

"Darius—"

"You can't deny it. It's true."

"He's not the only man in his life. Dad is in his life." I tried to take the heavy out of our conversation and quipped, "Lena's revolving door of boyfriends are in his life."

"Your father is a good man. I looked into him, and Tony's a good guy."

Interesting.

I tipped my head to the side. "You looked into him?"

"He's in your life, Liam's, so yeah. I looked into him."

"So he's not a secret agent?"

Darius's brows drew together. "What?"

I flipped out a hand. "Toni. She freaked out before the ceremony, worried she was getting into a *True Lies* situation."

"Was heading into the church, saw her Julia Roberts impression," he murmured. "Wondered what that was about."

"That's what it was about."

"She's a sneaky one, baby. She's crazier than you. Crazier than even Lena. She just knows how to hide it."

I started laughing, because I already knew this. He hadn't seen her version of incognito at his aunt's bar.

His fingers still at my hips dug in. "This is fucked up, what we're doing."

"But it works," I asserted.

He stared up at me.

"It might not be normal, but it's what you need," I stated.

That did it.

He couldn't have me doing that for him.

I should have known.

He made a move to stand.

I shifted my hands to his shoulders and put all my weight into keeping him where he was.

He gave up pushing, I knew, because he knew I didn't want him to.

"I'm not asking for that from you," he growled.

"You don't have to ask."

"You're wasting your life on me."

"We disagree on that, so much, I'm not discussing it. I know what I'm doing."

"Malia—"

"Darius, you were right."

His expression turned guarded. "About what?"

"I didn't try hard enough to tell you I was pregnant."

He shook his head. Firmly.

"Don't buy my shit, babe. I was full of it, lashing out."

"You were correct in everything you said. I was young and flipped out and feeling a lot of feelings, about me, for you, what happened with your dad."

He flinched.

Oh yes.

As suspected, he hadn't worked through the pain of losing his dad.

That was not for now.

I kept at him about what was for now.

"I made the wrong decision. If I couldn't get to you, I should have told Miss Dorothea. She would have gotten to you."

"What I made of myself isn't about what you didn't tell me."

"I'm not taking on what you made of yourself, even though I don't know what that is. I just know *you*. And I messed up. It's a mistake I'm not going to make again."

"We're never going to be a happy family."

*We'll see*, I did not say.

He saw it anyway, which was why he said, "I'm wrong. Toni isn't crazier than you. You are definitely the craziest of that crew."

"Whatever," I muttered.

Suddenly, he jerked my skirt up and I quelled a smile because I thought I was getting somewhere, especially when he yanked me to straddling his lap.

But we weren't going where I thought we were going.

I knew that when he said, "This is a dangerous game you're playin'."

"I'm not playing a game," I lied.

I so was.

The long game.

And I was in it to win it.

"I'm warnin' you, there's gonna be a time when I'm gonna have to set you aside. For your own good. For Liam's. And when I do, there won't be any going back."

"We'll see," I murmured.

"Yeah, we will," he murmured back, but his fingers belied his words because they went to my zipper. "Trust Toni to put you in sexy bridesmaids' dresses to make sure you all get laid."

"Am I getting laid?" I asked.

My zipper came down.

I smiled at him.

His eyes fixed on my mouth as his lips whispered, "Minx."

"You bet your bottom."

Those beautiful browns came up to mine. "Bottom?"

"I can't curse. Liam told his teacher he wasn't picking up the damned crayons other kids didn't put away, and I had to go to the school for a chat."

I worried, since his mood was mercurial anytime I brought up our son, how he'd react to that.

But he chuckled.

So I relaxed.

He also bunched the fabric of my dress at the hips, then up, and *boom*, it was gone.

He slid his hands up my ribs, watching their progress as they made their way to my lacy, black strapless bra.

I bit my lip, feeling it.

"I don't wanna fuck you up," he told my midriff.

"I know what I'm doing."

I cried out as he jerked me forward while falling back then rolled us so he was on top.

"No you don't," he said fiercely. "But I'm goddamned weak, and you're beautiful, and the only good thing in my life, and I can't seem to let you go."

Score one for me.

I made a noise that sounded like a purr.

His pupils immediately dilated.

Okay, *now* we were getting somewhere.

I slid a hand over his hip and in, cupping his hardness.

He growled.

Definitely getting somewhere.

"Am I getting laid, or what?"

Darius let it go and his grin was so wolfish, I felt in my vajayjay.

Then I got laid.

# Chapter Six

*Blinders*

## Rock Chick Rewind

*Still some time ago, but now even less...*

Toni threw herself in the lawn chair beside me, doing this without sloshing even a drop out of her mojito.

The girl was good.

"I am not feeling this," she declared, gaze aimed across my parents' backyard to Lena and her new fiancé, Kenneth.

"Hmm..." I replied.

She turned her head to me, lifting her drink to her mouth, but before taking a sip, said under her breath, "Darius get the skinny on him yet?"

"He's not a fan," I said under mine.

"Is that an understatement?" she asked.

I gave her big eyes.

"Shit," she said, turning back to Lena draped on Kenneth. "He got anything like those photos he got on Michael?"

"He's working on it."

"You know, Tony is a construction foreman," she told me something I did, indeed, know.

I confirmed I knew it and drew it out. "Yeeessss."

"He's not a master sleuth. He can't keep coming up with the dirty on Lena's boys. She's gonna start thinking it's weird."

"It only happened that once."

"We pinned nasty pictures on him knowing someone who knew someone who could look into things, which wasn't a total lie, since he knows you, and you know Darius. And you know, Denver's a big city, but it's also a small town. To her, Darius was your past, but everyone knows

Eddie Chavez is a cop, now he's made detective, and it wouldn't be hard to put those two together to get what you need to keep your sister from making shit decisions about the men she lets in her bed."

Uh-oh.

She'd been keeping my secret for a long time now.

Years.

And I had a feeling she was getting fed up with it.

"I won't pin this one on Tony."

"You need to tell Lena what's going on with Darius."

"*Are you high?*" I screeched.

Everyone looked at me.

I hid behind my mojito.

Toni let it die down before she said low, "I think more, you need to figure out what's going on with *you* and Darius."

I hated to admit it.

But she wasn't wrong.

I knew it'd take patience, but this was crazy.

And nothing I was doing was working.

Sure, we had great sex that never got old because it could be a month, even two, between times we could get together.

And no, it wasn't just sex. We talked. He ate up everything I could tell him about Liam like my words were mana from heaven. He asked about my new job at the law firm now that I'd finished my degree and landed a position as a paralegal. He asked about Mom, Dad, Lena, Toni.

He did not talk about himself.

He was a master at avoiding it.

Half the time, I was kissing him goodbye before I realized I'd had him again and gotten nowhere.

Liam was now nine. Toni and Tony had gotten pregnant and had a baby girl. Lena had been through five new guys before she latched onto this one.

And although I had Darius's number, and I texted him every day, and spoke to him just because on occasion, and he always took my calls and never left my texts hanging, we were no closer to the important things.

Like telling his family he had a child.

Like telling my family he was in my life.

Like introducing him to his son.

Oh sure, I had excuses.

First, it was having a kid and studying for my degree and having a full-time job, and those were all good excuses.

Then, it was my kid growing up and getting into activities, while I was still studying for my degree and having a full-time job while shuffling him to peewee football and junior basketball and piano lessons (don't ask me, my mom made us do it, Liam hated it, but we both promised her two years, and he was closing in on the end of year two, so we just had stick it out).

Then it was interning, and a full-time job, and a kid, and activities. Then having a new job and needing to put in the hours, which were extensive, to make myself part of the team.

In the mix of all that was keeping a house, groceries in the cupboards, good, cooked food on the table, time with my boy and his homework, laundry, the oil needing changed on the car, yadda, yadda, yadda.

I mean, life was life. It was full. Things got away from you.

But this was getting ridiculous.

"They're worried," Toni said.

I mentally shook myself out of my thoughts and asked, "Who's worried?"

"Your mom and dad," she said, eyes across the way on her hubby, who had little Talia on his hip.

"Worried about what?"

She looked to me. "That you don't date. That you work and hang with Liam. Hang with Tony and me. Hang with Lena. And go home alone. And you do it like it's all good for you, when they don't know it *is* all good, because the man you love is in your life in a super weird way, but still, he's in it. And I gotta say, they know you took a big pay bump when you got your new job, but you were living pretty large on a court reporter's salary, and they aren't dumb."

Oh boy.

She kept at me.

"Then you put the money down on that new build in Stapleton, *whomp!* Down payment on a brand-new house in a cushy development, and you didn't even blink."

Maybe I hadn't been as smart as I should have been about using Darius's support to take care of Liam and me.

On the one hand, if I'd made us go without to keep it from them, Darius would lose his mind.

On the other hand, no way was I going to accumulate tens of thousands of dollars in my panties drawer and make my boy go without.

Okay, so maybe that was the same hand.

But I probably should have pretended I won the lottery or something.

"I think they've figured it out," she muttered.

"Oh my God," I whispered, horrified. "You think they have?"

Slowly, she turned her head to face me. "I respect them, Malia. And I've been lying to them by omission for years."

I bit my lip.

"I love you," she went on. "And I gotta trust you know what you're doing, but something's going to break on this, and your family is good people. They don't deserve this deception."

I felt badly, I truly did.

But I knew what I was doing.

I hoped.

"I bought a nanny cam," I told her.

"Say again?" she asked.

"I bought a nanny cam. It's Eddie who breaks in and gives me the money."

"Whoa," she said.

"I left a note for him last time and told him to stop breaking in and stay for a beer. He wrote back, 'We'll see.'"

Toni's gaze was far away, keeping company with her thoughts. "Love my man, but I could do a beer with Eddie."

Yeah, via the nanny cam, I learned he just got better with age.

But we needed to focus.

"I can tell them that," I suggested. "If I tell them, they'll know what I know. It's from Darius. And maybe, when the time comes, they won't...have a problem with him."

"When the time comes for what?"

"When the time comes we can be a family."

A guard slammed down on her face, but her mouth didn't quit moving.

"Are you holding out for that, sis? Because, sure, I can see that. You love the guy. But also, no. He's got it made. He comes and gets his business, then he goes, no strings, no commitments."

Oh no.

Now I was getting mad at Toni.

Or maybe I was getting mad at the situation because it was dragging on forever.

But still, I was getting mad at Toni.

"You don't know how it is."

"Do you?"

That was the ten-million-dollar question.

I looked away and took a sip of my mojito.

"Unh-hunh," she mumbled.

"That envelope I get every month doesn't say no strings, no commitments," I sniped.

She got to the meat of it.

"It also doesn't say *Dad*," she told me. "He's even pulling away from Tony, have you noticed?"

I had.

Liam and Tony were tight, now it was like…not like he didn't love his Uncle Tony, just like he didn't need him like he used to.

Like he was getting accustomed to it being him and me and that was going to be all he had.

I looked around the backyard, trying to locate my son.

When I didn't see him, I knew where he was.

In the front drive, shooting hoops at the basketball goal Dad had mounted for him.

Shooting hoops alone.

I stood, saying, "I need to find my son."

Toni caught my hand. I looked down at her.

"I'm worried too," she said. "You were a teen mom, lost, but not alone. You found your way. Now you're twenty-six, living your life for a man who shows in your bedroom one night every couple of months for nookie with no promises." She shook her head and squeezed my hand before I could say anything I'd regret. "No, I'm not being cruel, I'm being real, because I'm worried. Don't say anything and don't get mad. Just think about what I had to say."

"I'll think about what you had to say," I said between my teeth.

She gave my hand a squeeze and let go. "That's all I ask."

I took off, trying not to feel all I was feeling, something that was getting tired.

Because I'd been feeling it now for years, along with putting in the effort not to feel it.

Mom and Dad were worried, I shouldn't be surprised.

Toni too, also not a surprise.

But I was too.

Because I'd had patience.

And it wasn't working.

I heard the dribble of the basketball before I made it to the front, the bang of it hitting the backboard, more dribbling.

When I got there, I saw my son setting up for a shot, and even with my thoughts in turmoil, my heart hurting—because if I allowed myself to admit it (and I wasn't there yet), I knew Toni was right, something had to give with Darius—I loved that even at Lena and Kenneth's engagement party, Dad wouldn't let anyone park in the driveway so Liam could shoot hoops.

"Hey," I called.

"Hey," he called back and let fly.

It whiffed the net.

I winced.

He needed to be taller, stronger, keep practicing, he'd get there.

Liam didn't show any emotion to the whiff. He just went after the ball and kept dribbling.

"I bet Tony would play horse with you if you asked," I suggested.

"Nah, he's got Talia with him," Liam answered, stopped, planted his feet and let fly.

It hit the hoop and bounced to the side.

Damn.

He went after the ball.

"I could confiscate Talia, no skin off my nose," I said.

Liam grinned while dribbling. "You spoil her more than her own momma does."

"That's what aunties are for," I said, bending to put my drink in the grass. I straightened. "Throw it here."

He stopped, tossed the ball to me, and I caught it.

I dribbled twice, set up, then tossed the ball. And in a dress and heels, I didn't do too badly, though it flew clean over the hoop from side to side, missing it altogether.

Liam chased after it.

"Want it again?" he asked after he nabbed it.

Out here, alone, shooting hoops.

My boy with no daddy.

"Is it upsetting to you?" I asked. "Talia, I mean. That Tony has his little girl now?"

Liam tipped his head to the side. "Naw. Why would it?"

"I think maybe he misses you a little bit," I shared.

His eyes wandered to the side of the house. "Ya think?"

"Heads up," I warned, then with two hands, I passed the ball hard. No problems, he caught it. "There are things you can't do with baby girls." I jerked my chin to the hoop. "And your granddad didn't put this up for you to hog it."

Liam grinned at me.

I then jerked my head to the side yard. "Go, ask one of them to hang with you."

"You sure?"

"Absolutely. I know for a fact your grandfather would kill for an excuse to get away from an engagement party he didn't want to have in the first place. He thinks Kenneth is touched."

Another grin, this one bigger, because Liam agreed about the touched part, then with ball under his arm, he dashed off.

This spoke volumes.

My boy, he liked his alone times. I'd noticed it more and more when he started to get older. He was just one of those people who were good in their own company. And he was like his mom. A reader.

Even so, he had those times where he wanted to be social.

But what boys liked to do together wasn't an awful lot like what girls liked to do, especially grown-up girls. I couldn't mix him a mojito and dish about Lena's boyfriends with him.

He needed a man in his life.

He needed his father.

And again, that was not for now, and I was getting fed up with the *not for nows*.

But that wasn't for now either.

I followed my son, and fast, because I had to be there to take Talia if he picked Tony first, because Tony doted on his daughter, and he loved Liam, but I wasn't sure he'd give her up for basketball.

Darius had been a great basketball player, though he excelled at football. Got a scholarship to Yale that was academic, but they scouted him for the team, and he'd had a place on it before he turned his back on all that when Mister Morris died.

He should be shooting hoops with his son.

But I couldn't do anything about that.

For now.

\* \* \* \*

I was in my nightie, putting lotion on my elbows, when the screen lit up on my phone sitting on the nightstand.

It said M.M.M. Calling.

When I'd programmed it in, I thought it was cute.

But now, it just reminded me not only that I could not type Darius's name into my phone, just in case someone saw it who shouldn't, but also, I couldn't type in what M.M.M. meant—My Main Man—because he was that, just no one knew it. And if they saw it, I'd have uncomfortable questions to answer that I had no answers I could give.

Questions about Darius.

And maybe among those no ones who didn't know who My Main Man was, was Darius.

I flipped the phone open and put it to my ear. "Hey."

"Hey, baby. I got nothing."

"Sorry?"

"About Lena's man. That Kenneth guy. White folk would call him a douche, and I gotta say, that works for him, but other than that, he's got nothing wrong with him."

I sat on the side of the bed, murmuring, "Damn."

"At least he's not a cheater or a low-level dealer," Darius tried to placate me.

"I guess we can count our blessings," I replied.

He chuckled.

"Okay, thanks for looking into it," I said, my tone flat.

He stopped chuckling, because he heard my tone, not that he could miss it.

"You okay?"

*No, I'm not! We're on the phone when you should be here with me and our son, so of course I'm not!* I wanted to shout.

"Worried about Lena," I kind of lied.

"That's not it."

When he said that, no clue why, but something broke in me.

"You know, Liam is pulling away from Tony."

"He is?"

Oh my God.

Was I reading him correctly?

He sounded...*happy* about that.

"That's not a good thing, Darius," I informed him.

"I didn't say it was."

"You sounded like it was."

A beat then, "Right. You're in a mood. Maybe we'll talk later."

"Easy for you to just hang up and not have to deal with anything real," I snapped.

Silence, but he didn't disconnect.

He got silence from me too, mostly because I *was* in a mood, and if I spoke, I was afraid of what I'd say.

Darius broke the silence. "Talk to me."

"About what?"

"About what's bothering you."

"How much time you got?"

"All the time you need."

I closed my eyes, clenched my fist, and dropped my head back, because...*why?*

Why, why, *why* did he have to be so good when I was so damned mad at him.

Why did he go out and discover Kenneth was a douche, putting that effort in, and he didn't play hoops with his son?

"Baby?" he called.

I opened my eyes and went for it.

What the hell, right?

I only had everything to lose.

"I need more from you."

"What? Money? Is it the new house? Are they screwing you over, pushing upgrades?"

"No, not money. *You*, Darius. I need more of *you*."

"Okay, so how do we manage that?"

I stared at my knees.

"Malia? How do we manage that?"

"I...you..."

I was having trouble speaking, mostly because I was so shocked he was giving in.

"I want more of you too, baby. It's frustrating as fuck trying to fit everything into a night every few months."

"I...really?"

Silence again, this loaded, like he was pissed.

I'd know why when he ground out, "You aren't a booty call, woman."

"I know," I whispered.

"So how do we manage that?"

"I don't know, but when I say I need more, I mean I need more of the important stuff. Not that what we do when we're together isn't important, but I need to know about you. Your life. What you spend your time doing. Who you spend it with. And Darius, Liam is going to ask.

One day, he's going to ask. It's a miracle he hasn't asked yet. And we need to have that figured out. What we're going to say when he asks about his father. And he's got a grandma and two aunties who live in the same town as him, and I think we're courting some serious future therapy for our son if we don't let him have all the things he's entitled to."

"I'll tell you, but only if you promise me he'll never know what I am."

That made me blink at my knees.

"Sorry?"

"You have to promise me."

"Darius, I can't make a promise without knowing what I'm promising."

"You're going to have to think on that, babe. Because this goes no further until you can give me that."

Fear was creeping into my veins. "What do you do?"

"Think about it, baby," he said softly, carefully. "How do I know Lena's ex was low-level?"

I turned my head sharply and said, "I'm tired. I don't want to talk about this now. We'll figure out a way we can spend some time together and talk then."

"You don't want me to run away from real, you can't either, sweetheart. I'm sorry, but it is what it is. I'll give you time to think about it, but I sense shit is coming to a head, and I've taken advantage of your denial too long. You're right. It's time to get real. And I'll make you a promise right now, when we do, whatever you decide, I'll honor it."

There was something wrong with his tone.

It sounded…

*Final.*

"You're scaring me," I whispered.

"I've been trying to do that from the beginning. You just believe in me so much, you wouldn't let it penetrate. I'll tell you, I thought I'd feel relief when you finally got it. But that's not what I feel. I feel the same way you feel. Except a lot worse."

"Darius—"

"Take the blinders off, Malia, think about it and call me. We'll talk."

Oh God.

"I love you," I blurted.

"I know," he said softly, gently, and uneasily. "And that scares me most of all."

I didn't know what to say, so I said nothing.

"Think, baby, and we'll talk," he urged, now it was just soft and gentle. "Try to sleep good."

"You too."

"Later."

"'Bye, Darius."

I said it and he disconnected.

I just didn't know when he disconnected, he was going to think too.

Think and act on what he thought.

Think and, to protect me, to protect our son, take the decision out of my hands.

So that goodbye was going to last a whole lot longer than I could ever imagine.

# Chapter Seven

*He's Always Been Darius*

## Rock Chick Rewind

*Also some time ago, but getting closer and closer to now…*

I sat across from my son at our table in the breakfast nook off the kitchen.

It was Saturday. That day, we were going to the new build to have a look at the progress and make some final decisions about what we wanted in the house.

It was also exactly six months since that phone call with Darius.

He no longer replied to my texts or picked up the phone, but the envelopes were still on my counter every month.

He'd made the decision for me, him, all of us.

Since then, I'd run the gamut of emotions. Anger, first. Fear, next (mixed with liberal doses of anger). Back to anger (of course). Resignation (also mixed with anger) after that.

Finally, acceptance.

And sadness.

"You okay, Mom?" Liam asked, watching me and shoveling pancakes into his mouth.

I tried to hide it, I really did.

I knew with how closely he was watching me, I'd failed at hiding it.

"Can we talk about something important?" I asked.

He swallowed. "Sure."

Was this right, what I was going to do?

Or was this about me and finding my way back to Darius, using my son as an excuse to do it?

No, it wasn't about me.

This was right.

He should know.

"You've never asked…about your dad."

He squirmed in his seat and looked out the window, plate of pancakes forgotten.

He was a growing boy. I'd given him three large, fluffy buttermilk pancakes and four strips of bacon. Grown men would have trouble putting away that much food. He'd score through all that, no problem.

"Liam?"

He looked back at me.

"No," he confirmed he'd never asked.

"Do you want to know?"

"Not if it hurts you."

Oh God.

My son.

I felt tears hit my eyes. "I loved him very much. I still love him very much."

"Mom—"

"You need to know that. He loved me very much too."

*And he loves you very much too*, I could not say, because he'd ask a question to which he was entitled to an answer, that being if he did, why he wasn't around.

And I didn't have that answer.

"We don't have to talk about this," Liam told me.

"I need you to know that."

"Okay," he said hurriedly. "I know."

"He lost his dad."

Liam straightened, his attention perking up. "He did? Like, his dad died?"

I nodded. "He was really close with his dad. He loved him. Admired him. It broke him."

Liam said nothing.

"I didn't…I didn't tell him about you," I admitted. "When I found out you were in my belly."

He turned his head and gave me the side eye.

"I tried," I assured him. "But honestly, not hard enough. He was dealing with big things. I was young. I made a decision. It was a mistake. He was upset with me when he found out I had you and he didn't know."

"It's okay. I got you, and Grandpop, and Grandmoms, and Auntie Lena, Auntie Toni, Uncle Tony and—"

"He would be here if he felt he could."

Liam looked out the window again, but this time, when he did it, I felt my small hairs stand on end.

Because this time, it wasn't avoidance.

It was cagey.

And what I'd said begged the question, why couldn't his father be here?

But Liam didn't ask that question.

"Liam?"

He straightened up again and looked at me.

I spoke. "I can't explain why he can't be here because I don't understand it myself. But it's something important to him. He gives us money. We wouldn't have," I threw out a hand lamely, "pretty much most of what we have if he didn't look out for us."

"A man's gotta do what a man's gotta do," he muttered.

I stared at him.

Was that it?

*A man's gotta do what a man's gotta do.*

"He doesn't know I know he gives us the money," I persevered. "I mean, I think he *knows*, but he doesn't want us to *know*."

Liam was again silent.

"But he, um...gives us a lot of money."

"Good. Everybody needs money."

"Do you want me to try to contact him, tell him you want to meet him?" I offered.

He shrugged and said, "Naw, I'm good."

Something wasn't right here, and it wasn't what seemed to be wrong on the face of it.

"Fathers are kinda important to little boys," I said carefully.

He forked into his pancakes. "Then it's good I got a daddy who takes care of us with money. I got friends whose daddies don't do anything."

I knew that to be sad, but very true.

"Do you have any questions?" I asked.

He shook his head and stuffed pancakes into his mouth.

This was too easy.

"Liam, honey, look at me."

He looked at me.

"If you ever have any questions—"

"I'll ask," he said with his mouth full.

"Don't talk with food in your mouth, baby," I admonished gently.

He nodded and turned back to his plate.

I guessed it was that easy.

Even so, I didn't like it.

I'd have to keep an eye.

Something I did for a long time.

And as I did that, it seemed it was what it was.

Just that easy.

* * * *

"No, you got to taste. Don't just throw the salt in. You gotta see how much it needs first," I heard Toni say to Liam.

They were in the kitchen, cooking.

I didn't know what they were making, it was a surprise.

I just knew it was going to be good.

Tony strolled to where I was sitting on their couch in their living room and handed me a fresh glass of wine.

"Thanks," I murmured, taking it.

He then sat down beside me in the couch.

*Right* beside me.

I froze, seeing as Tony had never done anything like this in all the years I'd known him, and I'd be very disappointed if this was what it seemed like it was going to be.

I gave him the side eye.

"Been piecin' shit together for years," he said low.

Hovering on the precipice of disappointment was gone, now I was confused.

"Toni doesn't want me to tell you. But I disagree," he declared. "You should know."

Right.

Now I was bracing.

"Know what?" I asked.

"Gonna preface this by saying, the war on drugs is bullshit, and we both know why."

We sure did.

What I didn't know was what he had to preface by saying that.

"Alcohol can fuck a family up. Chocolate and trans-fat can fuck a body up. The weight loss industry is making billions by fucking with people's heads. No one's locking anyone up for pushing that shit."

"Agreed," I said slowly.

"This is not to say I condone breaking the law. Condone doing the shit you gotta do to live that life."

I turned to him and started, "Tony—"

"What I can say is, my wife, my daughter, I'd do anything not only to keep them covered, but to give them more. To give them a leg up in life. To zero out the needs list and keep the want list low, so they know their man and their daddy worked his ass off to give them a good life."

Oh God.

My heart started hammering in my chest.

"Leon Jackson, he's an Ike," he announced.

Leon Jackson, Shirleen's husband, Darius's uncle.

"An Ike?" I whispered.

"As in Ike and Tina."

My stomach sunk.

"Oh God." I said it out loud this time.

"Darius Tucker is serious business. Leon, he's the kingpin, but even he's piss-scared of his nephew. I don't think it stops it for Leon's wife, but I know he doesn't put her in the hospital anymore."

I closed my eyes and dropped my head.

Yes, even in whatever he was involved in, Darius was Darius.

Protector.

Champion.

Good guy.

"Leon doesn't know about you and Liam."

I opened my eyes and looked back to him.

"If he did, he'd have something to use to control Darius."

Darius had said this same thing.

"But it's more," Tony went on. "You two would be targets if he let it be known you were who you are. I know it's been a while since he broke things off with you."

It had been a while.

Over two years.

"But I understand why he does it," he continued. "And Toni doesn't agree, but I think you should know what there is to know so you can maybe find your way to understand it too."

"He's protecting us," I whispered.

"Yeah," he said.

"He's a drug dealer." I was still whispering.

"Yeah," he grunted.

"He had a scholarship to Yale," I told him.

"Yeah. And it takes four years to get through college, and even longer to get sorted in life. And he might have had a scholarship, but his dad hadn't been allowed to live a long enough life to set up his family like they needed if he wasn't around. They didn't have the money to send him to Yale, because you can have a full ride, but it still takes money to be across the country at a university. They also didn't have the money to continue to live the life they'd been living. Darius had to step up. Darius had to look after his mom and sisters. He was a teenager. He got offered what he thought was an easy way to do that, and he took it. I don't blame him. Straight up, in that situation, I can see myself doing the same damned thing."

Straight up, I could too. Tony. Me. Anybody, really.

You didn't have the luxury of defending the high ground when food needed to be put on the table.

I looked away and took a sip of my wine.

"Lee Nightingale got honorably discharged. He's back in town."

My head whipped around to him.

"And Eddie Chavez is a maverick cop, but he gets the job done better than nearly everyone. It's all rumors, but those rumors say he's got an inside guy. This puts Darius out there, but it's him doin' the right thing."

"They're trying to pull him out," I breathed.

"They're trying to remind him who he really is. Lee in town again, I don't think it's gonna take very long."

Oh. My. *God*.

"What I'm sayin' is, don't lose hope, Malia. Let the man do what he's gotta do. If I had to steer clear of Toni and Talia, it'd kill me. But if it meant it kept them safe, I'd suffer a thousand deaths. It's killing him, but he still isn't dead. You get me?"

I nodded.

I got him.

He took me in, decided I did indeed get him, then he got up and moved to the armchair.

After he settled in, he shouted, "When's dinner? I'm hungry!"

Talia toddled out and shouted back, "Daddy!"

Tony grinned and winked at me.

I didn't have it in me to smile back.

I was holding on to hope.

With everything I had.

* * * *

I opened my front door and stopped dead.

Someone was in the house.

And I could smell…

Paint.

My heart tripping in my chest, my mind whirring, I forgot all about grabbing the book Liam called to tell me he forgot for school and marched up the stairs, straight to my son's room.

They knew I was there. I knew it when I stood in the doorway and stared at them staring at me.

Darius, Lee and Eddie.

My son's Transformer décor was in boxes in the hallway. His furniture had plastic over it. The walls were mostly painted a pretty, but masculine, blue. And there was a plethora of Target and Dillard's bags outside, not to mention a queen mattress resting up against the wall and a new, dismantled bedframe still bound in its delivery protective wrap leaned against it.

Where Liam's twin bed was, I didn't know. Just his dresser and desk were under the plastic wrap.

I ignored Eddie and Lee, looked to Darius, and ordered, "My room. Now."

I also ignored Eddie and Lee glancing at each other, lips quirking.

I marched to my bedroom.

I stood, holding the door, until Darius walked through it.

I slammed it behind him.

"So, five years, you've still been letting yourself in and checking things out," I said with false calm.

"Malia, he's growing up, and he's got a little kid room. He's gotta have a growing man's room."

"So you decided just to show up with your buds and make that happen without speaking to me?"

"It's been a while," he said cautiously, "so I see I gotta remind you that me stayin' away—"

"Fuck that!" I shouted.

His brows drew low. "Calm down," he growled.

"Fuck calm too," I retorted. "You can't waltz in here and give your boy everything he wants—"

"Wrong," he bit off and stabbed a finger at the wall through which, beyond the guest bedroom and the upstairs bathroom was our son's room. "Seein' as that's what I'm doing right fuckin' now."

"You made the decision it was nothing but envelopes and cash and no promises," I reminded him. "That wasn't me."

"It was the hardest decision I've made in my goddamned life."

"Seems like it was easy to me."

"Yeah?" he grunted, eyes flashing with rage.

"Yeah," I replied fake easily, swinging a hand out in front of me for good measure, then settling it on my hip.

Darius watched my hand move, then his eyes sliced to my face.

I glared at him.

He scowled at me.

For the life of me, I couldn't say who made the first move.

Though, I thought it was the both of us.

I went at him.

He came at me.

He was bigger, stronger. He had me up against the wall and then we were kissing and tearing at each other's clothes.

I couldn't tell you who gave up on the clothes-tearing thing first either, but I again thought it was the both of us.

He'd yanked up my skirt and pulled down my panties.

I stepped out of them at the same time I unzipped his jeans.

My blouse was half unbuttoned and his tee was misshapen, but we left them as they were.

I reached in, pulled him out and stroked…*long* and *tight.*

He groaned and I gasped when he lifted me up.

He pinned me to the wall then drilled into me.

My head flew back and hit wall.

*Yes.*

He thrust and grunted, "Mouth, baby."

I bent my neck, gave him my mouth, and wrapped him up with my arms and legs and held tight as Darius fucked me into the wall.

Eventually, all he was giving me overwhelmed me, and I tore my mouth from his.

"Harder," I begged.

"Can't," he gritted.

"*Harder,*" I demanded.

"Can't, baby. I'm close."

"Har—"

I cut myself off, whimpering and moaning through a sharp, sweet, long, beautiful orgasm. He went harder, faster, drawing out my climax, then he tucked his face in my neck and groaned, long and low.

I had my cheek against his temple, was fiddling with one of his short twists in my fingers and taking him in. His spicy, earthy smell. His strength surrounding me. His big cock still buried deep.

He moved his head so his lips were at my ear.

"He needs a growing man's room," he whispered there.

"Okay," I replied.

His arms around me got tight. "Fuck, I miss you."

I closed my eyes, and it was me who shoved my face in his neck.

It took me a second to build up the courage, but I did it and then it was also my turn to put my lips to his ear.

"Whenever you're ready, however long it takes, we're waiting for you."

"Don't," he grunted, the word hoarse, raw.

"Baby, you're giving him the room he's been begging me for. You don't think it's true. But you prove it. Over and over again. You're worth waiting for."

He pulled me off him, dropped me to my feet but held me to the wall until my legs were steady under me.

He also tugged down my skirt.

Only when I was standing on my own power did he step back and tuck himself away.

He didn't look at me.

"I know what you do," I shared.

His head snapped up and his gaze pierced mine.

"And I don't like it," I said. "But I understand why you do it. And we'll be waiting for when you're done doing that too."

He said nothing, just stood there looking into my eyes.

I said nothing more either, just stood there, drinking in the man I adored.

Then he made a move to go.

When he had his hand on the doorknob, I called out, "I love you."

He turned to me then and said, "You're beautiful. You're crazy. You're too damned loyal. And you're a huge pain in my ass."

I smiled at him.

He shook his head.

And then he was gone.

\* \* \* \*

It wasn't long after the incident against the wall in my bedroom when I found myself in the underground parking of an office building on 15th Street in LoDo.

I knew he showed because the cameras I saw everywhere caught me leaning against the door of my car and someone at Nightingale Investigations headquarters told him I was there.

Nightingale Investigations being Lee Nightingale's private detective agency.

Where Darius now worked.

This was not something Darius told me.

Oh no.

It was something Tony shared with me, seeing as he was surprised Darius had turned his back on the life that had kept him away from me and our son, and we were not together.

One could say, when I learned this, I was surprised too.

But that was only a very small part of what learning this knowledge made me feel.

Hence, why I was standing right there.

But I didn't move when he showed.

I didn't because I was drowning in sorrow, in disappointment. So much, I didn't even have it in me to feel rage.

He stopped in front of me.

"Malia," he greeted.

"You're out," I stated flatly.

"Malia—"

"You got out, you've been out for a while, and you didn't come to us."

"You don't understand."

"No, I don't. And that's tired, Darius Tucker. And you know it."

"You think my boy wants an ex-drug dealer as his dad?"

He asked that, and he wasn't done talking.

But I was done listening.

"I think it's clear you don't have the balls to find out."

His head jerked like I'd slapped him.

But…

Fuck that.

It was official.

It had been a good run.

But I was clean out of patience.

I said what I had to say.

I got in my car, started it up and drove away.

Darius, no surprise, didn't try to stop me.

* * * *

"Someone kill me," I said to myself as I drove up my driveway and saw Lee Nightingale and Eddie Chavez sitting in the cute, wicker chairs on my front porch.

I'd already hit the remote, so I drove right into the garage.

I then hit the remote to close the door, but I knew this wasn't something I could avoid.

So I didn't.

I went into the house, dropped my bag and attaché, and no matter that I was dying to kick them off, I didn't take off my pumps, because going up against those two, I'd need my height, even if it came in a three-inch stiletto heel and they'd both still tower over me. So I kept them on and headed to the front door to let them in.

I said nothing, just walked to the kitchen and put the island between them and me.

They followed me but barely came into the room.

I'd seen the newspaper articles. I'd bought but hadn't read the book.

I knew they were semi-famous. Also that Lee and Indy had finally gotten together (and I was glad for both of them) and Eddie had found his own woman, a lady named Jet.

But I didn't figure they were there to catch up.

I started it.

"I know why you're here."

"No, you don't," Eddie replied.

"He had chance after chance," I informed him.

"No offense, Malia, but this isn't about you. It isn't about Darius. It's about Liam," Lee reminded me.

That shut me up.

"He's nearly grown now. He's a smart kid. And he can make a mature decision," Lee said.

"He's sixteen," I pointed out.

"You got pregnant with him at sixteen, decided to keep him and…" he looked around, and really needed to say no more.

Yes, I had Darius's help, but even if I hadn't, we'd have been just fine.

Because I'd made my decision determined to be a good momma and give my son a good life.

And with the help of loving family and friends, I'd done that.

But I'd decided it at sixteen.

"I've already asked him if he wants to meet his dad," I told them.

"When?" Eddie asked.

I bit my lip.

Eddie sighed and quietly urged, "Ask him again."

I opened my mouth.

But Eddie beat me to it.

"He won't forgive himself. For the decisions he made. The things he's done. He's buried deep under that shit. He left that life behind, and it wasn't easy, extricating himself from all that. But he did it. Though, he's still mired in it. He needs forgiveness. He needs redemption."

"He needs to be reminded that he was always who his father raised him to be," Lee put in. "He made some shit decisions and did some shady things. But he's always been Darius."

*He's always been Darius.*

I held no hope for me. I was thirty-three years old, and I'd given the last seventeen years of my life to a ghost.

But I was also a mother.

And if I could give my boy what he deserved to have in this life, I was going to do it.

"I'll talk to Liam."

Eddie's dimple popped out.

Lee smiled the famous Lee Nightingale smile.

# Chapter Eight

*You Killed It. Dead.*

*Now…*

We'd been informed we could go in and see him.

And we were right outside his hospital room door.

I was anxious to get in there.

I was anxious about a lot of things. How Liam was going to react. Dorothea's new knowledge, sixteen years late. If there was going to be any lasting effects of Darius's head trauma.

I mean, a tire iron?

Bile filled my mouth.

Liam's fingers curled around my forearm.

I stopped and looked at him, saw the expression on his face and twisted my arm so he'd let me go, but only so I could take his hand.

"I know this is going to be hard," I started.

"Mom—"

"And we'll have a lot of chats, on your time, on your schedule at processing things."

"Mom, listen—"

"But now we have to—"

"Mom…*shit*," he hissed and looked away.

I got closer and held his hand tighter and decided, in the current circumstances, not to give him guff about his language.

"Baby, I know this is hard and confusing and—"

He looked back at me. "Mom. Dad and I've been hanging since I was seven years old."

I stood solid and immobile for a moment.

Then my head exploded.

* * * *

It was dark when he finally opened his eyes.

And as luck would have it (for me, not for Darius), I was alone with him in his room.

He turned his head, winced, and my heart contracted, but I stood strong.

No, I was sitting.

So I sat strong.

He looked at me and there was confusion, then softness.

"Baby," he whispered, and there was a rasp in his voice.

I felt that rasp in the heart of me.

Ugh.

"Ally's all right," I told him.

"Good," he murmured, still raspy.

"Do you need water?" I asked.

He was just awake after getting a tire iron to the head, two gunshot wounds to his thighs, a stab wound to boot, but he'd lived a certain life, so he shook off the stupor and was pretty damned alert as he studied me and nodded.

I got up and used the little plastic pitcher to half fill a little plastic cup with water then I put it to his mouth.

His hand came up, fingers curling around mine as he pushed up a bit in bed, again wincing, and on his own steam took the cup from me and sipped the water.

"The bed lifts up, it's one of those buttons," I told him. "You gonna do that yourself too, or do you want me to do it?"

He was still studying me, guardedly, even as he took another sip.

Then he nodded. "You."

I nabbed the control, figured out which button and pressed it.

"Tell me when," I said to the control.

The bed whirred.

"When."

I stopped pressing and dropped the control.

I returned my attention to him.

"Where's Liam?" he asked.

"With Toni and Tony, seeing as today, I disowned my mother, father and Lena."

"Baby," he whispered, but his mouth was twitching.

Fury boiled in my veins.

"Are you being serious right now?" I asked, my voice dangerous, my eyes locked on his gorgeous, full lips.

"Maybe when I'm not in a hospital bed with a caved-in head I can explain this to you," he said.

My eyes darted to his.

"Explain what?" I asked. "How you, for the last nine years, colluded with my sister, and then my mother and father, to be a part of our son's life, and you didn't tell me?"

"Lena caught me watching him on the playground one day."

"I know."

"She got up in my shit."

"You've been unconscious for a while, Darius, and cell phone technology was invented before you took that hit for Ally. I've had a few conversations since then." I leaned slightly toward him. "*Heated* ones."

His lips twitched again.

Of all the—!

"This isn't funny," I snapped.

"Maybe you'll get there one day," he murmured.

A tire iron, two bullets and a knife didn't kill him.

But I was going to.

"Taking us back, I know that too," I declared. "About Lena getting up in your shit. About you two striking a deal. About how she eventually roped my parents in. Even about the fact that when Miss Dorothea saw us in the waiting room of this very hospital and gasped, she didn't gasp because she didn't know Liam existed. She gasped because you were in surgery when it was all gonna come out that all of you all," I whirled a finger in the air, "were playing me *behind my back*." My voice was rising when I finished, "Even Miss Dorothea!"

"I know you wanted Liam to know his grandma."

"Not behind my back!" I shouted.

"We had to be careful."

I'd heard that refrain.

And I was sick to death of it.

So my eyes narrowed.

Darius got serious. "Liam didn't want you to know. He overheard me talking to your father about the precautions we needed to take, and he was adamant. You couldn't know. He thought, and he was right, that it might put you in danger. You'd push for more. We had what we could have, and it was Liam's idea, and I backed him, that we had to do it how we could to keep you safe."

"And you give your son everything he wants."

"Well…yeah."

Oh my God!

Why was he so awesome and such a pain in my neck *at the same damned time*?

Gah!

"Does he know you used to do what you did?" I asked.

"I think he suspected, with all the care we had to take with me being with him, but I came clean to him last year, when he was old enough to get it…and after I was out."

"So it was only me you kept in the dark."

"Sweetheart—"

"And when our son started to pull away from his Uncle Tony, it wasn't because he was settling into knowing it was him and me against the world. It was because he had his dad. Did you play basketball with him?"

"We had to make arrangements so no one would see us, but…yes."

"You didn't show to delete his Transformers and give him Tupac because he needed a growing man's room. You showed because he told you he wanted one."

"And he needed a growing man's room," Darius reiterated.

"Right," I said crisply. "And when I sat him down and shared about his father, the reason he told me a man has to do what a man has to do isn't because he didn't want to hurt me by talking about his dad, a man I confessed to him I still loved. It was because his father and him were lying to me. He didn't need me to seek you out and ask you to meet him. He'd been hanging with you for years."

"Malia—"

I turned stiltedly and grabbed my purse.

I turned back and said, "Fuck you, Darius Tucker."

He flinched.

"It took you a long, damned time," I shared. "But have to hand it to you, in the end you killed it. What I felt for you. You killed it. Dead."

With that, ignoring the expression on his face, I marched out.

# Chapter Nine

*My Own Damned Life*

When I walked into the kitchen the next morning, even if it was early, and summer, and a weekend, my son was sitting on a stool at our island.

He opened his mouth.

I lifted a hand, palm out his way.

"Nope. No." I shook my head. "I don't want to hear it."

"Okay, Mom, but you have to hear it."

I ignored him and went to the coffeepot.

There was a pot made. My boy started drinking coffee a few months ago. The beginnings of this slipped under my radar. By the time I cottoned on, it was too late.

Maybe *his father* introduced him to it.

I pulled a mug from the cupboard.

"I was going to call him. Figure out how we would come clean with you. And I did. Except, he'd been kidnapped by an asshole, so he couldn't take my calls," Liam said.

I turned to him then.

"Language, boy," I snapped.

I saw his jaw flex, and then, doggedly, he went on, "It needed to stop. We both knew it. I just couldn't get Dad to admit it. He felt...like, *unworthy* of you or something. So when you asked me if I wanted to meet him, I agreed like, well, uh..." he scratched his head uneasily, "like I hadn't met him yet when I had."

I'd poured my coffee, and after he finished talking, I turned to him. "That part, I got."

I moved to the fridge to get the creamer.

"Mom, it isn't like we *wanted* to keep it from you. You just, you know, still loved him. He told me you wanted to make us a family. And it wasn't safe to do that…yet."

"How did you know I still loved him?" I asked.

"You told me," he answered.

After pouring my creamer I turned to him again. "Yes, about seven years ago."

He looked uncomfortable. "Yeah, Mom, but you don't date. You're my mom, but I got eyes, I can see you're hot. You're still kinda young."

*Still kinda young.*

I was thirty-three!

Lord, grant me strength.

He continued, "You could totally land a guy. You never even looked. Because you're hung up on Dad."

Someone please explain to me why I suddenly wished I had a dull child.

I went after a spoon to put sugar in and stir my coffee.

"He's messed up," Liam said.

"A tire iron will do that to you," I told my coffee as I stirred it. "He'll heal."

"No. About you. About us. About what he did after his dad died. He's hung up on you too, you know." Weighty pause. "And he doesn't date either."

Shot…right through the heart.

I was correct when I walked in.

I didn't want to hear any of this.

I opened the cupboard to get a travel mug. "I'm going to the grocery store."

"Mom."

I poured my coffee into the travel mug. "Since you're up, I want the floors vacuumed before I get home."

"You can't walk away from this," Liam told me as I grabbed the keys from the counter and my purse, then I moved to the grocery list and ripped off the top sheet that had my and Liam's scratchings on it.

I then leveled my eyes on my boy.

"My son lied to me. His father lied to me. For years. I'm sorry, Liam, but you have no choice. You're going to have to give me some time."

"And Dad?"

"As angry as I am about how it happened and how long it went on,

I'm delighted you have a relationship with your father," I admitted.

"No. I mean and Dad, you, me, *us, our family*. We can be that now. For real."

"I love you, Liam, but you're old enough to understand it isn't your business as to how it came about when I say that ship has sailed."

He got visibly angry.

He was just going to have to get over it.

Actions had consequences.

He was going to have to learn that.

Starting now.

* * * *

The cars lining the street in front of my house told me I wasn't going to get to put the groceries away, throw together some peach salsa to put on top of the grilled shrimp tacos I was going to make later and put my feet up for a lazy Saturday with a book.

Even so, I pulled the car into the garage, went to the trunk, grabbed some bags and headed in.

Liam was standing at the island with his grandad. His grandma, one of them, was seated at a stool with my sister. His *other* grandma, who'd never stepped foot in my house in my life, looked like she was making cookies.

*Gah!*

I dumped the bags on the island and said to Liam, "There's more in the trunk."

Liam glanced at his grandfather, got a nod, then took off to the garage.

I started to pull out groceries.

"Darlin', we gotta talk," Dad announced.

Feeling a lot, too much, having just struggled all the way to the grocery store, and all the way home with not pointing my car in the direction of the hospital so I could check on Darius, managing to best that herculean task, I'd had enough.

And for some reason, I aimed my ire at the person who I felt betrayed me the most.

Darius's mother.

"I didn't expect this from you," I stated.

She stared right into my eyes, and sweet, quiet Miss Dorothea didn't back down. "I didn't expect it from you either."

"I was doing what your son wanted."

"You got a mind of your own, child," she retorted.

"So you thought the last sixteen years has been easy? All the decisions that needed to be made a breeze?"

"I didn't say that. In fact, since I hope you're listening, I'll say I know it was hard, terribly hard, for you, for my son, for my grandson, for all of us. We did the best we could with the lot we were cast. And now, praise the good Lord, it's over and we can heal."

I pulled out some bananas. "It doesn't feel over."

"That's because you're determined to hang on to hurt when the time for hurting is passed," Mom chimed in. "I get it. It's habit. But for everyone concerned, you gotta let it go."

I pinned her with a glare. "That's it? You all hiding secret visits with Darius and Liam from me for years, and I have to let it go?"

"He saw Liam at Toni and Tony's wedding," Lena put in.

"I know that," I snapped at my sister.

"Girl, it wrecked him," she whispered.

The tear in my heart from that time hadn't mended, so I felt that.

*I felt it.*

"He couldn't stay away," she said.

"Your mother and me already figured out you were getting money from somewhere, it didn't take Sherlock Holmes wading in to know where you were getting it," Dad shared (totally should have lied about winning the lottery, I was seeing that now). "Your mom dropped by Lena's place once when Darius and Liam were visiting. She wasn't expected. But we knew then, and we'd heard some things. We understood what he was about. But a boy needs his father. We did what we had to do to make that happen."

"A mother needs a partner," I returned.

"Now, baby," Dad said in his disappointed voice. "I know you're hurt, and I understand why you got that feeling. But you did not go this alone. Not even close. We had you. And Darius had you too."

Damn it.

I couldn't argue that.

I went to the fridge to put away the milk and cheese.

When I closed the door, I let out a squeak as I jumped back half a step, because Dorothea was right there.

"He's loved you since high school," she said.

I shook my head to shake her words out of my ears and rounded her to get to the groceries.

"Where's that boy with the bags?" I muttered.

"He's staying out there until we hash this out," Dad told me.

I looked to him. "Then he can put them away."

I turned to walk out of the room.

"Don't be stubborn," Mom called after me.

Right.

*Enough.*

I whirled on her.

On all of them.

"I know Darius gave me money. I know Darius bought us our furniture. I know Darius pretty much bought this house. I know he looked out for us. What you don't know is, it hasn't been over with him and me. It was stops and starts, and the last few years, he kept his distance. But in the beginning, when I moved back to Denver, he and I were together for years."

I could tell by the looks on their faces they didn't know that last part. Lena's expression, particularly, was hard to witness considering her shock was liberally mixed with hurt, as I knew it would be.

Even so, I lowered the boom.

"He could have told me. He had ample opportunity. He didn't tell me. He didn't tell me about the business he was in. He didn't tell me he was spending time with me and other times with his son. He didn't let me in. He didn't let me be a part of the conversation. Of the decision making. He didn't let me decide if I was willing to take the chances he wasn't willing to take so we could have a family. He kept us apart for his own reasons, and they might have been good ones, but he didn't give me a say."

I focused on my mom and kept going.

"I tried patience. Years of it. *Years.* He took my time and our boy's time, and he gave, but he didn't give enough."

I looked to my dad, and I wasn't done.

Far from it.

"Yes, we had your love and support, and it meant everything, Dad. *Everything.* I don't know where Liam and I would be without it. But you know damn well, it's not the same. It's not the same as a mom and dad living under one roof raising their child. You could take my car to have the oil changed, but you did so much, I couldn't ask you to, even though I had no time to do it myself, but it had to be done. You couldn't pop by the grocery store with a tired four-year-old to pick up something you forgot to buy when you were there the day before. I had to drag Liam to the store and heft him up into the seat and get what we needed and get my boy home and fed and in bed at a decent hour. Then, dead on my feet, hit my computer to do my coursework. I needed him. *We* needed him. And he was there. But he still was a ghost. So I'm mad. I get it. Your point is made. You think I need to get over it. But you've gotta let me be mad for as long as it takes, and whatever shakes out after that, you're gonna have to live with. Because for sixteen years, I've been living for whatever Darius Tucker felt was right. Now I'm going to make my own damned decisions about my own damned life. And he's gonna have to live with whatever those are too."

I got out what I wanted to say, then before anyone could utter a word, I hightailed it to my bedroom and slammed the door.

* * * *

Sometime later, when I sensed the hubbub was gone (and frankly, when I could no longer resist the lure of the smell of cookies baking), I went back downstairs.

There was a tin of cookies on the island along with a note from my son that said they'd all gone to the hospital to visit his dad, and it'd be cool if I joined them.

I didn't join them.

I ate one of Dorothea's cookies.

The instant it touched my tongue, memories flooded me. Of her, and Mister Morris, and lost youth, and wasted years, and dying hope, and as mad as I was, I hoped with all my heart these weren't the first cookies she made for my son.

I really wanted to cry.

But I didn't.

I grabbed two more cookies, made myself some tea and went up to my room with my book.

# Chapter Ten

*Stupid Stuff*

"Explain to me again why I'm doing this," Toni, standing at my side, whispered.

"Because I told you what I was doing, and you told me I was a damn fool, then I told you I was still doing it, and you said I'd be a bigger fool if I went alone, then I repeated I was doing it, and you made a big show of acting beleaguered, then you came with me," I reminded her.

"On the record, you are a damned fool."

"This client is hinky," I told her something else I'd already told her.

"How is that your responsibility?"

"I don't have a job if the attorneys I work for get disbarred."

"So move jobs."

"I don't want to move jobs. I like my job."

"So ignore the hinky."

"I'm curious and I have to know. If I have the information, I can make an informed decision. Are the attorneys I'm working for doing something illegal? If yes, look for another job, even though I like my job. If no, stay in a job I like without my headspace being taken up with a client who's hinky."

We both jumped a mile when a woman's voice remarked, "I know who can find out if your clients are hinky or not."

We were both staring at the two people who had snuck up to us in the dark hall of the office building where Toni and I were lurking after having hung out in the bathroom for an hour, waiting for the place to close down.

One of them was Ally Nightingale.

The other was a very well-healed Darius Tucker.

His gaze was locked on me.

He looked good, so good, *too good*.

Did God hate me?

What did I do?

Really, I wanted to know.

Ally made a move, which meant I was forced to rip my gaze from Darius and watch her jerk a thumb to herself, then over her shoulder at him.

"Private investigators," she concluded.

Not news since I already knew it, and now Liam talked about it all the time, proud as all hell Darius had gone to work at Lee's investigation firm after he got out of the drug business and now he was a hotshot PI.

"You take Toni home, I got Malia," he ordered low.

Uh-oh.

I wasn't at one with that plan.

"Wait," I said.

Toni didn't wait.

She took off toward Ally, Ally turned when she got to her, and Toni said while they walked away, "Girl, can we stop on the way home to get a drink? I'm parched. And by the way, you grew up badass. I'm impressed."

"Thanks. Now, are we talking cosmo parched, or beer parched?" Ally asked.

"You're drivin', you choose," Toni answered.

Their voices faded away.

This left me in a dark hall, alone with Darius.

It had been five months since his near-fatal run-in with Ally's stalker.

In those months, we'd negotiated a visitation arrangement, doing this using our son as an intermediary.

Yes, that was weak.

No, obviously, I didn't have it in me to do it differently.

Now, Liam shifted every week between his father's house and mine.

And it was Liam who delivered my envelopes to me. But it was no longer cash. It was a check, signed by Darius.

I had received reports about Darius's recuperation progress, but I hadn't seen him or spoken to him.

Until now.

"Follow me," he grunted.

"I have my car," I told him.

"You follow me to my truck, or I carry you to it, Malia. Your choice. Two seconds."

He couldn't be serious.

I guessed my two seconds were up, because he stalked toward me.

And he was serious.

I put both hands up.

"Okay, okay. Yeesh. I'll follow you."

He scorched me with a look, turned on his boot and prowled way.

I followed him.

When we got outside, he beeped the locks on a black Silverado and headed to the passenger side door, probably afraid I'd run if given the chance. He held the door while I grabbed onto the hold and hefted myself up.

He slammed the door on me and rounded the hood.

He angled in beside me.

I turned to him. "Darius—"

"Shut it," he ordered tersely, his focus on starting the truck.

Oh no, he didn't.

"Don't you dare speak to me that way," I hissed.

He turned to me. "Have you not heard of all the shit that went down with Indy, Jet, Roxie, Jules, Ava, Stella, Sadie and you gotta know what went down with Ally since I got a hospital stay from some of her shit."

"I read the articles."

Though, they hadn't included Ally's business, or whoever Sadie was.

However, Liam had filled in those blanks, also proud as all heck about his dad being the hero of those scenarios (because he'd also been in on Sadie's rescue).

I was proud too. I just wasn't admitting that to myself.

And scared to death, because all of that was dangerous, particularly Ally's situation, and he could have died, and I couldn't tamp down the fear, even though the bad guys got caught and the good guys were okay.

He jutted his chin to indicate the building we just vacated. "So what the fuck are you up to?"

"We were just going to look through a few offices."

"Breaking and entering is a felony."

"You'd know all about felonies."

He clamped his mouth shut, and I wished I could reach out and grab those words and shove them back in my mouth.

"I'm sorry," I said quietly. "That was uncalled for."

He turned, started the truck and put it into gear. He then twisted and put his arm behind my seat to look behind him in order to back out.

His arm that close to me gave me happy shivers.

I tried to ignore the shivers.

I failed at ignoring the shivers.

I decided to focus on something else.

"Darius, truly, I'm sorry. You just surprised me, showing like this. And I haven't seen you and emotions are still high."

"You got emotion?" he muttered like he was talking to himself, faced forward and put the truck in drive. "Coulda fooled me."

"That's not fair either," I said carefully.

He had no reply.

"Are you still watching me?"

"You're still my boy's momma. You're still prone to doing stupid shit. So yeah, I'm still watching you."

I decided it best at this juncture to ignore the "stupid shit" comment, so I targeted something else.

"Um...like...*personally?*"

"No, like I got tracking on your car."

What?

"And your cell," he added.

"You track my car?"

He again said nothing.

"And my phone?"

"Not your calls, just your location."

"Why?"

"I just caught you in an empty office building about to commit a felony to look into a client who's hinky. My experience, if someone acts hinky, they are. More experience, if they're hinky, they don't want people discovering why. More experience, they can do some pretty shitty things to people who poke around trying to find out what's hinky about them. You might be done with me, babe. But I didn't survive navigating the underbelly of Denver for fifteen years to stand at my son's side by his momma's casket at her funeral."

"I'm sure it wouldn't come to that," I murmured.

"Ask Jules how sure she was when she walked into a living room and got shot twice. And Sadie, when she was roofied, kidnapped and nearly taken out of the country. And Stella, ask how sure she was that her apartment wouldn't explode."

Yikes!

I decided to change the subject.

"My car—"

"Matt or Bobby will bring it to you."

"Who are Matt and Bobby?"

"They work for Lee."

"They don't have a key."

He was again silent.

Right.

They didn't need a key.

Interesting.

Although I wanted to know more about that (and, indeed, everything about the New Darius, though I wouldn't admit that to myself, and definitely not him), I decided it was time for another change of subject.

Though, the subject I picked was trying to learn something about the New Darius.

"So how is it…working with Lee?"

"You wanna be friends now? Catch up? Get to know one another?"

"I'm just carrying on a conversation."

"I'm good with silence."

Hang on a second.

Was he….

Mad at *me?*

"Are you mad at me?"

"The last time I saw you I was in a hospital bed with holes in my legs and a fractured skull."

"Yes, and I'd just found out you'd been deceiving me for years."

"Keeping something from you to keep you safe," he corrected.

"Toe-may-toes, toe-mah-toes, I guess. Am I right?" I sniped.

He sighed. "Let's not do this."

I strained the seatbelt to turn more fully to him.

"No. Let's."

"It's copasetic. You got Liam. I got Liam. It's working. Let's not rock that boat."

I felt like boat rocking.

I felt like tsunami-ing that motherfucker.

"You kept us apart, but you got the best of both worlds," I accused.

He burst out laughing, but there was zero humor to it.

It was the ugliest sound I'd ever heard.

"Stop it," I hissed.

"Yeah, walk in the park for me, babe," he bit. "It was awesome. Most of the time, I slept alone. You got to see him take his first steps. You got to go to the awards dinners at the school."

"It was your choice to be absent from that."

"It wasn't a choice. It was a necessity. This is what you're not getting."

"One thing I definitely get, it wasn't *my* choice. None of it."

Suddenly, he swung into a parking spot on the street, the move so unexpected, I automatically reached to the dash to hold on.

And then he turned on me.

"I had someone workin' for me. He was a pissant. I shook him loose. He didn't like that. He wanted payback. He asked around, don't know who talked, still wish I could find that motherfucker, but he found out about you and Liam."

I sat very still and stared at him.

"It wasn't to get something out of me. He didn't want anything from me, except for him to know he put the hurt on me. He was just gonna fuck you two up."

"Oh my God," I breathed.

"Yeah," he said sharply. "I don't know if he meant to kill you or beat you or rape you or all three. I just know he didn't get the chance. I also knew I couldn't let anyone else get the chance. So I crept around...*for fuckin' years*...to give the both of you the only things I had to give. A little bit of time and a lot of money. I'm sorry that wasn't enough for you, Malia, but that was all I had at the time. But when Liam was ready, fate fucked us over yet...fuckin'...again. And after I survived that, it was *you* who walked away. Suck it up. I lied to see my boy. Suck it up. I couldn't give you all you needed. You've made it clear you can't live with that, now I gotta suck it up. What I don't gotta do is like it."

After delivering that, he turned back to the wheel and pulled into the road.

I had a lot to process as he drove me home, and I didn't have enough time to do it.

I also hadn't found the words to say anything after all he'd said before he was in my drive and idling.

I found the words and said them. "I think we need to talk."

"Done talkin'."

"Darius—"

He shook his head. "I killed it. I get it. You move on. Our boy's old enough he can be our go between. It's working. Let's not fuck it up."

"I think...I need to buy him a car."

"Fine," he said tersely. "Have him pick what he wants, I'll go get it for him."

"Darius, I only said that to demonstrate—"

"Get out of my truck, Malia."

"Dar—"

His belt zipped back, my belt zipped back (and I didn't unbuckle it), and then I was crowded into the corner of the seat and door when he was smack in my face.

"Get out…of my…*fuckin' truck*…woman," he growled.

I stared into his cold, dead eyes.

And I didn't believe in that coldness or deadness for one single second.

"Do I…uh, talk to Ally about, you know, looking into the hinky clients?" I asked.

He sat back in his seat, rested his head against the headrest and said to the roof of the cab, "Jesus."

I put my hand to the door handle and said, "I'm just gonna…um, *go*."

He turned to me. "Yeah. Do that."

"Thanks for, like, you know, saving me from myself."

He just stared at me.

"'Bye now," I said.

He slowly shook his head like he didn't know what to make of me, but what he was making wasn't much.

I skedaddled out of his truck.

He sat idling in the drive while I made my way to the door.

Standing in it, I waved at him.

He just pulled out and drove away.

The wave was stupid.

What was I doing?

"Was that Dad?" Liam asked from behind me.

For the second time that night, I jumped a mile.

I turned to him.

He was looking over my head at the street.

"Move," I ordered. "I need to shut the door."

He didn't move.

He looked down at me. "Was that Dad?"

I scrambled. "Hey! Good news. Your dad and I decided to get you a car."

His brows knit. "You and Dad are talking now?"

Okay, not that I needed the proof, but his non-reaction to getting a car said just how much he felt about me and his father being together. Even just talking.

Dang.

"Can I get out of the door?" I asked.

Liam stepped back.

I stepped in and shut the door.

When I turned back to him, he had his arms crossed on his chest.

Ugh.

He was just like his father.

"Why is Dad bringing you home from going out with Aunt Toni?" he asked suspiciously.

"We ran into each other…"

Oh my God.

Now *I* was lying.

"…and I took that opportunity to discuss getting you a car. He agreed it was the right decision. So we're going to do that."

"Where's your car?"

"Um…well…"

"Mom, you can't be pissed as shit about Dad and me lying and then stand there and lie to my face."

"Your mouth," I warned.

"What are you doing with Dad?"

I didn't know.

What was I going to do with Darius?

And what was I doing with my son?

Time to pull myself together.

"Okay, your aunt Toni and I were out doing something we probably shouldn't have been. Your dad and Ally caught us, and he was kind of…angry we were doing something stupid. So he brought me home to lecture me. One of Lee's men is going to bring home my car."

"Matt?" he asked.

So he knew Darius's colleagues.

I loved that.

But I hated that I didn't know.

I nodded and said, "Him or Bobby."

"Right. What stupid thing were you and Aunt Toni doing?"

"The firm has a client I don't trust."

"Doesn't the firm have an investigator who can look into that kind of thing?"

Again, me wishing I had a dull child.

"We do contract with one when we need them, yes. I just don't know how deep this goes."

"So ask Dad and his guys to find out."

I sighed.

"I think I'm going to ask Ally," I told him.

"That'd be good too. She's a total badass."

His world had expanded a lot in five months.

I loved that for him too.

And it made me jealous as all hell.

"And don't do stupid stuff like that again," my child scolded *me*. "Dad's right. You and Aunt Toni got no business screwing around with that kind of stuff."

I arched a brow. "When did you become the parent in this scenario?"

"When you and Aunt Toni went out and did screwy stuff. Huh."

With that, he strolled away.

# Chapter Eleven

*What If*

I had to wait until Liam was back at his dad's to hold the meeting.

I sensed it wasn't going to go well when my sister strutted in, eyes on me, asking, "So, you're talking to me again?"

But it was Toni, who was stretched out on my couch with a martini in her hand, who answered.

"She might be, but I'm not. Everyone knows, it's sisters before misters."

"Spend two seconds with that man when he's with his son and get back to me," she retorted.

Toni rolled her eyes and sipped her drink, after which she mumbled, "Whatever."

"Not whatever. I did the right thing!" Lena cried.

I cut in. "We're not here to talk about that."

"So I'm not here to hear your apology?" Lena asked me. "Then I'm out."

"Lena, please sit down," I requested.

"I lied to you, babe, but you also lied to me," she declared.

"Yes, I did. I had my reasons. You had your reasons. I forgive you. If you forgive me, we can move past this and you can help me figure out how to win Darius back."

Lena's eyes went huge.

Toni took her legs from the couch and sat up. Such was her haste in doing this, she sloshed martini on her blouse. And such was her absorption in what I just said, she didn't go for one of the cute cocktail napkins I'd laid out to dab at the wet.

"Say what?" Toni asked.

"Pour me a martini." Lena was snapping at Toni. "I gotta catch up."

Toni's chin went into her neck. "When did I become your

bartender?"

"The pitcher is right there." Lena pointed to the glass martini pitcher that was resting in a bucket of ice and the empty glass I'd set out for Lena with two fat olives on the silver toothpick with its kick-butt swirly end already set into it. All of this was sitting on the coffee table right in front of Toni.

Yes.

Seriously.

Darius had set me and Liam up.

I had fancy silver toothpicks for my drinks.

And a sophisticated martini pitcher and ice bucket.

And no, I hadn't blinked before buying either of them.

"Holy hell, *I'll* pour your damned drink," I muttered, moving to do that.

Lena sunk into an armchair and accepted the glass I poured with a loaded, "*Thank you,*" and a side eye to Toni.

"Please, you two, let's get along while I use you to hash all of this out," I begged.

"You're going to try to get him back?" Toni asked.

"That'll take two seconds," Lena said into her drink before taking a sip.

"I don't think you're right," I told Lena as I sunk into my own armchair.

"Girl, he's crazy for you," Lena told me.

"I had occasion to be in his presence just a few days ago, and he ordered me out of his truck when I tried to talk to him."

Lena and her false eyelashes blinked rapidly.

I needed to get an appointment for those semi-permanent falsies. They looked great. Mine were always detaching mid-day so I either had to rip them off or do a re-glue over the basin in the employee bathroom.

Not optimal.

"Where do you get your lashes done?" I asked my sister.

"There's this place in Cherry Creek—"

"Hold up, hold up," Toni interrupted. "Are we talking about lashes now? And not the Great and Twisted and Entirely Fucked Up Love Affair of Darius Tucker and Malia Clark, who all of us thought had an unhappy ending, which turns out might not be the end?"

"I don't know," I said nervously, rubbing my hands on my slacks and then reaching for my own martini.

"I say you go for it," Lena chimed in.

"Liam told me that he was trying to get Darius to come clean and make a family out of us, but Darius refused to do it because, and this is Liam's word, he thought he was *unworthy* of me...or something."

"Huh," Toni said.

Lena's attention cut to her.

"He's not unworthy of anything," she snapped.

One could say, now that I was over The Great Deception (another such Great Deception I had committed myself, but we wouldn't get into that), I was glad I didn't have to clear the hurdle of talking Mom, Dad, Lena, not to mention Dorothea into not being mad at Darius and me for our, well, Great and Twisted and Entirely Fucked Up Love Affair.

"Calm down, sis. I didn't say he was," Toni replied to Lena. "I said 'huh.' That's got a lot of meanings. And in this particular instance, my meaning was, 'oh yeah, that tracks as to why he had his head up his ass for a long, long, *long* fucking time.'"

Lena sat back, crossed her arm along her belly, rested her drink elbow on it, and murmured, "Well, all right then."

I put my drink down and clapped. "Can we focus ladies?"

Toni looked at Lena. "Did she just clap at me?"

Lena looked at Toni. "She did. And she clapped at me too."

Oh my God!

Someone kill me!

I collapsed back in my chair.

"The drama, Malia," Lena grouched. "Really, just tell the guy you want to work things out. I don't know what happened in his truck, but he's head over heels for you."

Still in a slouch, I tried to reach my martini.

I should have put it on the side table.

I had to curl up, grab it, but then I slouched right back.

"I'm not sure he's over his father's murder," I noted.

"Well, duh," Lena said. "You never get over that. But I bet if he finally had his woman and his son under his roof, that'd help."

I bet the same thing.

"What's holding you back, sis?" Toni asked the pertinent question.

She didn't let me bat it away either. She kept at me.

"You love him. He loves you. You both love Liam. All that was keeping you apart isn't there anymore. He lied to you. Clearly, you're over it."

"As she should be," Lena cut in.

Toni threw her a look and came back to me. "So why the hesitation and the big show of martinis with the girls when you already know what you've got to do?"

"Because what if..."

I couldn't finish it.

"What if, without the obstacles and the danger and the history and the bullshit, you two can't hack it together?" Toni asked.

"Yeah, that," I said weakly.

She looked to Lena. "I see she forgot her big speech to me on my wedding day."

"I still don't know what she said," Lena replied.

"In a nutshell, woman up," Toni told her. "I was being a wuss. Go be with the man I love and make a life with him."

Lena turned her attention to me. "Right. Do that."

"Easier said than done," I muttered and sucked back some martini.

"You know, I know you all think Kenneth's touched," Lena declared.

Toni ducked her eyes.

I grew fascinated by a plant in the corner.

News: Lena married Kenneth.

Surprising news: they were still thick as thieves, loved each other bunches and had just started trying to make a baby.

Not surprising news: we all still thought Kenneth was touched, but he loved our girl, wanted to lay the world at her feet, so we found ways to get over it.

"And I didn't care," she continued. "I knew what I wanted, and it was him. So even though I respect all you all, and I can't say it didn't give me pause, I made the right decision for me. You don't have just you to think about, Malia. You have Liam. But I can testify that those two are two peas in a pod. They get along like a house on fire. Darius loves his son to his bones, and Liam feels the same way for his daddy. So yeah. I agree. Darius took a long damned time getting his head out of his ass. But now, I don't mean to be a bitch or anything, but it's you with your head in your ass, Malia."

Toni didn't say anything, which was tacit agreement with what Lena said.

"Okay then, how do I go about doing that?" I asked. "Because Liam can't be around. He caught his dad dropping me off, and it was all kinds of uncomfortable. I don't want his hopes up if things go south."

Lena shrugged. "No probs. Kenneth and me'll take him to a movie or something."

"Or Tony can ask him for a game of one-on-one."

"Or Dad can tell him he needs his help with one of his projects."

"Or we can ask him to babysit Talia while Tony and I have a date night."

"I see we've got the covert part of this operation covered," I mumbled before taking another sip of my drink.

"You say the when, we'll do the how," Lena declared.

She exchanged a fist-bump glance with Toni, them being too far away from each other for an actual fist bump.

I felt my belly being tied up in knots with nerves.

Could I be close to getting everything I wanted, everything I wanted for my son?

Could we be close to making a family with Darius?

"You hold a mean grudge," Lena noted. "What snapped you out of it?"

I shook myself out of my happy-terrifying thoughts and shared, "Darius told me to get out of his truck, but before that, he had a lot of other words to say that made me put myself in his shoes and see the truth of it."

"Glad that happened," Lena said quietly.

Toni shot me a small smile.

"He also told me about some guy who got angry with him for firing him, or whatever they do in that life, who found out about Liam and me somehow, and he was going to hurt us. Darius put a stop to it, but obviously, it really tweaked him. So I understood pretty well why he went to such lengths to keep us safe."

I was talking into my martini, wondering how I was going to finagle a meeting with Darius that he couldn't shut down, at the same time wondering if I needed another olive.

So when Toni said a vibrating, "Lena," I looked to my sister.

She was swirling her olives in her martini with acute precision and attention.

"You didn't," Toni whispered, her words still vibrating, now with fury.

Lena dropped the olives and looked to me. "He put it together, I didn't tell him."

Cold washed over my skin.

"Who?" I asked.

"Who do you think?" Toni ground out. "Michael."

My gaze flew back to my sister.

"I didn't tell him!" she exclaimed. "I swear. I was talking to you on the phone, I mentioned Liam. He asked who Liam was. I didn't think. I didn't *know*. So I said he was your son. He said, 'She's kinda young to have a son.' And since I didn't realize it was supposed to be secret, I told him you got knocked up in high school. That was it. He put together the rest. And seriously, it's a surprise other people didn't too. But saying that, you disappeared to Fort Fun, and this was around the time Mister Morris was killed, so I can see people not making the connection. Darius and you were well through before you vanished, and you weren't showing yet. And then you came back, and Darius found out, and then Eddie Chavez was everywhere, covering for you guys, laying it down to anyone who would listen that you met some asshole in Fort Collins, and he'd done a runner and what a dick guys could be, because you're a great gal and deserved better."

Eddie again, looking after his brother.

I had a feeling I owed those boys a lot.

"Whatever happened to Michael?" I asked.

"I know what's gonna happen to Michael if Darius knows he was the one who gave up the goods to that guy who wanted to go after you and his boy," Toni said by way of answer.

"He's not in that business anymore, and it's no longer a secret," I said.

"Tony isn't into any of this shit, but you know he's got friends who are. And I don't have to ask his input to tell you, beefs like that do not just disappear because you found the righteous path," Toni shot back.

"Well...*shit!*" I swore, because damn it, I did not need to be trying to figure things out with my man and for my family and have to keep something this huge from the man part of that.

"Maybe you can talk him out of whacking Michael," Toni suggested.

I gave her big eyes.

Did she *miss* the last fourteen years of our lives where he knocked himself out and scored his own soul to keep his woman and kid safe?

"Or, just tell Lee or Eddie," Lena put in. "They'll handle it," she snapped her fingers, "no sweat."

I slouched further in my chair.

"Sis, one thing at a time," Toni advised. "Go see him. Talk to him. Tell us a day, and make that day soon, so your chickenshit ass doesn't chicken out, and we'll see to Liam."

I sighed.

Then I sucked back my entire drink.

After that, I gagged.

Once I was done gagging, I ate both olives off my toothpick.

Then I got up to pour myself another martini.

When I was done with that, and speared two more olives from the bowl I'd thankfully made handy, I looked between my two sisters.

Then, before my chickenshit ass could chicken out, I said, "Wednesday."

Toni's smile was slow.

But Lena's was fast and bright.

# Chapter Twelve

*Wine Cellar*

I sat in my car, staring at Darius's house, thinking what a nice house it was.

It was a mid-century square with a long overhang that went out so far, it shielded the steps up to a front door that was set off to the side.

That had to be handy during a snowstorm.

The front door was painted a bright red, but it was mostly windows and had two panels of glass on either side. All of this was set into a white frame, but the rest of the house was two-toned brick, red on the bottom, some sandy colored brick at the top, with a thick red brick line close to the roof.

It had an old bungalow to one side of it and a classic Denver square to the other.

There was something very him about it. The fact it was unusual, made a statement, but managed to do this in an understated way.

And there was something very not him about it. The fact it was established and had a big tree out front that was probably older than the house, a house which had undoubtedly been built in the late 50s or early 60s.

I'd never allowed myself to think how, or where, Darius lived without us.

And this realization was so uncomfortable, it was painful.

I wondered, in all that I wanted from him, if I ever really thought about him at all.

So yes.

This meant, even though I knew Liam was hanging with Tony and Kenneth at T&T's house playing video games while Toni and Lena kept an eye and made sure Liam didn't get in his brand-new Charger and head home (no, his father didn't mess around, I got a text with a picture of his new wheels on day one back at his dad's).

I was wearing a new dress, which was not conducive to our current fall weather, seeing as it was bright pinks and oranges with mustard yellow and greens all in a flower and leaf motif, an orange leopard head with yellow spots here and there. It had a smocked waistband that went from below my breasts to upper hips, long, puff sleeves, and a barely-there frill of a skirt that showed off nearly all of my legs.

I wore this with green strappy high-heeled sandals that Lena let me borrow and some big, real gold hoop earrings that Toni loaned me.

It was an outfit to wear at a resort in the Caribbean, not during the mission I was currently on.

What was I thinking?

I couldn't go home and change now, as much as I wanted to use that as an excuse to get my behind out of there.

I had to do this.

I again let my eyes sweep Darius's cool house.

There was a light shining out of the long bank of the windows just off the front door.

So he was probably home.

I should check, though, before I knocked on the door.

Right?

The issue with checking was that it looked like a three-story house, except the first floor was kind of built into the earth, the second was a little elevated, and the third was super high.

This was smart, if you didn't want people walking by and looking in the windows.

My heels were high too, but it wasn't like the windows the light was shining out of were normal height and I could just walk up to them and peek in, even in my heels.

But…the house had surprised me.

What if the inside was immaculate? Say, designed by an expensive interior designer?

This visit was important. I had to stay on target. I didn't need to be blindsided by Darius's fabulous décor.

"Right, yes, just go peek in, make sure he's there and get the lay of the land. You aren't chickenshit and delaying," I told myself. "This is reconnaissance."

On my pep talk, I got out of my car, again lamented my choice of dress when the blast of cold hit me, and as casual as I could, I strolled up his lawn, in the dark, in a cute, bright, flirty, sexy dress and high heels and ducked to the side in hopes there were windows there (there were).

And then I realized I was right. The windows were high off the ground. I had to reach up with my hands, curl my fingers on the ledge and try to pull myself up to see inside.

This, I did.

"What the fuck are you doing?"

I squawked, dropped, turned my ankle and would have gone down if Darius hadn't shot forward and caught me.

I got my feet under me, pushed away from him, brushed my skirt in a nervous gesture since there was nothing to brush off, looked up at him and said, as nonchalant as I could, "Hey."

"There's a reason cat burglars wear black, woman," Darius drawled.

God, how embarrassing was this?

"And they don't sit in their car psyching themselves up for twenty minutes right in front of the joint they're gonna knock over before they go do a job," he went on.

Okay, we needed to move away from this. It was mortifying.

"Um…are you busy? Can we talk?" I asked.

He took a step back and did a top to toe.

As I mentioned, it was dark.

But that light was shining out of his window, and I could see all of him (and all of it looked good, just a red thermal (skintight) and jeans (that fit too well and had a fade mark that made me salivate a little), but it worked on me), so he could probably see all of me.

"You wanna try the front door?" he asked. "Or you want me to go in, open a window, come back out and heft you through it?"

All right, that was it.

"I was curious about your décor," I snapped.

"Good way to find out is knock on the door and say, 'Hey, Darius, got a second to show me your crib?'"

"Hey, Darius," I said sarcastically. "Got a second to show me your crib?"

He threw an arm out for me to precede him.

The ground was cold, not frozen (even though my legs were close to that), the trek to the side of the house had to be on my toes so my heels didn't sink in, as did the trek to the front door.

We finally made his walk, and I breathed a sigh of relief I hadn't made an even bigger fool of myself.

Once I hit the top of his steps, I stood aside so he could open the door.

He did but held back so I could go first.

When I did, moving through the entryway and into the living room, I really wished I had better sleuthing skills and upper body strength because I was blindsided by his fabulous décor.

I saw a boxy, creamy-beige couch with creamy-beige toss pillows with odd width black stripes running through them. Two square, low-sitting, black leather armchairs, and the leather looked soft and inviting. A massive fern on a stand. Interesting-based lamps. And a coffee table that looked like it was a slab shorn off a huge, gorgeous piece of wood, the top finished to a high shine.

There was a built-in low cabinet on the back wall on which was an African mask on a stand in the corner and an expensive-looking stereo with turntable in the middle. Over these was a triptych in blues and grays with a shock of white and some inlaid finished wood.

Last, there were stacks of hardback books everywhere.

"Meet your inspection?" Darius asked.

"It's very...stylish," I murmured my understatement.

"Yeah, Liam thinks it's the shit," he murmured in return.

I was sure he did.

I tried to decorate in gender neutral, but I'd pretty much failed (it was impossible, what could I say? I'd explained the dress I was wearing—I was all girl), and Liam had no choice but to live with it.

"Wanna see where he sleeps?" Darius offered. "He's got the whole lower level."

Every cell in my body which held the mother gene (which was every cell in my body) screamed, *Oh God, NOOOOOOOOO!* at the idea of my sixteen, nearly seventeen-year-old, who started casually dating last year, and now had his own car, having a whole level to himself.

I sounded choked when I asked, "Does it have its own door to the outside?"

"Yeah. It was once reno'ed to be an apartment. But he comes in the back, from the garage, like me, into the main house, and goes down the stairs."

I cleared my throat since it was clogged with all the words I needed to say about our son with his own ingress and egress on a level of a house his father didn't occupy.

"You need some water to hydrate since you're burnin' up so much fluid tryin' not to tell me I gotta keep a closer eye on our boy who's a teenager and probably pretty much lives for getting in pretty girls' panties?" he asked.

I retched.

Darius burst out laughing.

I froze, staring at him.

I didn't think I'd seen him laugh like that in seventeen (nearly eighteen) years.

When his humor died (though, not entirely, his eyes were still sparkling with it), he said, "One good thing about bein' in the business I used to be in, Malia, not much gets by me. You don't survive long in that world with people doin' shit you don't want them to do around you. Kinda like how I knew you were sitting in your car, psyching yourself up to come to my door and ask me to have a look at where your son spends every other week."

I was surprised.

"I…that's not why I'm here," I told him.

His head cocked slightly to the side. "Then why are you here?"

"I…" I brushed at my skirt again and lost track of my thoughts.

"Baby, you can swipe at it all you want, it's not gonna grow longer," Darius said in a sweet, sexy, teasing tone.

A sweet, teasing tone (the sexy was new, he was young back then, he hadn't developed that part yet) was so very *Darius*, every cell in my body that loved him (and that was all of them too) heated up.

Okay, I was there to talk, not jump him.

Talk, not engage in wild sex on his incredibly attractive Berber carpet.

"Malia?" he called.

Shit.

I tackled him.

His arms went around me as he flew back and landed in one of the low, black leather chairs, me on top of him.

I straddled him, knees in the seat and grabbed his head.

"Sweetheart—" he tried.

"We're gonna talk, just after you give me the business," I said.

He grinned.

It was cute.

I still kissed him.

He took over the kiss as, miraculously, he got us both out of that chair. He walked with me wrapped around him, his arm around me, one hand at my behind, all the while kissing me.

Then I was going down, Darius on top, in a bed.

*God*, I'd missed his weight on me.

I'd just missed him.

Only then did he break our kiss to lift his head and offer, "Fast and hard, or slow and sweet?"

"Fast and hard, um…first," I whispered.

His eyes darkened but he said, "Been awhile since I tasted your sweet pussy, baby."

"Okay, fast and hard after…um, *that.*"

I got another grin, a different one this time, one I felt right where he'd be giving me some attention, hopefully soon, then he dropped his head and kissed me again.

He left the dress on when he eventually went down on me.

But he got rid of it (though, not the shoes) when he fucked me.

Fast and hard.

But still.

It was all kinds of sweet.

* * * *

"What did you come to talk about?"

It was after.

I was lying on top of him, naked (he'd finally taken off my shoes). He'd pulled the covers up over my booty. And he was running the tips of his fingers up and down my spine.

I was gooey and warm and sated and happy, and his bedroom was even better than his living room (he had plaid wallpaper behind the bed and gold lamps and a tan leather bench at the foot of the bed with a buttoned top, and best of all, super soft sheets, and obviously he took care of his twists, the pillowcases were silk).

"Everything," I mumbled into his skin.

He had a smile in his voice when he asked, "Everything?"

I tipped my head back, stacking my hands on his chest, resting my chin on them and looking up at him.

My breath stopped.

His head and shoulders were propped up on some pillows and he was gazing down at me like I was the most beautiful girl in the world, and he was going to shelter me from every storm until the day I died.

"Everything," I whispered.

He pulled me up his body and rolled me so he was on top.

"Our boy is gonna be home soon," he reminded me. "And we haven't cracked the surface of this everything you need to go over, and I don't think either of us are ready for him to see us together, so why don't you whittle that down to your top two priorities."

"I never knew where you lived," I admitted. "Lena had to tell me."

"I didn't let it be common knowledge."

"I never asked. I never even thought about it. All I could think was that I wanted you to be with us."

"Ah," he murmured.

"I worry I was being really selfish," I said, my voice soft with shame and guilt.

His brows drew together. "Because you loved me and wanted us to be a family?"

"Because I didn't think much about you. Just about me."

"And Liam," he added.

"Yes, and Liam. But also me."

"And me, because you loved me."

"Well, yes, and you, because I loved you. But it was a lot about me."

His lips quirked. "You're pretty fuckin' determined to make yourself the bad guy."

"Darius," I warned.

He touched his lips to mine, lifted his head, and said, "Baby, this is what we got. We got a boy who wants us to be together, so you can be happy, and I can be happy, and we can be a family, which will make him happy. We gotta get our shit together so we can give him that. And we got two houses. I like mine, I suspect you like yours, and I hate to break this to you, but Liam likes mine way better than yours. Though he digs his bedroom."

He smiled.

I rolled my eyes to study my eyebrows.

I felt his body move with his laughter, and since I didn't want to miss it, even if it wasn't audible this time, I rolled them back.

Yes.

Totally worth getting over my mini-snit.

"But that's all we got," he declared. "Don't invent more garbage and slights and worries and bullshit. It's just not there. We got enough to figure out so we don't fuck this up. Because I don't ever want to hurt you again. And I want our boy to grow to know how solid we are. That it never ended, that we were always a family, even if we couldn't be together. It's just now, we can be together."

"You're right."

His gaze moved over my face, and something moved over his when it did.

"Do you forgive me?" he asked.

"For what?" I asked back.

"Any of it. All of it. Lying to you. Keeping us apart."

I put my hand over his mouth. "I thought all that just wasn't there anymore."

He pulled my hand away and said, "I need to hear the words."

I shook my head on the pillow. "There's nothing to forgive. You, me, our families, we were all just doing the best—"

I stopped talking when his body got tight.

Then I stilled when he pulled the covers up to my chest.

The door opened and I heard, "Dad? Mom's car is—"

Darius looked over his bare shoulder toward the door.

I realized, belatedly, that I'd left my purse, with phone, in the car.

Seriously, I was terrible at this.

"My eyes!" Liam shouted then I heard a thud like a body hitting the wall. "My eyes! I'm blind!"

Darius started laughing.

I took hold of the covers and pulled them over my head as I slunk down the bed.

"Don't go that way, baby," Darius whispered.

I groaned in mortification but stopped moving.

"I'll never see again! And I'm okay with that!" Liam yelled.

"Boy, get downstairs," Darius called, his voice filled with humor. "Your mother and I'll be down in a minute."

More thuds and, "I can't...find the stairs," Liam lied.

Did we go upstairs?

Boy, Darius could kiss really, *really* well.

I knew that already, but...yeesh.

"Open a bottle of wine for your mother," Darius called. Then to me, "Red or white?"

"I'm not here," I told him. "I've been swallowed by the black hole of humiliation."

"Then whose warm, silky skin is this?" Darius asked, his hand going up my belly to my...

I batted it away. "Stop it."

"Red!" Darius shouted. "Open a red! From the reserve!"

I pulled the covers from my face and tucked them to my neck. "The reserve?"

He looked down at me. "The lower floor isn't only Liam's space. There's a wine cellar down there."

Darius had a wine cellar?

"I'm totally moving here."

It was after I said that when I saw the most beautiful thing I'd seen since my son came out of me bawling.

The happy, carefree, sweet, tender loving smile of Darius Tucker.

# Chapter Thirteen

*Character*

I dressed.

Darius dressed.

And it was Darius who carried my shoes down the stairs, holding my hand on his other side.

We made it to the living room to see our son slumped, going extra, a wet washcloth folded over his eyes, his head resting on the back of the couch.

There was a bottle of red open and breathing on the coffee table, and two handsome, shining wide-bowled wineglasses.

Damn.

Darius had it going on.

Feeling our arrival, Liam told the ceiling, "I'm scarred for life."

I opened my mouth to say something when I was suddenly shoved behind Darius.

This was because we heard the front door slam open.

I peeked around him and caught Toni barreling in.

She skidded to a halt.

She was wheezing.

She put her hand to her chest, and it floated up and down as she tried to catch her breath.

Liam had taken the washcloth off, and he was studying her.

"Did you run here, Aunt Toni?" he asked.

"I…you…" She caught sight of me. "Girl!" she shouted. "I've been blowing up your phone!"

"I kinda left it in the car," I admitted.

Immediately, I thought it prudent to step back because it looked like Toni's head was going to explode.

Darius twisted to me. "Your phone is in your car?"

I nodded. "With my purse."

He sighed, then turned to Liam and said only one word.

"Boy."

I stared in marvel as Liam got up, no teenage-boy backtalk or grumbling, and headed to the front door.

"Hey, man," he said right before he disappeared into the entryway.

Tony strolled in and instantly said to Darius, "Sorry, brother. Tried to stop her."

Lena sashayed in, her gaze homed in on the wine, and she asked Darius, "Is that from the reserve?"

"Yup," he answered.

She moved to the couch and sat her round behind on it, mumbling, "When Liam gets back, he can get me a glass."

This was when Kenneth arrived.

His eyes went right to the triptych.

"Well, that's just stunning," he remarked, wandering to it like he was in a museum.

Toni and I exchanged a look.

Tony and Darius exchanged a look.

"What the fuck? My man appreciates good art. Get over it," Lena sniped.

"What?" Kenneth asked, like he just realized he wasn't the only one in the room.

Lena patted the couch next to her. "Come sit here by me, love muffin."

Dutifully, Kenneth padded to the couch and sat by his wife.

"When Toni couldn't get Malia on the line, they all piled in the car," Tony explained to Darius.

"Right," Darius replied.

"Parking around your place is for shit," Toni griped. "We had to park two blocks away."

Which explained the wheezing.

She was in heels too.

Yikes.

"Where's Talia?" I asked.

"She dragged our neighbor from having her feet up in front of her TV. She told her it was an emergency," Tony explained.

"It was," Toni asserted.

"Yeah, looks like things are dire here," Tony replied.

Thankfully, before this could escalate, Darius waded in.

"You guys want wine?" Darius offered.

"What I want is an update. Is shit good?" Toni responded, her attention pinging the short distance between me and Darius.

"She's got sex hair. Of course it's good," Lena put in.

My hands flew to my hair.

"Told you," Lena finished, aiming this at Toni. "All she had to do was show and *poof!* All good."

"Liam caught us in bed," I told Toni and Lena, moving my head each way and trying to forget the men were also there.

"Oh boy," Toni said.

"Fucking hell," Lena said.

"We were done, and I don't think he could see me. He still says he's scarred for life," I shared.

"I'm scarred for life, and I'm just listening to the story," Toni said.

"I'm not and neither is Liam. He knows his dad giving his mom the business brought him into this world," Lena said.

Even if she spoke truth, I fought gagging, knowing I'd prefer my son to live his life thinking a stork delivered him to us.

Toni looked to the side and warned an urgent, "Zip it," two seconds before Liam walked in with my purse.

And my keys.

For such a successful outcome, I'd really blown this operation.

Darius, who obviously didn't miss anything, didn't miss my keys.

He looked down at me and muttered, "Baby."

I stretched out my lips and shrugged.

His lips tipped up, and he slid his arm around my shoulders and pulled me into his side.

"Sick," Liam said, using that word as kids used it these days, meaning "awesome."

He was beaming at us.

Oh no.

I was going to cry.

"Hurry, pour the wine. You can't cry and drink at the same time," Toni announced.

"Liam, go get your aunties more glasses," Lena ordered.

"What now?" Darius asked right before the front door slammed open again and Ally stormed in, followed by Indy.

They halted and looked around the room, their eyes stopping on Darius and me.

Then their torsos swayed back.

In came Lee, and after him, the man who had pulled Ally away from Liam and me at the hospital.

But I only had eyes for Indy.

"Indy, girl, are you pregnant?" I asked a question to which the answer was obvious.

She put her hand on her big belly and smiled huge. "Yeah. Due very soon, in case you couldn't tell by how giganto I am."

"I'm so happy for you!" I exclaimed.

Her smile remained in place. "Thanks. We are too." She took in my dress and noted, "Killer duds, babe. That dress is *hot*."

I grinned. "Thanks."

"I told you it was all good and you didn't need to go crashing into Darius's house," Lee butted into our exchange to aim this at Ally.

"She was taking forever to get over it," Ally said back. "I thought she was over here, taking her sweet time to ream his ass."

"When has Malia ever reamed anyone's ass?" Lee asked.

Liam raised his hand.

"Put that hand down, Liam Clark," I snapped.

He smiled at me.

Darius gave me a squeeze.

Lee looked to Darius. "Roam and Sniff are in the control room. They saw her car here. They made a deal with Ally they'd tip her off if Malia got near you. They tipped her off. I tried to talk them out of it, but we were having dinner together and Indy fed into Ally, and you know how it goes."

Indy and Ally, everyone knew how it went, and for me, it had been nearly two decades, and still, I knew.

"Remind me to ream their asses next time I'm in the office," Darius said to Lee.

"I don't know, seems like an excuse for a party. I'll call Jet. She can bring the cashews," Indy said.

"Righteous!" Ally cried.

"Fuck," Darius swore.

"Best be gettin' your ass back down to the reserve, Liam. And break out some more glasses," Lena ordered.

Liam looked to his dad.

Darius nodded.

Liam headed out of the room.

I got up on tiptoe and asked in Darius's ear. "How do you do that?"

"I got a dick," he answered.

I scrunched my face.

Even so, he kissed me.

I could swear I heard someone sigh.

The problem was, I thought it was Kenneth.

"Girl, you gotta lose your pad," Toni, now examining the African mask, called. "It's alright. But this place has got character."

I looked up to Darius.

I leaned into Darius.

And then I smiled.

*　*　*　*

I was in Darius's attractive kitchen, which was bigger than mine (way bigger), had better…well, *everything* than mine (and I'd gone for a load of upgrades), and I was drying wineglasses.

With grave effort, Lee stopped Indy and Ally from calling in their crew.

We all had a glass of wine (except Indy, Darius got her some ice water).

Then Tony corralled his crew and got them out the door.

Lee corralled his (and I discovered Ally's man was called Ren, and he was as nice as he was fine) and got them out the door.

Which left me, Darius and Liam.

And I was hiding.

Darius walked in.

I aimed a smile at him, but it was trembling so much, it probably looked more like a grimace.

He took the wineglass out of one hand, the towel out of the other, put the first down, threw the last beside it, then shifted me with his body to fence me in facing him with his hands on the counter at either side of me.

"Right, sweetheart, so we didn't get down to planning how we'd ease into this with Liam, but we're here now, we gotta wing it."

"I just thought I'd give him a kiss and go home. He's got to go to bed. He's got school tomorrow."

"Baby, hate to break this to you, but he's in AP classes and football. When he's not doing something with the team, he studies so much, he sleeps about two hours a night. And he's sixteen. That's all he needs."

I begged to differ.

As such, I shook my head. "He's still a growing boy. I talked to the doctor about it since he won't stop. He said boys can keep growing into their early twenties."

"Good to know," he murmured, eyes on my mouth.

I put a hand to his flat belly, then wished I didn't because I could feel the hardness and ridges, and our son was in the next room.

"Darius, stop looking at my mouth," I demanded.

His eyes lifted to mine. "He's not six. He's not going to get confused."

I took my hand from his stomach so I could wring both of them together and looked around his shoulder at the door.

"Malia, baby, eyes to me."

I returned my gaze to him.

"Let's just sit him down, open a dialogue with him, and see where he's at."

I felt my brows inch together. "Open a dialogue?"

"Yeah. One of the guys at work, Vance, his wife is a social worker. Her name is Jules. She's got a job at a shelter for runaways. I talked with her about all this, and if you and I got to this place, how we'd help Liam deal."

Oh my God.

Could a body melt?

It could. I felt it happening to me.

"That was very sweet of you."

"I love my kid. I also talked to her about how to help him adjust to split custody. But he didn't need it. He was so relieved we were out about all our shit, he just settled in."

"I noticed that," I mumbled.

"Malia, our son is waiting for us."

Our son.

He was our son.

And he could be, officially, on the record, *our son* with us being *his parents* if I stopped hiding in the damned kitchen.

"You good?" Darius asked.

I nodded.

He unpinned me but took my hand.

He led me into the living room where Liam was sprawled in one of the black leather chairs.

In fact, he was sprawled in the one I tackled his father into a few hours before.

Eek!

*Work through it, girl!* my mind screamed.

Liam started it.

"You don't have to sit me down like I'm five and tell me Mom's spending the night. I think I got it earlier that you worked things out."

Darius led me to the couch and hesitated. I looked up at him in confusion, and his gaze went from me to the couch to me.

Oh.

Right.

I sat.

He remained standing and faced his son.

I stilled and my heart stopped in my chest.

Because Mister Morris used to do that.

At an event or gathering, he'd lead Miss Dorothea to a seat, made sure she was comfortable, but he was a stander.

He stood.

Usually close to his wife's side, sometimes so he'd be there if she needed anything, because he'd send Darius or one of his sisters to get their mother and him something, but usually, it was Mister Morris who saw to Miss Dorothea. Sometimes it seemed just so he'd be close, but she'd be comfortable.

Oh God.

Darius spoke.

"You do understand that we both love you and it's important for us to know you're processing this appropriately."

Man, he had this *down*. That Jules chick must be something.

"No shade, Dad, but again, I'm not five," Liam said, his manner relaxed, his face untroubled, his lips slightly tipped up at the ends. "I know how you two feel about each other. It's kinda hard to miss. So I guess how I'm processing things is to say it's about damned time." He looked to me. "No offense with the cursing, Mom, but it's warranted, don't you think?" Before I could answer (that would be in the negative), he returned his attention to his dad. "But you gotta talk Mom into moving here. Your place is where it's at."

"Your mother likes the wine cellar," Darius shared.

I hadn't even seen it.

Still, I'd had a glass of wine from it.

So, I liked it.

"I knew that'd get her," Liam mumbled.

I decided it was time to cut in.

"You seem very okay with this, honey. But maybe we should all take some time to get used to it."

Liam unslouched to put his elbows to his knees and level his gaze on me.

"I love you, Mom," he said softly. "But that's cracked. Stop wasting time. Be happy. Please."

Welp!

That did it.

I'd done well. I'd held them back, lots of times.

But I couldn't hack *that*.

I burst out crying.

"Oh shit," Liam muttered.

Darius pulled me out of the couch and into his arms.

"You got this?" Liam asked. "I got history homework."

"Got it, son. Go," Darius replied.

"'Night, Mom," Liam called.

"'N-n-night, h-h-honey," I blubbered.

"'Night, Dad."

"See you in the morning."

I cried and I cried some more, then a thought hit me, and I quit crying and looked up at Darius.

"I don't have any clean panties."

"Don't think I can send our boy out for those," Darius replied.

I slapped his shoulder.

He started chuckling.

Then he pulled me closer. "It won't kill you to drive home in yesterday's undies, will it?"

I sniffled and shook my head.

"Pack heavy when you come back tomorrow night after work," he ordered.

I stared up at him and condensed my "everything" discussion to one question.

"Are we really doing this?"

"We are absolutely doing this."

Happiness blossomed in me.

So, of course, my face crumpled, and I cried some more.

Darius held me through it.

Sheltering my storm.

# Chapter Fourteen

*Chicken Montana*

I woke, stretched, my wrist hit something, and I opened my eyes.

It was just dawn, the light coming in from outside was weak, but I could see I'd knocked the new toothbrush head that Darius had put on his pillow off said pillow.

I smiled.

Then I looked around, but Darius wasn't there. The bathroom door was open, so he must be up already.

I nabbed the toothbrush head, threw the covers back, and in Darius's thermal, which I put on after our second round last night (finding something good about Liam having a whole level to himself, with another one sandwiched in between), I padded to the bathroom.

I did my business, got dressed and headed downstairs, making a mental list of what to pack to bring over and wondering if I had time at lunch to run out and double up on some toiletries.

Once I hit the downstairs, I heard male voices coming from the kitchen and headed that way.

I stopped in the door.

So much was happening last night, I didn't get to take a moment to really watch father and son interact.

Now I saw Liam sitting at a stool at the long island that was the centerpiece of the big kitchen, eating eggs and bacon and toast with grape jelly, his back to me, but doing this like he'd lived there all his life, not just every other week for the last five months.

Darius was standing across from him wearing a long-sleeved Henley, this one in burnt orange, and jeans.

He had his weight braced into his hands at the edge of the counter, spread out to the sides, and his gaze on me.

He looked like the master of his domain, which he was, and that domain he'd created was amazing, like he was.

Liam caught his dad looking at me and peered over his shoulder my way.

"Carry on," I said softly. "I want to watch."

"You're not going to cry again, are you?" Liam asked.

"I make no promises."

He shook his head, a smile playing at his lips, and went back to his food.

"Come in, baby. I'll make you breakfast before you gotta head home," Darius invited.

"'Kay," I mumbled and wandered in.

I took a seat next to my son.

"Did you get good sleep?" I asked him.

"Dad bought me one of those hybrid mattresses. It's the shhhh-oot."

I bumped him with my shoulder and teased, "It's the shoot?"

"Cussing isn't such a bad thing, Mom," Liam informed me. "Dad and his buds do it all the time."

My eyes cut to his father.

Darius cracked an egg into a bowl, shrugged and agreed, "It isn't."

"A gentleman doesn't curse," I declared.

Father looked to son, son looked to father, and they busted out laughing.

Oh Lord.

We'd had an equilibrium, with one authority...*me.*

Now I was outnumbered.

"Are you two going to make a habit of ganging up on me?" I asked.

"Absolutely," Liam answered.

"Not on any important stuff, sweetheart," Darius assured.

"I think cursing is important."

Darius seemed perplexed.

He sounded it too, when he asked, "Really?"

"Maybe we should talk about this when the boy is not in attendance," I suggested sweetly.

Okay, not sweetly.

Fake sweetly.

"You're still not gonna change my mind. I don't buy that shit that swearing shows a lack of intelligence," Darius retorted. "It just demonstrates another way the establishment tries to control your behavior by making random shit wrong, like words."

"Or sex," Liam put in.

Darius nodded. "Or sex."

It felt like my eyes had bugged out of my head.

"We're definitely talking about *this* when the boy is not in attendance," I decreed.

"We've had the talk, baby," Darius replied. "A couple of years ago. He's got condoms."

I made a cacking noise then my forehead thunked on the stainless-steel counter because I couldn't hold it up anymore.

Though, it must be said, I was relieved they'd had the talk. I hadn't done it yet because I was committed to the task of avoiding it like the plague. Not smart for a woman who'd been a teenage mom but cut me some slack. That stuff wasn't easy.

And anyway, I'd been secretly hoping my dad or Tony had stepped in.

Fortunately, Liam's own father did.

"I think you broke her," Liam remarked.

"She'll be fine," Darius replied, and I heard him whisking my eggs.

I lifted my head and wheezed, "*Coffee.*"

"Get your mother a coffee," Darius ordered.

Liam left his plate and went to the coffeepot.

He then returned with a handsome mug that was a matte charcoal gray on the outside and a shiny robin's egg blue porcelain on the inside.

Right.

Now this was just weird.

I examined the cup then looked to my man. "Is everything in your house perfect?"

"Aunt Danni and Aunt Gabby bought everything in this place," Liam informed me. "They even put together my space. It's *sick.*"

"Danni and Gabby?" I whispered to Darius.

Those were his sisters, Danielle and Gabrielle.

"They own an interior design business together," he shared.

Now this was weird too, but not the good kind.

Because I realized how much I didn't know. How much I missed. How much I didn't ask about.

Even Lena last night knew about "the reserve."

But I hadn't even seen it and had just heard about it.

"Don't go there," Darius warned, reading my mind.

"It's impossible not to," I returned.

"We'll catch up. Mom'll have a dinner. It'll be all good," he declared.

"You can't catch up on eighteen years over a dinner, Darius," I informed him.

"You can make a start," he returned. "All we can do, the three of us, is take it one step at a time. We're having breakfast. That's this step. Let's focus on that. You with me?"

"Stop being rational when I'm on the verge of freaking out," I snapped.

"Get used to it, sweetheart," he shot back.

I felt something strange and turned my head to see our son's attention was bouncing between his dad and me and his grin was large.

When I witnessed it, I was sure glad I didn't make any promises about crying.

Liam saved me by stating, "This is the best fucking breakfast *ever.*"

Then he munched into his toast.

My son had just casually dropped the F-bomb in front of me.

I swung a killing look at Darius.

And again, he busted out laughing.

Liam joined him.

I didn't.

I drank coffee.

* * * *

I'd gone home, washed yesterday's makeup off, showered, dressed, and was on my way to work when the first call came in from someone I didn't know.

I had a son who was out in the world, and he had a new car, which was a muscle car, but even before that I'd lived a life where I knew anything could happen, so even if this meant I regularly had to hang up on marketers and scammers, I took the call.

"Hello?"

"Malia! Hey, it's Indy. We're putting together a Malia and Darius Are Together party. Obviously, since you're one of the people of honor, you gotta come. Are you free Saturday night?"

"I think so."

"Perfect. Text me Toni and Lena's numbers. We have to ask them. And your folks."

"Um...okay."

"So are you moving in with Darius, or is he gonna move in with you?"

"We haven't really decided yet," I semi-lied.

I was definitely moving.

And it wasn't about the wine cellar I still hadn't seen, nor was it about the décor.

It was the fact we'd shared our first breakfast as a family in his kitchen, even if Liam finished eating well before Darius and me, and it might be weird, but now, that felt like home.

"Oh?" She sounded disappointed.

"But I'm doubling up on toiletries," I blurted, because no one wanted to be disappointing.

"Really?"

"Yes."

"Rock on!" she cried.

I couldn't help it, I laughed.

She hadn't changed one bit.

And that made me happy.

"I gotta call Ally and tell her. Girl, you can't know how thrilled we are for you two. This is the best love story of them all."

I couldn't disagree.

"Thanks."

"And glad to have you back. Missed you."

"I missed you too."

"Right, letting you go. We'll catch up Saturday. Later!"

"Later."

She hung up.

I was smiling as I finished driving to work.

And when I got to my desk, I programmed Indy's number into my phone.

\* \* \* \*

The next call came when I was at the mall, dashing through the skincare and makeup sections, eating Wetzel Pretzel bites for lunch, multitasking.

It was another number I didn't know.

"Hello?"

"Hey, chickie. Ally."

"Heya, Ally."

"Were you at?"

"At the mall, doubling up on toiletries."

"I heard. Righteous," she said. "Listen, I know we're on for the party Saturday night, but you got some time during the day to meet me at Fortnum's?"

Fortnum's.

I'd avoided it for nearly two decades for fear Darius still went there, and more, because I couldn't face the happy memories that had seemed so bittersweet, with emphasis on bitter.

Now they could just be sweet.

I felt something settle in me because I had Indy back, and Ally back, and I'd have Duke back, and Fortnum's too.

"I can meet you, what time?"

"Eleven?"

"Works for me. And I didn't get to ask Indy, but should we bring anything to the party?"

"Just you and Darius and Liam. The guests of honor don't have to contribute. But get your recipes in order. We do this shit a lot."

Why wasn't I surprised?

"We'll bring a bottle anyway."

"Suit yourself. See you Saturday."

"See you then."

I hung up and the saleslady told me my total.

I then fought fainting (one never stocked up on it all, all at once, but doing so was sobering, it still wasn't going to deter me from my products, because I made bank, obviously so did my man, and I deserved them), and I handed over my credit card.

While she ran it, I programmed Ally's number into my phone.

When I got out to my car, I shoved it all in my trunk with a smile.

Because I had to lug it all out there.

But Darius would order Liam to go out and get it when I got home.

\* \* \* \*

That night, after going to my house and packing, I drove down the alley behind Darius's house and used the remote for his garage he gave me that morning.

But even after the door was completely up, I didn't pull in.

Because the Charger was in the garage, and the Silverado was parked in the spot beside it, open to the elements.

He gave his son and his woman his garage, and he was going to get into a cold car tomorrow.

I took a deep breath so I wouldn't get caught by one of his neighbors sitting in my car in the alley sobbing, and I pulled in.

Since I'd gone gung ho, I opened the back door and heaved the massive suitcase out of it. No need to waste a trip.

That big case didn't fit in the trunk with all my bags and the other suitcases.

Luckily, it had rollers, but still. I had some steps to get up, which wasn't easy.

I made it to the back door, entered a mudroom/laundry room that looked like an advertisement for Crate and Barrel, and then Darius was there.

He looked to the huge-ass suitcase, to me, the suitcase, back to me.

"Jesus, babe," he said, lips twitching.

"There's more in the car."

That's when he started chuckling, and the light that hit his eyes was humor, for sure, it was also something else that I loved with every fiber of my being.

He then shouted, "Liam! Get your mom's shit from the car!"

"On it!" Liam shouted from the bowels of the house.

Darius strong-armed me away from my suitcase and rolled it in.

I followed him into the kitchen then into the living room and stopped there to get a kiss on the cheek from my kid and a "Hey, Mom."

"Hey, honey."

He kept going.

Darius left the suitcase at the foot of the stairs and came back to me.

"How much is out there?" he asked.

"You might want to help him."

That look in his eyes came back, he wrapped a hand around the side of my neck, and he kissed me.

It was wet, and it was thorough, but it was far too short.

"A red is breathing for you in the kitchen," he murmured when he was done with my mouth.

"Okeydokey." I was breathing too (I still wasn't over the kiss).

He shook his head, gave my neck a squeeze and took off.

I went to the kitchen and poured a glass of wine.

I was taking my second sip (I really needed to tour the cellar, last night's wine was excellent, tonight's was superb) when my two boys came back.

"Jeez, Mom, did you leave anything at Nordstrom?" Liam asked.

"No," I answered.

He shook his head like his father had not much earlier and disappeared into the living room.

Darius, rolling my medium suitcase (Liam had all the bags, and was rolling my carryon), followed him.

Darius came back quickly, meaning Liam got the job of lugging that all up the stairs.

"Did you make room for my stuff?" I asked.

"Babe, I'm not a clotheshorse like you. Three quarters of my closet is empty, and there's inbuilt drawers in there I've never used."

"So I'm set," I said before my next sip.

"Did you bring hangers?

I frowned.

"I'll hit Target tomorrow," he muttered, going after his own wineglass.

This wine thing was another surprise. I'd always thought Darius would be a beer drinker. He was when we were partying in high school.

I guessed he grew up.

Like me.

I noticed it.

And yet part of me was stuck back in time.

Learning these new things about him, I found, was pretty damned awesome.

"I'll head out at lunch and go to the Container Store," I said. "I'm persnickety about my hangers."

He poured as he replied, "You tell me what you want, I'll get it. I'm out of the office most of the time. It's easier for me to swing by than it is for you to get away. And you need a break for lunch, not hitting a store."

"It'd be appreciated."

"That's nice, but it really isn't a problem."

Okay, maybe I could take them ganging up on me, if I got this diva treatment on the regular.

But we still had to have a conversation about the cussing.

"Did you hear about the party on Saturday?" I asked.

"Brace, baby. They're gonna suck you into the Rock Chicks."

The Rock Chicks.

That's what the book was called that someone wrote about Indy and Lee.

It was apropos. They'd always been Rock Chicks, and from what I could tell, that also hadn't changed.

"Is that bad?" I asked curiously.

"Not even a little bit. They're good people," he muttered as Liam strolled in.

"We got a decision?" he asked. "I'm hungry."

"Oh, are we deciding on dinner?" I inquired, and my stomach inquired too. Those pretzel bites wore off several hours ago.

"Kind of," Darius said then turned to me. "You wanna go out? A family celebration. Our first dinner together. Or do you want me to cook us something and have it lowkey here? I got a reservation at Carmine's on Penn, but I can call and cancel if you want lowkey."

I watched him get wavy as the tears filled my eyes.

"Dad, she's gonna blow," Liam warned.

Darius got close, bent to me and cupped my face. "Sweetheart, we don't have time for this. Liam is hungry and our reservation is in half an hour. If we're staying home, I need to call so they can seat our table. If we're going, we have to leave in fifteen minutes. You can lose it when we get back."

"We-we're going out," I forced out. "It's a celebration. Nobody does dishes after a celebration."

It was still watery, but I caught his smile.

I lost it when he touched his lips to mine.

"Rad," Liam said. "Can we get Chicken Montana?"

With his arm around my waist, Darius tucked me into his side.

And then he said to his son, "You can get anything you want."

I blubbered into my wine.

My boys looked down at me.

I lifted a hand. "Fine, fine, I'm fine." I took a deep breath and let it out. "Totally fine."

"She's not gonna make it through dinner," Liam said to his dad.

"Go get some Kleenex from the bathroom and shove it into her purse."

"Gotcha."

Liam took off.

Serious.

It was like magic.

I looked up at Darius. "Is it really just because you have a dick?"

"No. It's because he's happy and he wants us happy. In a week, he's gonna return to being a teenaged kid."

"So you have times were he grumbles and moans and backtalks under his breath?"

Darius's brows went up. "He backtalks you?"

I shook my head quickly. "No. No. Never. Not ever." And I hid my lying eyes by looking away and taking a sip of wine.

Darius nabbed his glass and sipped his.

Then he stated, "You're a shit liar."

"Whatever," I said into my glass. After another sip, I told him, "I want Chicken Montana too."

He turned me fully into his arms and bent his neck to look down at me.

"Anything you want, baby. Always."

I rested against him in his beautiful kitchen held in his strong arms, thinking this was working out great.

For me.

For Liam.

But especially, for Darius.

# Chapter Fifteen

*Any Means Necessary*

I walked up Broadway toward Fortnum's, Toni at my side, and I didn't have sidewalk pavement under my feet.

I was walking on a cloud.

Suffice it to say, our first family dinner was perfect. So much so, I knew with no doubts I'd remember every second of it for the rest of my life.

Sure, my boys teased me mercilessly, but I didn't care.

I got to watch them together.

How easy they were in each other's company. How Liam looked at his dad with pride and respect and love all over his face. How Darius seemed so in his element with his woman and his son in his space. It was natural, relaxed, we laughed a lot, conversation flowed. It wasn't like our first family meal out ever; it was like we'd been doing it for years.

When we got home, I finally got a full tour of the house.

A tour that cemented the fact I was moving.

The main level had the fabulous kitchen and living room, and it also had a handsome study, a family room (there was no TV in the living room, but there was a huge comfortable sectional, and an equally huge flat screen TV, replete with games console, in the family room), a dining room and full bath, which would come in handy if we had a house full of people visiting (and with the amount of extended family Darius and I had, this could happen), and someone had to bunk in the family room.

The upstairs had Darius's room with big walk-in closet, his extraordinary bathroom that had a mix of teal floor tiles with an interesting design, white subway tile above the basin and in the shower, slate gray walls and a clean-lined, modern, wood vanity under a double basin with brass fixtures. There was also an open shower and a statement bath.

There were three other bedrooms up there, one larger, with a smaller walk-in and en suite bathroom, two smaller that shared a Jack and Jill bath.

None of those had any furniture.

So I guessed Darius hadn't had any company.

But I knew that would change.

The lower level wasn't as bad as I thought it'd be.

In other words, it didn't look like a bachelor pad.

If there had been a kitchen down there, there was no sign of it now. Liam's space had another huge sectional with a TV mounted on the wall and a games console and DVD player with a long shelving unit filled with DVDs underneath it. This sectional was less stylish than the one upstairs (but still stylish), built for comfort and hours of lounging with a massive removable ottoman that fit snug in the U of the couch, so it resembled a bed.

His bedroom area was all grays and blacks, and there was no fourteen-year-old boy there.

It was a man's room.

That didn't mean there wasn't any personality. But it was in the art and the lighting (including a cool blue glow that crept from under the bed).

It was perfect for him.

He had a full bath that was all chrome and dark gray block tiles and an interesting bowl sink sitting on a rich wood bureau.

This only took half the downstairs.

The other half was divided between four rooms, two being storage that were mostly empty, except some crates at the back of one, in which, among other things, I saw Darius's high school yearbooks.

The other one was a big room that had a treadmill, an elliptical machine and weight equipment.

And the last was the wine cellar, which was a true wine cellar with walls of wine shelves, innumerable dusty bottles of wine, two large, tall, restaurant-quality wine coolers, and even a grouping in the center of four leather armchairs with attractive tables in between. There was another small fridge that looked like it had fruits and cheeses in it, set into a bar cart with a full bar, and above it, a set of display shelves with a selection of gorgeous glasses.

It wasn't just a place to store wine. It was a place to hang out and appreciate wine.

I loved it.

The whole house.

It was very masculine.

But I wouldn't change a thing.

After I'd oohed and aahed and smiled and giggled and put my official stamp of approval on the place, Darius asked after Liam's homework, and our son set off to his room.

I set off to do whatever unpacking I could do, which was emptying my Nordstrom bags (and putting my stuff around the unused basin next to Darius's made me decidedly giddy). Liam had taken the suitcases into the walk-in, and I located the empty drawers and put away anything that could go in them and on shelves.

I discovered Darius's clothes were hanging on wire hangers, and I couldn't even, so I didn't, and I decided to deal with that too when Darius grabbed some the next day.

Though, he'd been wrong. His stuff didn't take up a quarter of the space, it maybe took up a sixth. It was clear it was casual gear he wore to work, but my man needed more clothes.

It looked like no one loved him.

And that wouldn't do.

After that, Darius and I finished off the bottle of wine he'd opened earlier while sitting cuddled together on his creamy-beige couch in the living room, with me asking questions I'd been dying to ask, and getting answers I loved to hear.

Yes, he liked his work at Nightingale Investigations.

No, it didn't feel like Lee was his boss. Lee didn't manage his men that way, or he wouldn't have the men he had. They were a team, Lee was just their leader.

No, it wasn't as dangerous as I'd feared it would be. It was just that the Rock Chicks were magnets for disaster. All their shit was outlying (I wasn't sure he told the whole truth about this, but since my cloud of happy goodness was forming around me, I was letting that be).

Yes, he bought and paid for all of this during his drug dealing days. And yes, he had money safe and tucked away so Liam and I were set for life. Also yes, Lee paid well for the work he did. But no, the ties to that life were completely severed. It hadn't been easy, but he and his Aunt Shirleen were out and there was no going back.

Shirleen, by the way, was Lee's receptionist.

So yeah, those men always took care of their family.

And it wasn't lost on me when we got to the "set for life" part that this was likely, if possibly unconsciously, why Darius stayed in the game as long as he did.

His father could have no clue he'd be murdered, but when he was, his wife and children were nowhere near set for life.

But even though nothing was going to happen to my man (God willing), Liam and I were.

Eventually, the bottle was empty, and I was tired, so we called down our goodnights to Liam, went upstairs, made love, and I passed out.

I woke up to breakfast at the island with my boys. It was an unusual gray, blustery day for Denver, but it shined bright for me in that kitchen.

I went to work, and after work, I went to my place with my big and medium suitcases and filled them again.

Yes, I was moving fast.

No, I didn't care.

The writing was on the wall. I'd waited years for this.

And anyway, I needed more shoes.

I got handed guff from Darius when I rolled one of the suitcases up to the back door, and he sent Liam out for the other one.

He took the one I rolled up to the closet, where I followed him, in which there were three bags filled with hangers.

I changed into some jeans and a warm sweater that hung off one shoulder and got down to work unpacking, but also taking Darius's clothes off the wire hangers and switching them out with the new.

I ran out of hangers, counted how many more I needed and added a few in my mental calculations for growth purposes, deciding to sandwich a trip to the Container Store (and the mall, Darius needed a new shirt for the Rock Chick party, and new jeans, and boots) between the meet at Fortnum's and the party.

I then went downstairs to the kitchen to find Darius cooking.

"I was gonna cook," I announced.

"You can cook Monday," he replied.

It was Friday. The party was tomorrow.

So…

"Monday?" I asked.

"We're having dinner at Mom's Sunday."

"Oh boy," I said.

"It's gonna be fine."

I wanted to believe that, and I kinda did.

We weren't months deep in this situation, far from it, but so far, no hiccups.

So far, it was nothing but clouds of happy goodness.

We'd been through years of strife and strain, and everyone knew it.

Maybe now, I could believe.

Maybe now—enduring bouts of rocky times, the kind that life always eventually threw at you—we could be normal.

We could be free.

I went to the wine Darius had opened and poured myself a glass as he asked me, "You good with that?"

I nodded.

"Danni and Gabs are gonna be there," he shared.

I'd liked his sisters. They were sweet. We'd been close. In fact, Gabby was in my grade and had been my friend before I'd started going out with Darius.

I was looking forward to seeing them again.

I took my wine to a stool, reminding him, "They always liked me."

"Sorry, babe," he said low, "but so you don't walk in blind, you gotta know, they weren't huge fans of you being angry at me and laying it out when I was in a hospital bed."

Oops.

I caught his gaze over my wineglass while taking a sip.

When I was done with that, I said, "They're going to have to get over it."

His lips curved. "Yeah, they are."

Liam sauntered in. "What's for dinner?"

"What's for dinner is you getting on the corn, son," Darius ordered. "The cast iron skillet. Melt the butter. Medium heat. Pour in the whole bag of frozen corn when it's melted. Salt and lots of pepper. And watch that shit. I don't want it burning. And let's get a move on. You gotta get to the field."

Liam had a game that night, and Darius was right. We were cutting it close.

"Gotcha," Liam said, heading for a drawer and pulling out a Le Creuset skillet that had a matte blue around the outside.

"What can I do?" I asked.

"Drink wine," Darius answered.

It hit me then, like a bullet.

All this spoiling. No lugging suitcases and shopping bags or running out into the cold to get the purse and keys I left in my car my own self.

This wasn't Darius making up for lost time, going the extra mile to show he was a protector and provider.

This was Mister Morris.

Miss Dorothea was *A Mom*, in caps, through and through. She cooked. She kept her house immaculate. She checked homework. She did school runs.

But she did not carry the groceries from the car.

She didn't even waste a trip and bring in the first load.

She came in with her purse, and Mister Morris or Darius went to get the groceries, not a word spoken, it just happened.

And Danni nor Gabby did that kind of thing.

Just Mister Morris or Darius.

Back then, I thought it was sweet.

Now, I got it.

I got all of it.

Including the drug dealing.

Mister Morris was a protector and a provider.

He taught his son that.

And the way he did, it was by any means necessary.

I didn't realize I was staring at my man until he asked, "What?"

I jerked myself out of it and took in his beloved face.

There was only one thing I could say.

So I said it.

"I love you."

His expression grew soft. I noted out of the corner of my eye our son ducked his head.

But I was wildly elated when, for the first time since forever, our child was right there when Darius said it back.

"Love you too, baby."

Happy…

Cloud…

Of *goodness*.

Darius got his son fed, and his woman, and Liam took off to the field. Darius and I followed later, and there was only a bit of uncomfortableness when Miss Dorothea joined Darius, my mom and dad, Lena, Toni, Tony, Talia and me (Kenneth didn't do sports).

But she smiled brightly at us and kissed my cheek.

So I guessed it was water under the bridge, and I was glad for it.

And one could say I was fucking *ecstatic* that Liam's cheer block was expanding.

Second best to our night at Carmine's? (Okay, third best, after our first breakfast together.)

Sitting beside Darius, watching our boy play ball.

I'd never forget that either.

Not a second of it.

By the way, our team won, and Liam scored a touchdown.

So, yes.

Walking toward Fortnum's after breakfast number three with my kid and my man, this meal longer, more laid-back, with all of us cooking together and eating together and lingering over coffee and giving each other stick and cleaning up together, I was walking on air.

We turned the corner to the door to Fortnum's that was angled there, and I suddenly couldn't wait to walk into my past that was also my future.

I shot Toni a bright smile that had her eyebrows reaching for her hairline before I pushed in, and the familiar sound of the bell over the door rang.

But once I got inside, I stopped dead.

Toni stopped dead beside me.

And we stared.

She was the first to break the silence.

And she did this by drawling, "Welllllll...*shit.*"

# Chapter Sixteen

*Swatches*

Things had changed over the years at Fortnum's.

There was an espresso bar against the side wall where the tables and chairs with the games had been back in the day.

There were new, but still worn-in and comfortable couches and armchairs scattered around, with some tables and chairs at the front.

And there were a lot more patrons than there used to be, and although some high-school-aged kids were there, they were no longer the majority.

But the field of books stretched off to the back just like they used to, and that musty smell I remembered so well mingled with coffee filled the air, permeating me with nostalgia.

The good kind.

The happy kind.

The wondrous kind.

However, sitting in the seating area in front of the large plate-glass window was what could only be every beautiful white woman in the Denver Metro area.

And, if my eyes weren't deceiving me, among them was Dolly Parton, traveled forward through time, or a much younger lookalike, replete with a huge head of platinum blonde hair not even close to being contained by a wide pink Alice band. She was wearing a pink lace bustier out of which was bursting so much cleavage, entire sects of fundamental Christian churches had her on their watch list. Over this was a denim blazer, its lapels adorned with diamanté rivets. On the bottom were skintight, stonewash jeans, her calves and feet covered in bubblegum pink, patent leather, platform stripper boots.

She looked like she was going to pop up and start singing "Two Doors Down."

She was a lot.

And I wanted to be her best friend immediately.

But there was more.

The man behind the espresso counter had an ultra-long russet beard, a wild head of graying blond hair, and the aura of a serial killer. He was wearing a flannel shirt and looked like Grizzly Adams gone bad.

I wasn't sure I wanted to be his best friend, but he looked interesting.

Duke, unfortunately, was nowhere in sight.

Indy was waddling over to us, but it was the guy behind the espresso counter who boomed, "VIP! VIP!" He turned to a blonde woman behind the counter with him and hollered, "Froth, woman! Froth! She's here!"

"I'm frothing, Tex, I'm frothing," the woman said, smiling a smile that was so dazzling, I was stupefied for a moment, but she was doing it while frothing.

And then Indy was there. "That's Tex. He's loud. He's annoying. He's also sweet and makes great coffee. And that was his way of saying he's happy to meet you."

"Do I get froth, my man?" Toni called to him.

"Who are you?" the man named Tex boomed.

She tilted her head at me. "I'm her best bitch."

"Then fuck yeah!" Tex shouted, and I felt my eyes widen at his language shouted across a place of business where the women at the front section, clearly Indy's crew, weren't the only people in the place.

However, oddly, it didn't appear like they heard it, or they were regulars and it was nothing new.

"Sit your ass down," Tex ordered on another boom. "I got you."

He then, no other way to put it, appeared to be *attacking* the espresso machine.

Indy took my hand and thus began the introductions.

I kinda recognized them from that time Liam and I spent in the hospital, but for obvious reasons, I couldn't say I was paying a lot of attention then.

In fact, I couldn't have been, because I hadn't noticed Tex or the Dolly Parton lookalike, and even with the Darius situation, I would have remembered them.

First there was Roxie, who was Hank, Lee and Ally's older brother's wife. Then Jules, who was married to Vance, another one of Lee's men, the woman Darius had talked to about Liam. And Ava, who was married to a guy named Luke, also one of Lee's men. Sadie, a fairytale-princess-looking gal who was married to Eddie's younger brother, Hector (who, too, worked for Lee). Stella was semi-kinda famous. I'd heard of her before she hit the papers with her story with her guy. She was in a popular local rock group. Her man was another of Lee's team, his name was Mace. Then there was Jet, who came out from behind the counter. She was Eddie's wife.

Ally was there too.

And the Dolly Parton lookalike was called Daisy. I learned she worked with Ally, and when I was introduced to her, she said, "I sure am glad to meet you, sugar. It's high time. Welcome to the tribe," and then she emitted a laugh that was gorgeous. It sounded like tinkling bells.

The final two were a hippie chick named Annette who greeted me with a "Yo, bitch!" and I learned, unsurprisingly, she owned the head shop down the way.

And Shirleen, who was studying me tentatively and holding herself uncomfortably.

I knew why.

Darius hadn't given me the whole story yet, but I did know she blamed herself for her nephew getting sucked into a world where he didn't belong.

It was just, she held no blame.

So I stood in front of her, a bevy of Rock Chick eyes focused on me, and I said softly, "Come on, Aunt Shirleen. It's been a long time. No hug?"

She caught my eyes and relief saturated hers, right before she surged out of her chair and gave me a hug.

I remembered it right.

Her hugs were the best.

"Stop hugging. Sit your ass down. Drink." Tex was close, his booming even closer, so I let Shirleen go, but made sure I gave her a smile before Toni and I were bumped and prodded into sitting beside each other on the couch.

Jet assumed the arm of the couch by me, Indy wedged herself in beside Toni, and Jules was perched on the other arm. Roxie and Ava lounged in the two armchairs across from us, Daisy sitting on an arm of Ava's chair. Shirleen sat in the one at the end, Sadie in the other. Annette sat cross legged on the top of a table between Jules and Sadie with Stella straddling a turned-around chair she'd pulled over from a table, doing this between Sadie and Roxie. Ally doing the same thing between Roxie and Ava.

The gang was all there.

A mug topped with foam was shoved in my hand.

"Don't know what you like, so I threw everything good at it," Tex low-boomed. "Vanilla, cinnamon and a hint of almond. Tell me what you think."

I sipped it.

My eyes rolled back into my head.

He'd shoved a mug into Toni's hands too, and I knew she had her sip when she whispered a reverent, *"Motherfucker."*

"I'll take that as approval," Tex declared then he clapped his hands, the sound so loud, I jumped, nearly sloshing coffee and foam over my hand. He then rubbed them together, saying, "Right. What we talkin' here? I gotta dust off my grenades? Smoke bombs? Or dig out my brass knuckles?"

Slowly, my head turned to Toni to find she'd already turned to me, and I was pretty sure we wore identical surprised/confused/terrified expressions.

"We've never needed brass knuckles, Uncle Tex," Roxie put in.

"Don't mean you shouldn't have them," Daisy replied in her adorable country twang, studying lethally tipped nails embedded with so many rhinestones, you could barely see the pearly pink polish underneath. "I got me some years ago. Between Jules and Ava. Or was it Roxie and Jules? Don't matter. Pink lacquer. They're cute."

Cute brass knuckles?

I was under the impression this was the chilled-out, hang-with-some-coffee-and-girlfriends-before-the-onslaught-of-a-big-party-in-order-to-get-to-know-each-other portion of shifting into the life that I hadn't shared with Darius until then.

How were we talking about brass knuckles?

The bell over the door sounded and I looked that way to see a tall slender white man with a brown crew cut and a shorter, handsome Hispanic man walking in.

The taller man had what looked like a scrapbook in his arm tucked to his chest.

"I'm out," Tex low-boomed, and immediately lumbered away.

Even as crazy as that man seemed, I should have taken this as the warning it was.

Alas, I did not.

The crewcut guy walked right into the seating area, dropped the scrapbook on the coffee table with a loud *funf*, then lifted his hands, forefingers and thumbs in L-shapes, tips of thumbs touching to create a frame through which he squinted.

*At me.*

"Ummm…" Toni mumbled.

My thought exactly.

He dropped his hands and announced to the store at large. "I can't. I don't know her, but this is impossible. Every color looks good against Black skin. I'll never be able to pick."

I wouldn't quite agree. The color they named "flesh" didn't quite work.

Toni and I exchanged another glance.

"This is Tod," Jules shared. "And his partner Stevie. Tod's the Rock Chicks' officially unofficial wedding planner."

I choked and I hadn't even sipped my coffee.

Darius and I weren't even living together officially.

We were on *day three*.

Yes, I loved him, and he loved me. Yes, we were *doing this*. Yes, we shared a son who we were both devoted to.

But with all that had gone on before, and it being so heavy, I'd never even thought about us getting married.

Never let myself dream that far ahead.

Something around the region of my heart shifted, and it didn't feel bad.

No.

It felt very, very good.

"I've got it!" Tod shouted on a snap. "Amethyst!"

"My man," Toni butted in. "My bridesmaids wore aubergine."

"I approve," Tod told her, then asked. "Who are you?"

Toni hiked a thumb at me. "Toni, her best bitch. And as such, she was my maid of honor."

"I approve of that too, since it's clear you have good taste," Tod replied.

"Well, thanks," Toni said. "But see, she's got a framed picture of us at my wedding. She's gonna obviously have framed pictures of her wedding. And aubergine and amethyst clash. She couldn't put those pictures close together, and everyone knows, best bitches put their wedding pictures close together in their family rooms."

Tod hooked a finger on his cheek and rested his chin on his fist, murmuring, "This is true."

I turned my head and stared at Toni like she'd done what she'd obviously done.

Lost her damned mind.

"What did you wear?" Tod asked Toni.

"Ivory. Off the shoulder. Kickass ruching at the midriff," she answered.

"Structured ruffle at the hip?" he pressed.

"You got it."

"De la Renta?"

"You got that too."

"Saks?"

"Yup."

"Excellent choice."

I'd lost Toni, so I turned to Jet. "What's happening?"

She smiled her dazzling smile and urged, "Don't fight it. Tod's crazy, but he's really good at it. He won't do that first thing you don't want. And swear to God, he works his ass off so all you have to do is show up, get your hair done, your face done, put your dress on, drink champagne, marry your guy and be happy. He's a miracle worker."

"But Darius and I aren't engaged," I pointed out.

"Excuse me," Tod called me.

I looked to him.

"It's been what? Three years? Not even that. Two and a half, at most," he said then pointed at Indy. "Married and pregnant." He pointed at Jules. "Married and has a kid." His finger bopped between Roxie and Ava. "Married. Married." Then to Sadie. "Engaged." Then another bop between Stella and Ally. "Shacked up." Then Jet. "Married, new baby." He looked at me. "Any questions?"

"Holy crap," I whispered.

"Yeah, strap in, sister. The Hot Bunch don't fuck around. *Comprende?*" Daisy declared.

"The Hot Bunch?" I asked.

"Lee, and Eddie, and Vance, Hank, Luke, Hector, Mace, Ren and *Darius*," she explained. "The Hot Bunch."

Oh man.

But, I was seeing this.

And there was me, packing my own damned bags, doubling up on toiletries and essentially moving myself in *before day three.*

"Holy crap," I repeated.

Tod waved his hands beside his head. "I can't work like this. I need a season. What's it gonna be? Spring? Summer? Winter? Fall? I don't see you as a fall. Maybe a summer. So? What's it going to be?" he demanded of me.

"I'm not sure what you're talking about," I admitted.

"The season you're going to get married," he explained.

"Again, I'm not engaged."

"Leave it to me, my man," Toni told him. "I'll get you what you need. Give me a day or two."

*What?*

"Are you free Tuesday?" Tod asked Toni.

"I can be," Toni answered.

"Martinis at the Cruise Room. Stevie and my treat. Get a season. And thoughts on venue. And a theme. I'll bring swatches."

"You got it, brother," she said, clicking her teeth, squinting her eye and pointing at him.

Tod snatched up the scrapbook and turned to his partner. "Come on, honey. We gotta go get some swatches."

And with that, he swanned out, the bell ringing his exit.

"Bye, girlies," Stevie called, all smiles, clearly used to this crazy. "Lovely to not quite meet you Malia and Toni," he finished as he followed.

The bell rang again, and Stevie was gone.

"Drink the coffee," Stella advised. "It helps."

I took a sip of coffee thinking, after all that, she'd be wrong.

After the sip, I realized she was very right.

Even so, when I dropped my mug, I asked, "Is a man I don't know planning my wedding to a man I'm not engaged to yet?"

To this, for some bizarre reason, Annette threw her head back, whooped to the ceiling, then dropped her chin and looked at me. "This is sofa-king *phat*! It's been a long time. Too long. This is gonna be awesome."

"It's been five months," Ava pointed out.

"That's too long. God, I hope there's another car chase," Annette said and again looked at me. "Do you think there's gonna be a car chase?"

"Um, I hope not," I replied.

"Snipers?" she asked.

Oh my God!

"Lord, no," I said.

"Well, I hope Darius's house doesn't get bombed. I haven't partaken, but I heard about that wine cellar, and it'd be a shame that went sky high," she shared.

Good Lord.

Regrettably, Annette wasn't done.

"At least I won five hundred bucks off you. Thanks for that. I didn't know you, but I thought, things came to a head when the dude was in a hospital bed. You needed to let him heal before you started the Rock Chick Sex-a-thon. And I was right."

I was speechless.

Annette continued not to be. "You gotta give me something to add to the tour. We need new blood."

I turned my attention to Ally. "Can you explain what's happening?"

Ally was fighting a smile. "First, don't get offended, we all went through it starting with Ava. But we take bets on when the Hot Bunch wears a sister down and the Rock Chick starts getting the business."

I heard Toni's chuckle.

I was sure I'd find it funny.

Someday.

"Second, after the books started coming out, Annette started doing Rock Chick Tours, taking fans around to all the places everything went down," Ally went on.

"Cheese and wine in the Reserve would be a good place to end a tour," Annette noted.

I considered for a nanosecond how I'd feel about Rock Chick Fans in Darius's house.

I then considered for less than a nanosecond how Darius would feel.

Then I said, "That's not gonna happen."

Annette looked to Daisy and said, "Worth a try."

Daisy laughed her tinkly-bell laugh.

"Last," Ally carried on, "I asked you here to talk about what you and Toni were doing in that office building."

"Oh," I mumbled. Then I glanced around and said, "I kinda can't talk about that in company. This is a client. I'm bound by confidentiality."

"Got a dollar? Or a quarter, a quarter would work," Daisy put in.

"I got one," Toni said, digging in her purse.

She fished it out and Daisy treated us to a bird's-eye-view of her cleavage when she leaned forward and took it, and I had to admit, my eyes started burning.

She shoved the bill in her cleavage then said, "Right. You just hired Rock Chick Investigations. And we got confidentiality too. Carry on."

"Okay, but..." I slid my gaze through the crew.

"I hear you," Daisy said. "And Ava's our graphic designer. Roxie is our website coordinator. The rest you can consider associates."

"It's okay," Ally cut in. "No one is going to breathe a word. Honestly. Shoot."

I looked to Toni.

She nodded in encouragement.

I returned to Ally. "Right, so I got this folder on my desk. Except, when I opened it, there was nothing in it but a Post-it that said 'Remostros Engineering,' and that address we were at."

"The vacant offices?" Ally asked.

"What?" I asked back.

"I did some preliminary checks. On that floor where you were, there were four office suites. Three taken. One by an accounting firm. One a data processing organization. The last, an architect. The only other suite of offices, the one around the corner from where you two were lurking, was vacant."

Again, Toni and I exchanged a glance before I went back to Ally. "That should be an engineering firm."

"Well, it isn't. I went in. There's nothing there. Not even a desk. But there is a listing for it on a commercial rental site, and it's been vacant for twelve months."

"Whoa," Toni whispered.

My skin started feeling funny.

"That's it, child?" Shirleen spoke for the first time, watching me carefully. "An empty folder?"

I shook my head at her. "No. I didn't know what was up, so I typed the number on the tab into our system, thinking maybe the paperwork had been misplaced. It's the case file number. And it came up locked. The message said I had to ask the network engineer for access. I've never run into that before. We have three named partners, four senior partners, six junior partners, and four associates. I do work for all of them. I have all access to everything because I need it."

"Okay, we're getting fishier," Ally said. "What else?"

"I asked the network administrator for access," I told her. "And he was acting all kinds of shifty and said that only Jeffrey, one of the named partners, has access to that file."

"And let me guess, you got curious, and it didn't stop there," Ally deduced.

I nodded. "Especially since it was a named partner. They don't do any of the grunt work. They pass it off to the paralegal pool. Or an associate. So I looked up Remostros Engineering. And it exists, and I'm no forensics accountant, but from what I can tell, it's a shell company."

"Well, damn," Daisy whispered.

"And that's owned by what appears to be another shell company, that's owned by another one, that's owned by yet another, and that last one is owned by a tiny LLC with only one director," I went on.

"This Jeffrey," Ally concluded.

I nodded again.

She turned to Daisy. "Extortion?"

Daisy shrugged. "Maybe." She gave her attention to me. "This Jeffrey married?"

Oh my God.

Why hadn't I thought of that?

"Office gossip has him banging one of the junior partners," I shared.

"Yup," Daisy stated. "Hiding assets. He's gonna scrape off the wife for the side piece."

He totally was.

"After I talked with our network administrator, Jeffrey called me into his office," I told them. "He asked me to bring the file, the one with nothing in it. He's usually very professional. Friendly, but a be-a-good-team though work-is-work, get-the-job-done type of guy. Except, when I brought the file, he was being super outgoing in an oily way that felt dirty, telling me the Remostros deal was highly confidential, they were important clients, would mean a ton of billable hours, and the firm had promised them his individual attention."

"And you didn't buy it," Ally said.

"That was when I started digging deeper. But my bad feeling was helped when he ordered me in no uncertain terms not to speak to anybody about it. Not anybody. Not even the other partners."

"Well, stop digging," Ally ordered. "I'll get Brody on it so we can make sure this isn't extortion, and your firm isn't going to be vulnerable to whatever he's doing. But if he's preparing to fuck over his wife, you got a decision to make. That being, does she somehow learn, anonymously, he's screwing around on her at the same time setting her up just to screw her?"

"That would be my vote," Ava said.

"Me too," Sadie put in.

"Totes," Roxie added.

"Malia, you do any of that research on a work computer?" Shirleen asked me.

More shaking of my head. "No. I did it at home."

She nodded once. "Smart girl."

I smiled at her.

"I think we all know everyone's vote, but it's gotta come from you," Ally said to me. "If it's him ramping up to fuck over his wife, do you want her to know?"

I thought about Jeffrey.

I didn't really know him. The underlings didn't pal around with the partners, but he was even more removed.

Though I did know he was in his early fifties, he and his wife had three kids, all of them in college. They'd been married since college themselves. The junior partner he was possibly sleeping with was in her mid-thirties, smart, gorgeous and a shark. And Jeffrey's wife planned all of our office parties.

She was the perfect attorney's wife. She didn't work, except the onerous jobs of making his life and family run smoothly so he could make his mark, and she bent over backward to make him look good to colleagues, staff and clients.

I didn't really know her either.

I just knew she didn't deserve to be screwed over while her husband lived the high life with the next young thing.

"Yes," I answered. "Definitely."

Ally pushed up from her chair, muttering, "We're on it."

She walked away, putting her phone to her ear, now all business.

Wow.

She *was* kinda badass.

"This isn't gonna amount to anything." Annette sounded disappointed. "This Jeffrey guy gets it in his head to kidnap you or car bomb you, and he gets one look at Darius, he's gonna tuck his tail between his legs and move himself and his fuck buddy to Panama."

"Good riddance, I say," Jet muttered.

It was then, I caught movement across the way, at the entrance to the shelves.

Duke.

My heart warmed, my lips formed the words, "Excuse me," and I put down my coffee mug and got up.

He turned around and disappeared into the shadows of the stacks.

I followed him in.

But he'd vanished.

Except, he hadn't.

The books were in three sections, the middle one containing tables with milk cartons on top, filled with vinyl.

On the edge of the one closest to the aisle was a plastic-covered album.

*Bridge over Troubled Waters.*

On it was taped a note.

I picked up the album and read the note.

*My Boxer,*

*I know Darius has a turntable.*

*You did good.*

*Proud of you.*

> *Duke*

I closed my eyes to fight the sting in them and hugged that album to my chest.

Once I got myself together, still hugging the album, I walked back to my coffee.

And my friends.

The old.

And the new.

\* \* \* \*

It was a couple of hours, and a couple of coffees, later, when I was hoping we'd have enough time to get hangers and a new outfit for Darius before we had to head home and get ready for the party, when Toni and I were walking to my car.

Before I opened my door, though, she was suddenly in my space.

Surprised, I turned to her.

Her arms closed around me.

Shirleen's hugs were the best, truly.

But Toni's gave them competition, partly because she put her all into them, mostly because she was choosy about doling them out, and they didn't come often.

"Happy for you," she whispered in my ear, and as fast as the hug started, it ended, and she headed to the passenger side.

I had to fight the sting of tears again, but I was getting good at it.

Anyway, I had hangers to buy and an outfit to pick out for my man and a party to get ready for.

There was no time for tears.

# Chapter Seventeen

*The Only Dream I Had Was You*

"C'mere, baby," Darius murmured.

My eyes went to him first.

Looking up those ridged abs and swelling pecs to his handsome, lazy face, I had no choice.

Even though I was into what I was doing, I slipped his cock out of my mouth, and kissing my way there, I crawled up his body.

Once I got there, both his hands went into my panties at my behind, those and my bra the only things I was wearing (sunshine yellow, like my mood of late), and he muttered, "These off. You on."

I felt my eyes go hooded as I dipped to the side, wheeled off my panties, then climbed back on.

I positioned him and took him, sinking down, Darius sinking in, filling me, and my spine arched, my head falling back.

I started moving and Darius spanned my hips with his hands.

"Slow. Look at me."

I looked to him and moved slow.

"Christ, you're so fuckin' beautiful," he murmured.

"You are too."

His mouth curved, then he caught his lip in his straight, white teeth when I tilted my hips on a downward slide.

"Fuck," he bit.

"Okay?"

His fingers dug in. "Fuck yeah."

I moved and watched him, felt him, smelled him, reveled in him.

He watched me, the tensing and releasing of his fingers encouraging my movements, controlling my rhythm.

Finally, his hand slid over my hip and in, his finger hitting the spot, and I had no choice. I bounced faster, harder.

"That's it, baby," he growled.

"I wanna kiss you," I told him.

"I want your show," he replied.

His finger put on more pressure.

My head fell back again.

He got his show.

"Yeah, arch into it, Malia," he grunted, his hips now thrusting up.

"Baby, I'm gonna—"

I yelped because I was flying off.

Before I could blink, he was behind me, hand in my back pushing me down, then both to my hips hauling me up to my knees, and he pounded back in.

"*Yes*," I hissed, bucking into him, searching for it again, finding it again, I shoved my face in the sheets and whimpered.

I was so, *so* close.

Hands at my ribs, he pulled me up to impaled on him, thrusting up as I bounced, his hand cupping my breast, the other one narrowing in on the exact right spot between my legs.

My head fell back to his shoulder.

"Can't get enough of you," he growled into my ear.

"Same," I pushed out.

"Never get enough," he grunted.

"Same," I breathed.

"Go, baby," he encouraged.

I bucked against him as the orgasm roared through me.

He set me down gently so I was genuflected before him again, but then drove into me relentlessly until I heard and felt his take him.

He stroked slow and sweet through coming down, his thumbs moving over the swells of my booty, before he pulled out, used my hips to turn me to my back, and carefully, he settled some of his weight on me, some into his forearm in the bed.

"Yeah?" he asked.

Still drifting through my aftermath, I only had it in me to nod.

He kissed me, deep and wet.

Then he ran his nose along my jaw before he asked, "You want me to clean you up, or you wanna do it?"

"I'll do it."

"In a bit," he ordered.

I felt my soft smile, but those same lips said, "Bossy."

He chuckled then lifted his head to look at me.

Shifting his weight a little more to the side, he put his finger to my face and grew fascinated with tracing every curve and swell and hollow. My eyebrow. Cheekbone. The edge of my lower lip. My cupid's bow.

I didn't want to break the mood, which felt like a warm cocoon of Darius's brand of sweet, but I also felt a niggle of worry, so I asked, "Are you okay?"

His gaze came to mine. "I still can't believe you're here."

God.

My man.

I clenched my teeth, shook off his finger and used his shoulders to pull myself up so I could hide my face in his neck.

It was after the Rock Chick party. It had been fun. Everyone came, including my parents and Miss Dorothea (but not Danni and Gabby, and I didn't ask why they weren't there, if they weren't invited, or if they refused to come, like I didn't ask why they weren't at Liam's game…maybe they didn't like football, or at least, for now, I was going with that).

I got mildly tipsy.

I got not mildly concerned by how captivated Liam was with the extreme testosterone brigade floating around (one could just say, Darius fit Lee's team really well, if the Rock Chicks were the most beautiful white women in Denver, the Hot Bunch were the most beautiful men, though they weren't all white).

However, they were all nice men who were openly pleased that Darius had Liam and me, free and clear.

So even if they looked like they could topple an entire government in their spare time just for shits and giggles, and that was why Liam was captivated by them, I let it go.

I was down to let everything go because I was residing on my happy-goodness cloud, and I liked it there.

And with what Darius just said, that happy goodness got happier.

I pulled it together, dropped back to the pillow, and blurted, "Tod's planning our wedding."

I was preparing to endure a major flip out that I'd let that slip.

Because…too soon.

*Way* too soon.

But Darius just said, "Good. Roll with that. Eddie said, once Sadie maneuvered their mothers out of the process, Jet didn't lift a finger. And Luke told me Tod treated Ava like she was a queen, got her everything she wanted. They only had an issue because Luke told her he wouldn't dance at the wedding with her."

This was a surprise. The man I saw with Ava that night seemed besotted with her, in a badass, super-macho way, of course.

"He didn't dance with his bride at his wedding?"

"He told her he wouldn't, but he absolutely did."

"This doesn't scare you?" I asked. "Tod already planning our wedding, I mean."

"Why would it scare me?"

"Because we're on day three."

He grinned. "Baby, I just came hard. I don't got it in me to do the mathematic gymnastics. But even so, I know three hundred and sixty-five times eighteen does not equal three."

What was he saying?

"What are you saying?"

He appeared bemused. "What do you think I'm saying?"

"It sounds like you're saying you're okay Tod is planning our wedding."

"That's what I'm saying."

"But we're not engaged."

He shifted so he could look down at our (mostly, I still had my bra on) naked bodies in his bed, then he looked around his bedroom, lingering on my night cream, lotion and book on what had become my nightstand.

For good measure, he announced, "I got all new hangers, three new shirts, two new pairs of jeans, five new sweaters, and two new pairs of boots."

"Winter is coming," I mumbled. "I want you covered."

His body started shaking as he asked, "What do you think we're doing here?"

"Figuring out if we can hack it after all the heartache and drama."

"No. We're gonna hack it. Liam took your cue, sweetheart, and after watching films with the team this morning, he went to your house and packed two big bags and brought more shit here. Tomorrow, we're gonna go back and get more of your shit and his shit and bring it here. We're gonna hack it. We're gonna go the distance. And you're both gonna take my name. Now, you can do that just by asking a judge to change it. But I want to see what dress you got in store for me at a wedding."

The fluffiness of my happy-goodness cloud got exponentially fluffier, but still, I said, "I got an earful of stories tonight."

I knew by the light in his eyes he knew what stories I was talking about, even if he asked, "Yeah?"

"Indy was living with Lee the first day her troubles started. He was living with her a couple of weeks later when they were done, and that was it. They've never been apart since. Much the same with Jet, Roxie, Jules, Ava—"

"I was around for all this, babe."

"Is that what's happening with us?"

He shrugged a single broad shoulder. "Naturally."

"Should I be worried this is going so fast?"

I could tell he was fighting laughter when he replied, "Again, we disagree that three hundred and sixty-five times eighteen is fast."

"This is different, Darius, and you know it."

Something shifted in him. I could feel it in his body, and I could see it on his face.

This wasn't lighthearted, after-sex talk, even if that talk was about a wedding.

Now this was something very different.

"I was your first. Was I your only?"

"Yes," I answered truthfully, if a bit mortifyingly, but that mortification flew out the window with the hot flash of possession that sparked in his eyes, making those long, long, *long* dry spells totally *worth it*.

"You weren't my first. But after you, you were my only."

Wait.

*What?*

Oh.

My.

*God.*

"Darius—"

"It's me for you, it's you for me. You were right all those years ago, Malia. We were meant to be. Not one woman would put up with what I put you through, grasping hold of the shit ton of love she has for me to get her through, except you. No other woman would wait for me to sort out my fucked-up life so I could come to her clean and redeemed. Except you. Part of me burns. I hate it that you gave up so much of your life waiting for me. But the rest of me, babe, the rest of me knows, if I didn't know I had your brand of love waiting for me, I'd still be in that life. I'd be lost to it. I'd be someone no one would want to know. I would have lost everything. My mom. My sisters. My brothers. Everything."

My heart was beating wildly as I refuted, "That isn't true. Everyone believed in you. Everyone, Darius. Indy. Ally. Lee. Eddie. Your mom. My mom and dad—"

"That means a lot, Malia, but you know." He dipped his face to mine.

"*You know*, it was you who saw me through. You and Liam."

"Oh no!" I exclaimed, because they were coming so fast, I couldn't hold them back, so I covered my face with my hands to hide them.

Darius wrapped his fingers around my wrists and pulled them away.

"No hiding," he growled. "No burying this emotion. You know it. Don't you?"

I shook my head, fighting his hold on my wrists.

"I saw myself in your eyes every time I was with you," he pushed. "The only time I felt like me was when I was with you. You grounded me. You anchored me to *me*."

"Stop it," I pleaded.

"I love them, all of them, and the faith they had in me. But you sacrificed your life and your dreams to wait for me."

"The only dream I had was you."

"You wanted to be a lawyer."

I twisted from his hold and framed his face. "Darius, if I wanted to be a lawyer, I'd be a lawyer. Look where I am. *The only dream I had was you.*"

After I finished speaking, it felt like a concussion of emotion buffeted us, like the room had imploded, but it had not.

"I want you to take my name," he said, his words raw, guttural, so much so, they scraped across my skin in the most insanely beautiful way.

"I'll absolutely take your name."

"I want Liam to have my name."

"Can he keep Dad's name too?"

"One in the middle?"

"Agreed."

"Deal."

Then he kissed me, pushing my legs open, and he was inside me.

This time, it was fast. Rough. Fiery.

It wasn't making love.

It wasn't fucking.

It was a branding.

I was his, Darius was searing that into me with his hands, his lips, his teeth, his cock.

I took it, my back arched, my thighs pressed tight to his sides, my arms around his shoulders holding on as each thrust jolted my whole body.

And I came for him on a loud mew of his name before he buried himself deep and came for me.

He stayed planted as he grunted, "I hurt you?" in my ear.

"Not even a little," I whispered, still clamped on tight.

He was still at my ear when he said, "I want you to think about giving me another baby."

"I don't have to think about it. I want a little girl. Talia is getting older. I need a princess to put in frilly dresses." I paused then added, "Though, I'd take another boy. Boys are the best."

He shoved his face hard in my neck.

The tears gathered in my eyes again.

"You won't miss the first steps this time," I whispered.

"Quiet," he groaned.

I fell silent.

Darius covered me, keeping me warm, shutting out the world, making it just us.

Eventually, though, he had to shift. We had to sleep. We had a big day the next day. Not only dinner at his mom's, but I'd just decided we were filling his truck, and my car, and Liam's.

We could rent my place furnished for a while.

See how that went.

And then decide if we wanted to sell.

So yeah, there it was.

I came up the rear.

But it was official.

I was a Rock Chick now.

"I'm gonna clean you up," he said.

"Works for me."

He lifted his head to kiss me.

Then he set about taking care of me.

Although Liam had undoubtedly learned his lesson that first night, since then, neither Darius nor I slept naked. So when he came back after taking the washcloth to the bathroom, he brought my nightie from the hook on the back of the door. He nabbed my panties from the floor. He gave both to me then went to get his plaid pajama bottoms.

I didn't exit our bed as I shimmied into my nightclothes.

Darius turned off the lights and joined me.

We cuddled in the middle.

"So what do you think?" I asked him in the dark. "Spring wedding? Summer?"

"I don't give a shit, if, when it's done, God and country know you're mine, I'll be there. And we're gonna do a lot of dancing."

I smiled into the shadows.

"Summer it is."

# Chapter Eighteen

*Family Dinner*

"I understand what you're saying. And obviously, when he's a grown adult, he can do what he wants, but right now, it's about respect," I said to Darius.

"He can respect you, and me, by keeping his room clean. By doing his chores. By getting his homework done without us havin' to ride his ass. By helpin' with dinner and cleanup after. Him not saying shit and fuck is bowing to the bullshit, baby," Darius said to me.

"Yeah, what Dad said," Liam said, also to me.

We were in Darius's truck on the way to Miss Dorothea's. Even though my son's legs were longer than mine, like when we went to Carmine's, Darius wouldn't hear of me giving Liam the front seat. He was in the back.

And we were again on the subject of cursing.

"Also by offering up no grumbling or backtalk," Darius added pointedly.

Liam didn't pipe up to that.

Even though Darius had scored one for me with that last bit, I crossed my arms and groused, "I'm obviously not going to win, but whatever. Let's see how Miss Dorothea feels about Liam dropping the F-bomb and the S-bomb and the D-bomb and the H-bomb all over her doilies."

And yes, that was Darius's mom. Sweet. Quiet. Loving. Made great cookies. And she collected antique doilies.

"It isn't about winning, sweetheart. I can tell this is important to you, and I'd roll over for you in just about anything, if it wasn't important to me too. Who said the woman's place was in the home? The establishment. Who said a Black man couldn't fall in love with a white woman, or vice versa? The establishment. Who said gay people were unnatural? The establishment. Who said dealing drugs was worse than rape so the sentences for those offenses are longer? The establishment. Fuck that. And fuck them for telling me, or my son, or you, or anyone they can't say fuck."

That was a great speech.

And the best part about it?

"You'd roll over for me in just about anything?" I asked.

Darius was silent for a beat, then he busted out laughing.

I enjoyed it then I turned to look at my boy in the back. "Just temper it, okay? And please, be careful with your mouth around both your grandmothers." I shot him a jaunty smile. "They're not as cool as your mom."

I saw the white flash of his teeth in his handsome face before he said, "'Kay, Mom."

Darius reached out a hand to me.

I took it.

And the rest of the way to his mom's, we held hands.

I was surprised to find she didn't live in the same house, at the same time unsurprised.

Mister Morris was all over their old house. He'd put in the landscaping. He'd sacrificed his garage by making it into a rec room for his kids. He'd built the back deck.

There were some who would find those constant reminders of a lost loved one a balm.

And some would find them torture.

I was glad she'd moved, because I'd loved Mister Morris, and I would find them torture.

Obviously, Miss Dorothea did too.

There were two spiffy cars parked at the curb in front of her house when we pulled into the drive, and I reckoned Danni and Gabby's interior design business was going well. They had talent, that was clear.

I'd also learned, after we'd moved our carloads of stuff to Darius's that day, and Liam was relaxing with a video game, and Darius and I were upstairs, cuddling after an afternoon quickie, that he'd put them through school and put up the money for them to start their business.

I also wondered if he'd given them the money for those spiffy cars.

For sure he bought Dorothea her house (something else he told me), which was a tidy bungalow in Washington Park, one of the most coveted neighborhoods in Denver, so it had to cost a fortune.

The front door opened before we were fully out of the truck, and

Miss Dorothea was standing in it.

While her sister, Shirleen, was a tall, curvy, proud Black woman with a gorgeous, full Afro, tawny eyes and mocha skin, Dorothea was a less tall, but still curvy, bundle of femininity with a becoming hairstyle of flips and curls and subdued makeup. And I didn't think I'd ever seen her in anything but a stylish dress and heels, flats or classy sandals. Some were more casual than others, but she always turned herself out in subtle, impeccable ways.

And now was no exception.

Liam forged ahead swiftly, and I knew why when her arms opened up before he got there. They closed around him, and she swung him side to side, saying, "My boy. My boy."

"Hey, Grams," he greeted.

She let him go and he stepped inside. Darius pushed me forward, and I, too, walked into her open arms.

"Malia, the first time of many to have you back home," she whispered in my ear. "A celebration."

I relaxed into her even as I hugged her back.

We let go and she gave the same treatment to Darius, her eyes closing, love washing through her face, and I wondered if she noticed in him the things Mister Morris had left behind like I did.

Then again, she couldn't miss them.

She shuffled us in and there they were. I couldn't help but smile. Pinned precisely, framed and artfully arranged on a gallery wall, somehow looking cool rather than old-fashioned and dated, were Miss Dorothea's doilies.

Yes, it felt like I came home.

Danni and Gabby wandered in from the kitchen.

"Get over here, kid," Danni said to Liam.

He loped over.

She gave him a hug.

Gabby stared blazes at me.

Uh-oh.

Liam moved for a hug from Gabby, and she wiped her face clean when he did.

But then Danni stared blazes at me.

One could hope Darius had fallen into a perusal of the doilies, but he was Darius. Not only had he seen them before, and probably didn't give a damn about them, he was Darius.

And I was me.

"Wipe that shit off your face," he growled to Danni.

Yep.

He wasn't in perusal of the doilies.

Dorothea came abreast of us, asking, "What?"

"Nothing, Ma," he said, scowling at Danni.

"Yeah, nothing," Danni said then cried a fake happy, "Malia! So good to see you!"

I endured two fake-happy hugs from Darius's sisters, with Gabby adding, "What can I get you to drink? Wine? Beer? Sweet tea?"

"Wine, if you have it," I replied.

"I live to serve," she said, whirling and making no bones about escaping my presence by going to the kitchen.

"I'll help!" Danni called and followed her sister.

"Sit down, darlin'," Dorothea ordered. "But first, let me get a good look at you." She took my hands and held them out to the sides. "You always were such a pretty thing, with such great style."

Considering I'd had some nerves about this dinner, like most women when something important was going down, I'd worried about what to wear.

I was glad I got it right.

I'd worn a midi-dress in tiny yellow, purple and green flowers, sleeveless with a ruffled shoulder and a v-ruffle on the full shirt. The mock turtleneck was smocked, as was the waist. I was wearing a cropped jeans jacket over it and fawn-suede, peep-toe, sandal-back, stack-heeled booties. And I'd smoothed my hair into a fluffy-bunched topknot.

Darius, by the way, was in one of his new shirts.

Which was what Dorothea commented on next. "Son, that shirt looks fine on you." Her gaze coasted between us. "Such a handsome couple."

Darius draped an arm along my shoulders.

"Family," Liam corrected, sliding up next to us and popping his collar. "Handsome family. What do you say Grams? Are the girls gonna fall at my feet in this new button-down Mom got me?"

Okay, so Toni and I got a bit carried away at the mall. We were in the men's department at Nordstrom.

Sue us.

"Liam Edward, I hope you're more worried about your studies than girls," she chided.

"Get on this planet, Grams, and get ready, 'cause Dad bought me new wheels, so it's date night every Friday and Saturday night for Liam

Edward Clark Tucker."

Yes, we had the conversation with Liam that morning over breakfast.

And yes, he was all the way down with taking his father's name.

And yes, when Dorothea's gaze raced to her son's after her grandson's announcement, a nanosecond later, her eyes filled with tears.

Darius pulled her in his arms and said over her head to his boy, "Smooth, son."

Liam grinned unrepentantly. "Surprises are the best."

"What's going on?" Danni asked.

She was carrying two glasses of wine.

It looked like Gabby had a glass of Coke, which I frowned at. My son didn't drink pop. There weren't a lot of things I refused him, but a beverage that could break down a nail over time was one of them.

"I'm taking Dad's name as soon as he gets it sorted to go before a judge," Liam announced.

The real Gabby came out when she exclaimed, "Oh my God! That's amazing, honey!" as she handed him the Coke and gave him another hug.

Danni didn't even look at me when she passed off the glass of white wine, and I didn't think it was just because she was all about Liam as she added, "Totally! That's great."

She definitely looked at Darius when she handed him his glass of red.

I actually preferred red, but she didn't ask, and I didn't say anything.

"Liam," I said softly, dipping my head to his Coke.

He didn't hesitate. "Yeah, Aunt Gabs. I don't drink Coke."

"It's a special occasion," she replied.

"Mom doesn't like it. And I don't really like it either." He looked to his grandmother. "I'm sorry to waste, Grams."

"That's fine, love," she said, sending a side eye to Gabby, telling me that Liam had told them this already, including the part that I didn't like it. "I got you cranberry juice and some of those sports drinks you like. The blue ones. Your favorite."

"Thanks," he mumbled, then hustled to the kitchen.

"Okay, now, let's sit," Miss Dorothea said.

Darius led me to the couch, and I sat, but he didn't. He stood at my side, arms crossed on his chest, eyes tracking every move his sisters made.

Oh boy.

He hadn't missed the Coke thing either.

Dorothea sat on the opposite side of the couch to me.

I shrugged off the strap of my purse, placed it by my feet and settled in.

Because it was time to thaw the iced-over ramparts.

"So, Liam tells me you two designed Darius's house. It's gorgeous," I said to his sisters who were sitting opposite us in armchairs.

"It's not like he gave us free reign. He picked everything. We just gave him choices. He's got good taste. A real eye," Danni replied.

"Well, of course. Obviously, he'd have the final decision," I muttered. I drew in a breath and glanced at the doilies before saying to Dorothea. "You know, all through the years, every time I saw a pretty doily, I thought of you."

"Too bad her thinking of Mom didn't get her ass with her kid over to Mom's house," Danni said to Gabby in a loud whisper just as Liam came in with a bottle of Gatorade in his hand.

Gabby pulled an *oh shit* face.

Dorothea's head jerked Danni's way.

Liam's brows shot together, so I knew he heard.

But I had other things to worry about.

Principal of which being the burning wall of fury that moved through the room from my left.

Everyone felt it, including Danni and Gabby, who looked right to their brother.

Gabby had the good sense to quail.

Danni lifted her chin.

Darius's voice was deceptively quiet when he asked, "Is my woman's business your business?"

"He's our nephew and Mom's *grandchild*," Danni snapped. "And we didn't meet him until he was *eight*, and even then, barely saw him *at all*."

"I'll repeat," Darius said slowly. "Is my woman's business your business?"

"It's family business," Danni retorted. "And I'm sorry. I'm not down with this whole pretending everything is okay crap. We can't sit on this. We need to have it out."

"You don't know what the fuck you're talkin' about," Darius clipped.

"I know she took your money and kept her son from his family," Danni returned then looked at me and commented snidely, "Nice dress, Malia."

"Eyes to me," Darius ordered.

Danni sneered at me.

"*Eyes to me!*" Darius roared.

Danni jumped.

Oh boy!

I stood and turned into him, putting a hand light on his stomach. "Darius, let's talk outside, baby. Okay?"

He didn't take his attention from his sister.

And so, when he spoke, it was right to her. "You have the fuckin' balls to sit there wearin' the dress that the money I made off *my* back and sellin' *my* soul got you the education and set you up in the business you can buy it, and you talk shit to my woman about the money I gave her to keep her in a good house and nice clothes while she's raising *my son*?"

"Darius—" she tried.

"No, girl," he bit. "You started this, answer me. You got those big a' balls?"

Danni squared her shoulders but said nothing.

"I'd like to hear the answer to that question too," Dorothea chimed in. It was quiet, but it was firm.

Danni looked to her and there was a slight whine in her, "Mom."

"You disrespect the mother of my grandchild, the love of my son's life to her face in *my* house?" she asked. "Who raised a child to do that?" She shook her head. "Not me."

"Darius was lying in a hospital bed," she slashed a finger at me, "and she gutted him like he was the bad guy in this scenario."

"Drop your hand, girl," Darius warned on a terrifying purr that gave even me a shiver, and it wasn't directed at me. "Do not *ever* point at Malia like that."

She was smart enough to drop her hand, but she threw both up. "I'm just saying, Gabs and I don't think we should all pretend like everything is happy and awesome, when for sixteen years, it was *not*."

"And who do you think felt that the most? You?" Dorothea asked.

"I'm just saying—" Danni repeated.

"I heard what you were saying," Dorothea cut her off. "And I cannot believe in all the heartache we've all endured you'd want to keep that going for another *second*." Her hair shook on her last word. "Not another *second*." More hair shaking. "I did not cook for the last three hours to have my family all around me for the first time and have my girls act like harridans."

Gabby threw Danni right under the bus with her, "It wasn't me!"

Then again, Danni had already tossed herself there.

Still, Danni shot angry eyes to her sister.

"Maybe we should all just take a breath," I suggested.

"Naw," Liam said, putting down his drink. "I think we should go home. This is bullshit."

Dorothea's face froze.

As did Gabby's and Danni's.

"Honey—" I started.

"When they apologize, we'll come back. But not before, Mom." He'd come to me, and he swung an arm to the door. "Get in the truck."

I looked up at his father.

"You heard your son," he said. "In the truck."

Totally ganging up on me.

"Darius, your mom has cooked for hours."

He looked down on her, his face blank, eyes cold. "Sorry, Ma. But you know the statement has to be made."

God!

I whirled.

"I'm not leaving. I'm eating your food." I said to Dorothea. Then to Gabby and Danni. "Be mad at me. I don't care. Darius is right. You don't know what you're talking about, and our business isn't yours. I appreciate your loyalty to your brother, but really, you should have thought this through. If you had something to say to me, you should have found some other time to say it. I would have listened. I might not agree with you, but I love your brother enough to listen. But you didn't do it like that. You did it like this. That's not on me. It's on you."

I switched the wineglass from hand to hand as I took my jacket off. I swung it on the arm of the couch, then I sat back down, took a sip, thanking the good Lord it wasn't sweet, because sweet wine was from Satan, and I went on.

"I've got a great job. But yes, this dress is not Walmart and it's highly likely some of Darius's money bought it for me, and I'm proud of that. My man takes care of the ones he loves that are under his protection. As you both know *very* well."

Gabby had the good grace to look ashamed.

Danni couldn't meet my eyes, so I figured she felt the same.

I turned to Dorothea and finished with, "What's for dinner?"

"Chicken and dressing, pureed carrots and turnips, sauteed green beans, mashed potatoes and rolls. Carrot cake for dessert."

Damn.

I shouldn't have eaten lunch.

"That sounds great," I replied.

She stood. "I think it's time to sauté the beans and finish sorting the table. I was going to ask my girls to help me, but would you do it, Malia?"

I stood too. "My pleasure."

She started to the kitchen with me following, and she didn't look at anybody when she ordered, "Sort it out before your behinds sit at my table."

I turned and gave Darius a *work it out!* look then transferred it to my son before I lost sight of them when I turned the corner into the kitchen.

That said, before I lost sight, I didn't miss their identical stances (feet planted, arms crossed on chests) nor their identical scowls.

Both of them aimed at me.

Eek!

\* \* \* \*

My family and I trooped through the back door and laundry room into the kitchen.

The ride home had been silent.

The night had been great…for Dorothea and me.

We caught up and her food was just as I remembered it, stick to your ribs, soul food delicious.

Danni and Gabby tried to make up for blowing it, but Darius and Liam were having none of it. They were warm and respectful to Miss Dorothea and me, but it was like their sisters/aunts weren't in the room.

And I knew I was in trouble for defying the men in my life on the ride home. They made that perfectly clear the entire silent ride in the heavy atmosphere of the cab of Darius's truck.

The instant Darius switched on the light, he turned to Liam.

"Downstairs, son," he ordered.

"With respect, Dad, I got things to say too."

A muscle in Darius's jaw jumped.

Then he jerked up his chin.

I put my purse and the tin of cookies Dorothea sent home with us on the island and rounded on them.

"You two can't be mad at me," I stated.

Two sets of beautiful brown eyes turned to me.

Beautiful *angry* brown eyes.

Yes.

They were mad at me.

"Before we got there, we were talking about respect. That was not respect. And you took it then ate dinner with it," Darius bit off.

"I didn't take it," I slapped back. "But I wasn't going to walk out of a house where your mom had spent hours cooking and totally ruin the night for her."

"Someone disrespects you, you make it so they don't do it again," Darius retorted.

"Your sisters didn't buy that food and cook it," I returned.

"Right, then, you made me and Liam take it and eat dinner with it," Darius shot back.

Well, hmm.

I did do that.

"It was the right thing to do," I stated.

"So, Aunt Lena talked trash about Dad, you'd sit down to dinner with her after?" Liam asked me.

Uh-oh.

I caught my lip between my teeth.

Because...no. I would *not*.

"Yeah," Liam grunted.

"Ma would have got it," Darius declared.

She probably would have.

Aw, hell.

I lifted my hands and pressed down. "Okay, okay. I get it. You're right. And I'm sorry I put you through that. Though, I was really happy to have some time to catch up with Miss Dorothea. But yes, I'll have other opportunities and we should have come home."

The doorbell rang.

"*Fuck*," Darius clipped, then prowled out of the kitchen.

"It's gonna be Aunt Danni or Aunt Gabby," Liam said, staring at the wall between kitchen and living room like he could burn holes through it with his laser beam eyes.

"*Fuck*," I snapped and followed in Darius's footsteps, noting he'd switched on a lamp by the couch on his way to the door.

I was getting close to the front door when I heard him say, "You need to back off and let me cool down."

"I'm here to apologize," Danni said.

"I hear you. You still need to back off and let me cool down."

I stopped in the archway to the entry and Danni, who Darius was barring at the door so she was still outside, looked to me.

"Malia, get him to let me in," she demanded.

I shook my head. "I'm sorry, Danni. I intervened for your mom, but you have to work this out with your brother."

I turned to move out of eyesight and nearly ran into Liam.

"Liam, honey, I'm so sorry," Danni said pleadingly.

"Not me you should apologize to," Liam replied.

"Malia, seriously. I'm sorry," she called, and I stopped and turned back. "You were right. I should have connected with you so we could talk things out. That was fucked up."

"It's not me you should apologize to either," I told her.

Her eyes went up to her brother.

"Darius—"

"What would Dad say to that shit?" he asked.

*Ouch.*

Low blow but deserved.

She suffered it, her face crumbling.

"Yeah, that's what he'd say," Darius whispered.

"We lost her when he *died*," she cried.

I froze.

Darius froze.

Liam froze.

She looked to me. "I was mad at you then. Even before we knew about Liam. *He needed you. I* needed you."

"Oh, Danni," I said softly.

Yes, Darius's sisters had liked me.

She dashed the back of her hand under her eye and pulled breath into her nose. "You were dealing with a lot. I know you called. I talked to you. I know you were trying to get to him. But all I was feeling got twisted up in all that happened, and I acted like a bitch. I'm sorry." She looked again to her brother. "I *am* really sorry, Darius. It just all came back when you got hurt, and suddenly Malia was back, and everything was out with Liam, and I got wound up in being pissed instead of being scared because you got *shot* and *smashed in the head.* And I was *scared.*"

Her face crumbled again, and Darius swore, "For fuck's sake," hooked her behind the head and pulled it into his chest.

"Get her in out of the cold, honey," I urged.

Darius pulled her inside, shut the door and led her to the couch where he sat her down, going down with her, his sister still held close in his arms.

I switched on another couple of lamps before I asked, "You want wine? Or something stiffer?"

"How can you be nice to me?" she wailed into Darius's shirt, "I'm such a bitch!"

"Danni," Darius said to the top of her head. "This is why you do what Malia said and talk shit through instead of being a bitch. Yeah?"

"I think I learned that real good," she snuffled into his shirt.

"Kleenex, son," Darius murmured to Liam.

Liam took off toward the bathroom.

"Now Gabs is pissed at me," she mumbled.

"Can't help you with that. She was tryin' to contain it and you swung her ass right out there. You gotta work that out with her," Darius told her.

"Huh," she told his shirt. She blubbered some more, then muttered, "Work is gonna be interesting tomorrow."

"Bed you gotta lie in," Darius muttered in return, but did it rubbing her back.

"Babe, wine, or something else? I make a mean martini," I pushed.

She sniffled and then Liam was there shoving a wad of about fifty tissues (the same amount he'd stuffed into my purse before we went to Carmine's) in her face. She took them and about ten of them drifted to her lap because she couldn't handle them all, but she pulled away from Darius and blew her nose with some, dabbed her face and under her eyes with others.

She glanced at Darius.

He nodded.

She looked to me.

"I'd murder a martini."

I smiled at her then turned to Darius because I hadn't yet discovered the full lay of the land at his house.

"Vodka, freezer. Vermouth and olives, Liam's gonna have to get those from the cellar," he answered my unspoken question.

Liam took off.

So did I.

"Grab the shaker too, boy!" Darius called.

"Got it!" he shouted back.

I wasn't real big on them shouting at each other all the time.

But whatever.

We'd just surmounted another obstacle, and we were still standing, and together, and we understood each other better, which meant we'd come out of it stronger.

So I could deal with a little shouting.

# Chapter Nineteen

*Big Events*

I was in a conference room at work, surrounded by boxes and stacks of files, working with two other paralegals and highlighting and taking notes like a highlighting-and-taking-notes fool.

We'd just received the discovery on a huge case that the judge for some reason refused to give us a continuance on, so we had tons to get through and about two months less time than we needed to get through it.

It was exactly three weeks since Darius and I brought our family together.

And it had been three weeks heavy with big events.

First, within days of our drama at Miss Dorothea's, I came home to two fully-kitted-out guest bedrooms upstairs, seeing as Darius called "his guy" who went and packed up all my bedroom furniture, and all Liam's, and moved mine into the guest suite, Liam's into the Jack side of the Jack and Jill.

Liam and I had already done a cursory packing of all our most personal items the Sunday before we went to dinner with Darius's family, but we headed back the next Saturday after Liam was done watching films with the team. We carted over boxes of books, picture frames and other essential items, including packing up all the food in the kitchen.

The next day, Darius and I went back and got all the sheets and towels and bathroom accessories to stock up the guest spaces.

By this time, I'd done a full perusal of what Darius had and found there was nothing of mine I needed to fill the gaps. There was also nothing I needed to make the space mine.

Liam was thriving in Darius's lair. It suited him, like it suited his dad.

And after not having Darius for so long, being surrounded by him at every turn, well, that totally worked for me.

Darius was surprised I didn't want to make my mark on our place, but when I explained why, we had to take a break from putting away towels so we could fuck on my old bed in the guest room.

Thankfully, Liam was out with some friends seeing a movie.

At that juncture, Darius called "his guy" again, and he went and packed everything else up—dishes and pots and pans and knickknacks—and stacked those boxes in Darius's storage room downstairs.

Darius then called a cleaning crew to go in, and after that, a management company to ready it for the market. We dropped some cash on some nice, middle-of-the-road bedroom furniture, and got word a few days ago it had rented, furnished.

In the meantime, I'd extended an olive branch to Danni and Gabby by explaining I did need someplace to put my books, as well as new frames for my pictures that would work in Darius's space.

They took hold of that olive branch like their life depended on it (they really did love their brother, and actually me, not to mention Liam), and now we had three new handsome shelving units, one in the living room, another in the family room and the last in the study, where I put my books and arranged my newly framed pictures.

And with that, I was good.

Liam and I were firmly in Darius's home, so it was no longer just his.

It was ours.

In that time, Ally called to confirm that Jeffrey was indeed hiding assets, not extorting them from the firm, and advised that was the last she'd report to me about the situation. She was going to "take care of it," and she felt the less I knew, the better.

She said that, considering it was a high probability that the only people who knew about it were me, Jeffrey and our network administrator, who was the one who probably mislaid the file on my desk, I should act like handing it over to Jeffrey was the last I'd thought about it. Especially since his shit was soon to hit the fan.

I thought this was good advice, so I took it and asked her to send me an invoice for her time.

"Chickie, Rock Chicks get my services for free," was her response before she hung up on me.

I wondered how often the Rock Chicks needed investigative services, then decided I didn't want to know.

Toni met with Tod and Stevie for martinis and wedding discussion, and I let them have at it...for the preliminaries. I'd butt in as soon as things heated up (that being, when Darius put a ring on my finger).

I was busy with work, catching up with my man, solidifying my family, and picking and choosing from the whirlwind of invitations that swirled around the Rock Chicks (we'd all had brunch this past Saturday, I'd been to Daisy's castle for a facial with Ava and Roxie (and it was *a castle*, in the middle of Englewood, Colorado, for goodness sake, complete with moat), we'd pimped ourselves out and gone to watch Tod perform (he was one of Denver's premier drag queens) the Saturday before (Lena getting initiated that night, Toni was already there when I got there), and select Rock Chicks and Hot Bunch were always at Liam's games, even the away ones, with Indy and Lee, Jet and Eddie coming to every one of them).

And in quiet times, in fits and starts, Darius shared with me about his years away from us.

He did this like he was confessing, and I couldn't say it was fun to hear, nor could I say he shared it all, or ever would.

What I knew from how he told it was that, even if Shirleen was always there, throughout that time, he felt very alone and very lost, and the shame he carried was extreme.

However, he explained that shame was tempered by an epiphany of redemption he felt when he'd saved Ally from certain dangers that, if she'd survived them, would haunt her for the rest of her life.

He didn't seem to realize he was on the periphery, helping where he could, having the Rock Chicks' backs through all their trials and tribulations. Not to mention, he did, indeed, work with Eddie on keeping the underbelly of Denver organized and controlled, weeding out "players" who didn't know the game and made things messy so people who didn't choose that life wouldn't get caught in the crossfire. On top of that, he often worked on the sly with Lee on jobs he was doing.

But it was Ally's situation that he felt washed him clean.

Which meant he felt he was finally free to come to me.

I could see that. Lee was his brother, so Ally was his sister. It didn't happen, thank the Good Lord, but he was willing to sacrifice his life for hers.

He almost did.

And she came away from it unscathed, while he had puckered scars in the skin of both of his thighs, and jagged ones on the left side of his head under his twists and up his right side.

These, I could tell, he carried like badges of pride. And although I didn't like them all that much (say, *at all*), for Darius, they were the marks that signified the life he felt he had to live, but had always hated, was a life that was no longer his.

He still carried some baggage from that, and as much as it hurt my heart, he was that man, so he always would.

But when he'd saved Ally, the weight had grown a whole lot less heavy.

As for me, I'd been to the grocery store only twice since I moved in with Darius, and I didn't carry the bags in from the car.

I paid my mortgage, but Darius switched the utilities at my old house to his name (though he'd soon lose those expenditures when our tenants moved in). He paid all the other bills and said we'd discuss it "later" how I would contribute. And I knew the way he said this that "later" would never happen. I also knew how important it was for him to take care of us, so I determined to find my ways to spoil him (evening out our closet was part of that), and I'd let him.

He also cooked most nights, but if I did, he helped, and so did Liam (Liam also helped his dad, but Darius didn't let me when he was cooking, I could tell he got off on me sitting with them and drinking wine while they provided for me, and I got off on it too). The same with doing the dishes.

And he had a cleaning lady, so I no longer had to clean the house.

He and Liam took care of raking the leaves in the yard one Sunday while I stood in the window sipping tea and watched father and son working side by side, doing something mundane and normal, feeling my fluffy cloud of happy goodness shroud me.

I sometimes had to work late and loved the fact that I had a family text string where I'd tap in that info and send it to my boys so they'd know where I was and when I'd be home.

And Darius never said a word about me arriving an hour or two after I normally did. He knew I loved my work. He also warned me that Lee was keeping him on jobs where his work hours were normal so we could all settle in. But eventually, his hours could be anything.

I encouraged him to tell Lee he could remove those barriers. Because Darius also loved his job. And although it was very clear that team would move mountains to give one member what he needed (because, from what I'd heard, they'd done a lot of that in their time together), I got how Darius didn't want to be someone who would slack.

But the bottom line was, my life had changed significantly, and it wasn't just that I came home to a different house and slept every night beside the man of my dreams.

It was because I'd discovered Mister Morris lived on in his son. And the way Darius was guiding Liam, he'd live on in his grandson.

This meant I had time to bake my molasses cookies, just because.

I had time to curl in the club chair in the study and read, because I didn't have groceries to buy or bathrooms to clean or bills to pay.

After a sweater of mine turned up four sizes smaller than it used to be, I firmly set the boundaries around laundry. But I'd long since taught Liam how to do his own. It was just Darius who needed to stay well away from the laundry room. So that was my only big job.

I didn't just have the family I always wanted. I had a partner who more than shouldered his share of life's burdens.

I was living the dream.

The only gray edge on the silver lining of the cloud I resided in was the fact that I hadn't found the time to share with Darius that I knew who was the likely suspect that told someone about me and Liam.

Or, more to the point, I hadn't figured out *how* I was going to tell him.

That and the fact Miss Dorothea and Mom were going head-to-head about who was going to host Thanksgiving this year.

I had a feeling Miss Dorothea was going to win. Danni and Gabby were now kitting out the last bedroom in our house. This was because everyone on Darius's side was descending on Denver, mostly to meet Liam and look me over, and we were going to have a full house.

"*You told me you had this covered!*"

I jumped when I heard these words shouted somewhere in the office. I glanced at my two colleagues, then looked over my shoulder through the wall of windows into the bustle of the office, across from which, through another wall of windows, Carrie, the junior associate Jeffrey (it was now in no doubt) was sleeping with was shoving Jeffrey in the chest.

"*Easy for you!*" she screeched. "*But shit like this can derail my whole fucking career!*"

She probably should have thought of that before she climbed into a partner's bed and fucked over his wife.

With that, she flounced out of his office, slamming the door behind her.

I kept staring, because, Lord, I couldn't help it. That was *a scene.*

Everyone in the office was staring.

But Jeffrey was glowering at the door.

Until his eyes moved to the window. I could see from all the way across the office his face was red, probably with anger and embarrassment, but unfortunately, as his eyes scanned the space, they eventually locked on me.

Oh hell.

I didn't know what to do, but turning my head quickly like I was guilty of something I didn't think was smart. So I held his gaze for a beat, before shifting my attention back to my work.

"We knew *that* was gonna happen," Samantha, one of the other two paralegals in the conference room with me, said under her breath.

"Fuck around and find out," Robin, the other paralegal, replied.

"Literally," Samantha added.

The door opened and we all looked that way.

Jeffrey was in it.

"Malia. My office. Now."

He turned on his heel and stormed through the cubbies toward his office.

With Samantha and Robin staring at me, I got up and followed him.

"Close the door," he snapped when I made it to his office.

I closed the door and stood in front of it.

"Did you defy my direct orders about our client, Remostros?" he asked.

"Sorry?" I asked back.

"Remostros. I told you to let that lie and keep it confidential. Did you speak to anyone about it?"

"I…" I faked confusion. "Wait, you mean that empty file?"

"Yes," he said through his teeth.

"Honestly, I didn't think anything about it. I mean, it was empty, and you said you'd handle it and I've been busy with other things." I looked to the door behind me, still faking it, then back to him. "Did I mess up? Is something wrong? Did you need my assistance with something on that?"

He visibly ground his teeth before he kept talking through them. "No. It's fine. Get back to that discovery."

I nodded, but still faking it, I asked with concern, "Are you okay?"

"I'm fine," he forced out. "Thank you. But that discovery needs your attention."

"Of course," I murmured, then lit out of there trying not to look like I was lighting out of there.

Samantha gave it some time after I returned before she asked, "What was *that*?"

"My guess, he fucked around and found out," I told her.

She smiled.

I got to work.

I'd learned to keep the Bluetooth bud in my ear when I was in the car, considering I was a Rock Chick now, and they knew I didn't have time at work to field calls, but they were rabid communicators. And it wasn't all just invitations. It was also that they needed style advice, or to complain about their hot guys and how their overabundance of testosterone made them behave, or just to shoot the shit.

I liked it.

I'd missed it.

I'd had a big posse in high school, and I loved having that back.

But this time, on my way home that evening, it was me who called Ally.

"Yo, chickie," she answered.

"The shit hit the fan today at work."

Now she was faking it. "Did it?"

"Ally, after Carrie, the woman he's cheating on his wife with, shouted at him in his office, he came right to me and asked about Remostros."

"What'd you say?"

"I pretended I forgot all about it."

"Good."

"But he latched right onto me," I told her.

"Assholes like him need someone to blame, considering, in their minds, they can do no wrong. He's looking for someone to blame."

"Should I be worried?"

"It's impossible for this to blow back on you."

"He can fire me, Ally."

"He has to have cause, Malia."

"It's an employment-at-will state."

"That's bullshit, and you above everyone knows it. That protects an employer only so far. And when you're lashing out because you got caught with your dick in a woman not your wife at the same time you're moving marital assets to hide them from said wife, you best not be firing a valued employee in retaliation for some slight you have zero evidence she gave you."

I blew out a breath.

Because she was right.

"Just be cool. He'll turn his attention to someone else," Ally advised.

"All right."

"See you at Liam's game on Friday. Ren and I are coming."

"Great, see you then."

We hung up and I'd almost made it home without another RC

interaction before my phone rang.

Tod.

I smiled and answered, "Hey, Tod."

"Fuchsia, tea rose and lilac blue," he replied.

I thought about it.

"Don't answer now," he said into my thoughts. "I found a bouquet. It...is...*life*. I'm inspired. I'll text you a picture. Byeeeeee." With that, he hung up.

I smiled again, and as I was pulling into the garage, I got a bing on my phone that I had a text.

Once I parked, I pulled it out and looked at it.

Tod was right.

That bouquet was *life*.

Now *I* was inspired.

And excited.

My fluffy happy-goodness cloud grew even fluffier.

I texted, *Roll with it.*

Then I texted, *Does it have Toni's approval?*

I hit the remote to lower the garage door, grabbed my purse and headed to the house.

Halfway there, I got a return text from Tod that read, *Of course it does! You'll be a goddess. I swear. It's perfect!*

I'd seen some of the pictures of the other RCHB weddings.

I trusted him.

I hit the back door, the laundry room, but stopped dead in the doorway to the kitchen.

Because Darius wasn't cooking.

Darius wasn't doing anything but sitting at a stool by the island, a full wineglass and an open bottle beside him, staring at me like he wanted to murder me.

# Chapter Twenty

*Scrapper*

"Did you forget to tell me something?" he asked in that dangerous voice he'd used when things first sparked off between him and Danni weeks ago.

God, in the ten minutes since I talked with Ally, did she call Darius and fill him in on my work situation?

They were tight, but why would she do that?

Cautiously, I moved forward and put my purse on the island.

Then I said, "Ally doesn't think it's going to be a big deal."

His eyebrows shot up. "Ally knows about it too?"

Okay, wait.

What was he talking about?

"What are you talking about?"

"You first," he retorted. "What are *you* talking about?"

"The shit hit the fan with my cheating boss today."

"And why does Ally need to assure you it's not a big deal?"

"Because he came right to me and asked me questions about that file I found."

I'd told Darius all about it.

At the time, he seemed unconcerned.

Then again, he'd trained Ally to be the investigator she was, so he would be.

"You think he's gonna target you?" he asked.

"He came right to me. And he's a jerk. And a narcissist."

"And what can he do to you?"

"Fire me."

"Can he blackball you?"

I shook my head and rested my weight into a hand on the island. "The firm isn't that big. He doesn't have that much power. Not even within the firm. The other partners are better liked, well-respected, and thinking on it, more successful attorneys when it comes to winning cases. Though, he thinks he does. Have the power, I mean."

"Can he act on his own in the position he holds?"

Reflecting on this, I realized I'd panicked too soon.

I worked for attorneys. They knew the law. They also knew what could happen if you did whatever you wanted regardless of it.

Even if Jeffrey wanted to be an asshole, the other two partners would never let him put them in an untenable position.

"I don't report to him," I told Darius. "On the cases I work, I report to the attorney who's handling them. But strictly, I report directly to the HR Director. She does my performance evaluations. And she reports to the partners. He might share with her he has an issue with my work, even if he has to make it up, but it would have to be really bad to terminate me immediately, without warnings or official writeups. There's office politics and gossip, but it isn't a toxic environment. They've let people go since I've been there, but not without cause. I can't imagine the other partners would allow him to do something maverick, especially in a retaliatory manner when he was in the midst of hiding assets. That's fraud. He could be disbarred for that. Even serve jail time."

"So you're good."

"I think so."

"Right, then now I wanna know, what'd you think? That I'd kill him?"

What?

"Who? Jeffrey?"

"No, Malia. Michael."

All the air went out of me in a whoosh.

So it was breathy when I asked, "How did you know?"

The mood in the room, already not great, deteriorated.

"So you were keeping it from me?"

"No. I just…we were busy and…"

"Bullshit."

"Darius—"

"I'm not that man. Not anymore."

*Not anymore.*

"You've killed people before?" I whispered.

"You will never know." Still seated, he leaned toward me, and his tone was awful when he said, "*Never.* What I will say is that I made an example of the man who wanted to hurt you, so anyone who might find their way to something they thought they could use to fuck with me, they thought twice. That's all I'll say."

Okay.

I was reading this as the fact there was a good possibility that he'd killed people.

This was not knowledge I wanted, but it also wasn't surprising. He'd been at the top of his game. Shirleen's husband had been whacked years before, he was a kingpin, and they took over his kingdom when he was gone.

Darius did it to keep earning until he knew the ones he loved would be taken care of even if he was gone.

Shirleen did it because it was all she knew.

You didn't get to that place in that world without doing what had to be done.

"Love me still?" Darius asked, but there was snideness to that.

Snideness that was hiding fear.

I stared at him.

Then I said, "Yes."

He shook his head. "You know the man I am. That shit is gonna haunt us for the rest of our lives."

"It's gone. Over," I returned.

"Really? So why, when Liam always wanted to be a lawyer so he can get into politics, is he now talkin' about going to work for Lee?"

"He is?"

"Yeah."

Wow, my boy sure shared a lot with his daddy.

"Well, probably because all you all are badasses, and he thinks that's cool."

"No, it's because he knows he'll never become a senator when his daddy's an ex-drug dealer."

I started toward him. "It's not that. He's sixteen. He doesn't really know what he wants to be. But he'll go through a lot of things he's sure he wants to be before he figures out which path to take." I stopped in front of him, but I didn't touch him. "He's proud of you."

"I'm an ex-thug who fucked his momma when he was asleep and had to sneak around to shoot hoops with him."

"Stop that," I hissed.

"It's true."

"That's not who you are. It's what you had to do."

"So why didn't you tell me about Michael?"

"First, how did you know about Michael?"

"You answer."

"No." I said firmly, but then shared, "I didn't keep it from you." I threw both hands out beside me. "You've been around the last three weeks. I've been kinda busy."

"And we've been doin' a lot of catchin' up, baby, and no mention of Michael."

"You're right. Because I didn't know how to tell you because you're insanely protective."

Before he could retort, I held a palm in front of his face and his head jerked back when I did.

I dropped it and continued.

"And that's not a complaint. I love that about you. Do I love you did what you did? No. Do I love why you felt you had to do it?" It was me who got in his face then. "*Yes.* One hundred percent." I leaned back. "I wish you didn't carry the burden you carry because you made decisions at seventeen years old no seventeen-year-old should have to make in order to take care of your family. But you made those decisions. You carried them through. They weren't great, but you are far from the first person to make those same decisions, and you won't be the last. But you're not Tony Soprano, for goodness sakes, and I'm not Carmella."

"Malia—"

I shook my head again. "Unh-unh. No. I'm glad we're talking about this because we need to have this conversation so we can be done with it...*forever*. And I'm glad Liam is out on a date so we can do it, even though you two are *still* ganging up on me, and I don't think he should date on weekdays. But whatever. That's obviously going to be my lot. I've decided just to go with it. Like you two shouting at each other all the time. It drives me nuts. You both have feet. Walk to the other person and say what you have to say like you have manners. You both have phones, if you're being lazy, text. But all this shouting, *Lord.* It does my head in."

"As cute as you are, babe, you might wanna stay on target," he warned.

Good advice.

"You're Mister Morris."

His whole torso shot straight, and his face closed down.

I didn't care.

I kept at him.

"I know you think you let him down. I know that's what's eating at you. That's the baggage you refuse to let go. I also know I didn't know him near as long as you did. I still know you're wrong. He'd be proud of you."

"Careful, Malia," he whispered.

"He would," I pressed. "And he's all over you. You raking leaves and bringing in the groceries and paying the bills and opening the wine before I get home so it can breathe. Also you taking care of your mother and sisters, your woman and your son, tearing strips off your soul so we wouldn't do without. Putting yourself out there to work with your brothers, taking their women's backs. That's Mister Morris, Darius. That's *you*."

He started to get off the stool.

I moved to get in his way and keep him where he was, and thankfully, succeeded.

"When your mom hugged you, you should have seen the love that washed over her face. That's because you're hers. And that's because you're what she has left of *him*."

"Quiet, woman," he growled.

I didn't get quiet.

I put my hands on either side of his neck and kept going.

"I honestly don't care if you don't believe me. I have what Mister Morris left for me. Liam has you teaching him the lessons Mister Morris taught you. I'm *all* good. And to answer your question, no. I did not think you'd whack Michael. Did I think you'd be pissed? Yes. Did I think you'd hunt him down and shoot him? No." I flipped out a hand then put it right back to his warm skin. "Maybe rough him up a little. But that's all."

"Michael got tagged trying to sell a crate of AKs. At that time, he also had a key of coke and five pounds of pot. And this was when pot was illegal. The dumb fuck resisted arrest and broke the nose of a police officer. He's been in prison the last five years. He tried to play the big man when he got there, ran up against the wrong guy, and now he's the buttboy for a brick shithouse named Onyx. There's no doubt he's the one who told, but he's broken. He's learned his lesson. When he gets out, he wouldn't mess with me, or Lee, if his life depended on it. Because he knows if he did, me, Lee, Eddie and a dozen other men would stop at nothing to give him right back to Onyx, who's serving life without parole, and reportedly, he really likes his bitch."

I winced, because…yikes.

I wasn't a fan of Michael's, but that was harsh.

Darius kept talking.

"And how I knew you knew about Michael is that Kenneth's sister is running with the wrong crowd. He's worried, Lena's worried, and she came to the offices today to ask me and Lee if we could intervene. And she let it slip, thinking you'd already told me. I didn't disabuse her of that thought."

I stepped back. Miffed.

"Why didn't she tell me?"

"You're missing the point here, Malia."

"No," I said sharply. "I didn't tell her we were together for years, and she was mad at me. She didn't tell me about you and Liam, and I was mad at her. I thought we got beyond these lies."

"None of you have accepted Kenneth. I can't speak for her, but if I had to guess, she doesn't want to give you more ammunition for keeping him out of the pack."

"I like Kenneth!" I exclaimed.

"You think he's touched."

"I still like him."

He dropped his head back and whispered, "Jesus Christ," to the ceiling.

"Darius," I called.

He looked at me.

"I love you, heart and soul, and honest to God, I wasn't keeping the news about Michael from you because I didn't trust you with it. I'm living in a cloud of happy goodness, and I wanted to just hang here for a while, and I like you being here with me."

"A cloud of happy goodness?"

"It's fluffy."

He stared at me.

I stared at him.

"Fuck, I love you," he said.

"Are we going to have sex on the kitchen island?" I asked hopefully.

"Absolutely," he answered.

I could tell he was going to make a move to initiate that.

Except he couldn't.

The doorbell rang, and when I say that, I mean someone was leaning on it so it didn't stop.

Alarm sizzled over the surface of my skin.

"Stay here," Darius bit, and avoided me standing frozen right in his space as he got off the stool and went straight to the laundry room.

He came out of it with a gun.

"Where'd you get that?" I asked, my eyes rounding.

"Gun safe."

"There's a gun safe in the laundry room? I didn't know that."

"I know," he said as he moved into the living room.

By the way, through all of this, the doorbell didn't quit going.

I went to my purse, nabbed my phone, and was wondering if I should have 911 ready, or Lee, or alternately Eddie, when I heard Tex boom, "About fuckin' time. I was out there forever."

I dropped my phone and went to the doorway between the kitchen and living room to see Tex walking in with a pet carrier in one hand and a massive Petsmart bag that looked heavy hefted over his other shoulder, like he was Santa Clause.

"Yo, woman," he said to me, shrugged the bag off his shoulder and set it down with a *thunk*.

He then put the pet carrier down and unlatched the gate.

Tentatively, an utterly adorable, teeny, tiny, black and white tiger striped kitty slunk out of the crate, gazing around curiously.

"*Kitty!*" I squealed and dashed forward.

The kitty froze at my motions so I caught her (or him) before she (or he) could retreat to the crate.

I picked her (or him) up and cuddled her (or him) to my face.

Her (or his) fur felt just like *silk*.

Oh my *God*.

Instant *love*.

I looked to Darius. "Oh my *God*, honey. *Kitty*."

"See I picked the right one," Tex said, watching me contentedly.

Darius swung disbelieving eyes to Tex.

"Get over it," Tex told him when he caught them. "You got a family now. Every family needs a cat."

"Maybe you'd wanna ask first?" Darius suggested.

"You might say no," he returned. He then jerked his head to me. "Though, she says yes. Anyway, quit bitchin'. I gave you time to settle in." He lightly kicked the Petsmart bag with the toe of his boot. "Litter. Kitten food. Kitty pâté." He turned to me. "They need a little bit a' wet. Better protein delivery. But it fucks up their teeth. So they also need dry." Back he went to Darius. "Toys. Treats. I got the litterbox in the car. And a litter mat is in the bag because they track that shit everywhere."

Darius sighed.

Tex kept talking.

"Got his shots." So it was a he. "And you'll have to take him back in to be fixed. Also got a good vet. I'll get you the number."

He walked to me and scratched the kitten's head with his big, rough fingers, and the kitty squinted his eyes with happiness.

*God.*

I loved him with *all my heart.*

"Named him Scrapper," he told me. "'Cause he's a scrapper. Found him alone in my alley. Scrawny as all get out. Barely alive. Bottle fed him. He pulled through." He stopped scratching and said, "Also knew I was givin' him to you, and it's perfect. Because you and your man are definitely scrappers. Life sucker punched both a' you, neither of you went down. Even if it kept hitting you, you kept your feet and carried on scrappin'. Found your way back to each other. Got yourself the lives you deserve. That means nothin'll ever get you down. Because you two are scrappers."

I stood motionless, staring at him, but even as moved as I was by what he'd said, I realized Darius was doing the same as me.

"Obviously, you can name him whatever you want," Tex concluded. Then boomed, "Welp! Gotta go get the litter box then I'll be out of your hair."

And with no further ado, he lumbered out the front door.

I looked to Darius. "Can we keep him?"

He was looking at me and I knew with the way his face got soft what his answer would be.

"Look at you, woman. What do you think I'm gonna say?"

"The same thing Mister Morris would say."

He closed his eyes and dropped his head.

I held my breath and waited.

He lifted his head and opened his eyes.

When he did, I knew he saw what I saw when I looked at him, and maybe, just a little (it was a start and I'd take it), he believed what I already knew.

He proved my thoughts correct when finally, *finally*, he said…

"Exactly."

# Epilogue

*Riding a Cloud*

I was pouring coffee when Darius came in the back door with a stack of donut boxes from LaMars.

"Well, don't mind if I do!" his Uncle Samuel said, leaning back on his stool at the island and patting his big belly.

"Lord Jesus. He ate a whole sweet potato pie at Dorothea's yesterday, and he's eyeing those donut boxes like he hasn't had food in months," Samuel's wife, Miss Regina, sitting next to him, said.

"Donuts! Awesome!" Liam exclaimed, strolling in with Scrapper where Scrapper often spent his time. Tooling around on Liam's wide shoulders.

I didn't know how those two did it. How Scrapper stayed balanced while Liam did whatever Liam was going to do. But they worked it.

Yes, my kid stole my cat.

It took him two seconds after he got home from his date. They took one look at each other and both of them were gone. If Liam was home, they were inseparable.

The good news about this was that Darius wasn't annoyed at Tex anymore for springing a cat on us.

There was no bad news.

Except I wanted to be a good momma and think it was cute my kid stole my cat.

But I was peeved.

I saw him first!

Darius put the boxes down, spread them out on the island and flipped up the lids.

After he did that, he said to his son, "Round up the cousins, son. Breakfast is served."

And what did Liam do?

He walked two steps to the doorway to the living room and shouted, "Richie! Jacqueline! Donuts are here!"

I looked to Darius.

He was fighting a smile.

I fought grabbing a donut and throwing it at him.

Mister Sam leaned long and nabbed himself a cinnamon twist.

"One, Sam," Miss Regina warned. "Thanksgiving is over. You heard what your doctor said."

"Thanksgiving lasts four days, woman," he retorted then munched into the donut and spoke through cinnamon and dough. "No doctor worth his salt would deny me this donut."

She turned beleaguered eyes to me.

I stretched my lips out to say I couldn't help her.

Anyway, I agreed with Mister Sam.

Liam sat by his father's uncle, his grandfather's brother, and reached for his own donut, and I reveled in watching them so close, soaking in the similarities.

Soaking in the fact not only Darius had the full force of his family around him, we were now able to give it to our son.

Scrapper sat down on Liam's shoulder, and with interest, studied my boy as Liam bit into a custard-filled, chocolate covered.

Liam tore of a tiny bite and offered it to his cat, who investigated it with his teeny black nose, then turned that nose up from it.

"More for me then, bud," Liam said to his furry friend.

Darius got close to me where I was leaning on the back counter, dipped his head and whispered in my ear. "Better get what you want. Richie's worse than his dad. And Jacqueline will hoover through a box on her own. She may be skinny as a meth head, but the bitch can put it away."

I'd noticed that yesterday at Dorothea's.

I stifled a giggle then hid my smile behind my coffee mug.

"Did someone say donuts?" Richie, Sam and Regina's son, asked, strolling in, eyes homing in on the boxes.

Darius's hand darted out and he stacked up a lemon filled, a cinnamon roll and a Boston cream.

He leaned back, set the cinnamon and Boston cream on the counter by his side and handed me the lemon.

My man.

Always taking care of me.

Jacqueline swanned her tiny behind in, body swathed in a short robe, face perfection, hair still in curlers.

Her gaze went to Darius. "Bad timing, cuz. You don't interrupt a girl in the midst of her daily preparations."

"You didn't have to come down," Darius pointed out.

"And let Richie and Dad eat them all?" she asked.

She leaned over the boxes delicately, perusing the selection like her decision would take hours, then snatched a jelly from right under Richie's fingers.

"Hey!" he snapped.

"Snoozers are losers," she said before making a show of biting into it, not taking her eyes from her brother.

"No wonder Tyler didn't want to come to Denver with you for Thanksgiving," Richie verbally slapped back.

"Oh, Lord," Miss Regina called to the ceiling.

Jacqueline swallowed her bite of donut and sniped, "My man is tight with his family."

"He'd reach for a turkey leg, and you'd gnaw off the poor brother's arm," Richie returned.

She smiled sweetly, and with experience from the last two days, I knew Richie was in for it.

"At least he doesn't break up with me before every holiday because I'm too chickenshit to commit, even after six years together." She lifted her hand and wriggled the big diamond on it in his face. Unexpectedly, her expression turned horrified, and she whirled on Darius and me. "I'm sorry. No offense. You all had extenuating circumstances."

"No offense taken," I told her.

"Kimberly understands a man needs to be ready," Richie huffed.

Jacqueline whirled back to him. "Kimberly right now is checking out Chester because he's a man who can commit."

"Yeah, he's proved that, with two divorces, and the brother's my age, thirty-two fuckin' years old."

"Richard! Language!" Miss Regina shouted.

The front door opened.

"Yoo hoo!" Miss Dorothea called.

"In here, Ma!" Darius yelled.

Gah!

The shouting.

I blew out a breath.

She showed in the doorway, balancing a baking pan in one hand, holding her handbag at her shoulder with her other, and her mother,

Grandmoms Beverly, who was up from Phoenix, was at her side.

"Well, look at you. You got donuts. And here, I woke up early and whipped up a batch of my cinnamon rolls."

*Whipped up a batch.*

It took three hours to make her cinnamon rolls.

She held them forward and Liam and Jacqueline ran into each other in nabbing them.

But Scrapper, being the scrapper he was, held on.

"I love my life," I said.

Darius grabbed my hand, and I started to smile at him, but he lifted it in a weird way as he shoved his other hand in his jeans pocket.

He then slid a cushion-cut diamond, surrounded by more diamonds, with even more diamonds embedded in the band, on my ring finger.

And the main diamond was way bigger than Jacqueline's (she was sweet, and I liked her, but, as Toni would put it...*huh*).

Miss Dorothea gasped.

So did Miss Regina, Grandmoms Beverly and Jacqueline.

"Well, all right," Mister Sam crowed.

"And I love my soon-to-be wife," Darius whispered, staring into my eyes.

Oh well.

Fuck it.

I wasn't holding these back.

I threw myself in his arm and burst into tears.

\* \* \* \*

Two hours later, after a bunch of other calls, and a bunch of other family showed, I called Tod.

"Heya, girlie," he answered. "What's shakin'?"

"All systems go," I replied.

I giggled when I had to take the phone from my ear because he hollered so loud.

\* \* \* \*

I walked in the back door, put my coat on the hook, looped my purse and the strap of my attaché on top, then went through the laundry room to the kitchen.

I'd already smelled the fact that someone had lit my evergreen candles.

It smelled like Christmas.

And my kitchen was dripping in it (that was something from the old place we definitely used, my Christmas decorations).

My man was at a cutting board, cutting vegetables. My son was at a tray of yeast rolls, brushing melted butter on the top. Scrapper was where Scrapper was not allowed to be, batting the lid of a water bottle around the island about two feet away from the rolls.

"Son, your cat," I said.

"He's so tiny, I can't see him when he's on the floor, and I don't wanna step on him," Liam replied.

I looked to Darius.

"I don't want to step on him either."

These two.

Someone. Kill me.

No one was going to kill me, so I did the next best thing.

I went to the wine and poured.

"Woman, mouth," Darius ordered.

I went to my man and gave him my mouth.

He didn't take his time, but he still did it right.

My wine and I moved to a stool and asked them, "Wanna know what happened at work today?"

"Sure," Liam replied at the same time his dad urged, "Shoot."

"Jeffrey's office was cleaned out before anyone got in this morning. Nothing in there. Just his desk and other furniture, which the firm owns."

"Whoa," Liam said, turning to the oven to set the temperature for the rolls.

"And Carrie was canned. I guess we have a no-fucking-named-partners policy." I took a sip of my wine. "I must have missed that when I read our employee handbook."

Liam looked to Darius, grinning. "Mom said fuck."

Darius grinned back.

"Boys!" I called. "This is big news."

"I know. You never say fuck. Or you don't say it very often," Liam replied.

Scrapper batted the cap my way.

I caught it, flicked it with my finger, and he scuttled after it, booty up in the air, tail swaying, front legs reached out, paws slapping the stainless steel, head jerking side to side, totally missing the danged thing.

Adorable little rascal.

Liam put the bowl he'd melted the butter in in the sink and then grabbed Scrapper and put him on his shoulder.

Scrapper instantly draped himself over the curve, close to Liam's neck, front paws dangling forward, back paws dangling down his back, apparently deciding chasing caps was hard work, and it was time for a nap.

It totally sucked my kid stole my cat.

"Can you dump a named partner that easily?" my son asked.

"No. Unless he did something very, very wrong."

My gaze went to Darius.

His eyes were alight.

"Is Ally that good?" I asked.

"What do you think?" he asked back.

I didn't have to think.

I knew.

I smiled at him.

He winked at me and then turned with the cutting board to dump the veggies in a pot of boiling water on the stove.

\* \* \* \*

We sat in the four armchairs in the Reserve, Toni across from me, Tony across from Darius.

The table between the chairs had a board covered with cheeses and cured meats and olives and nuts and fruit.

I held a glass of an exceptional red in my hand.

Toni decided tonight, like many nights, was a martini night.

Tony and Darius were talking about something. Sports. Current events. I didn't know.

I didn't care.

I loved that they got along. That they could carry on a conversation without their women, like we could do the same.

Toni's eyes came to me, and I read in them what I felt in the hug she'd given me outside Fortnum's a few months ago.

I got it. I lived it.

My happy-goodness cloud never went away, and I knew now it never would.

"Daddy!" Talia shouted from the door.

I twisted to look around my chair at her.

She seemed peeved about something.

She didn't make us wait to share what that was about.

"Liam is cheating!" she accused.

"I am not!" Liam yelled from the lounge in the other room.

"Liam isn't a cheater, baby," Tony said.

She glared at him, then shifted targets.

She walked to Darius, put her hand on his forearm, turned her ankle, looked up at him with wounded doe eyes, and pouted, "Uncle Darius, Liam keeps winning at the TV games."

Instantly, Darius pushed out of his chair. "All right, sweetheart. Let's go have a chat with him."

She smiled a gleeful smile, took his hand, and they walked out.

"When you give him another kid, you are gonna be in a world of hurt," Toni warned.

"I already know that," I said blithely, then took a sip of my wine.

And I did know it.

I just didn't care.

\* \* \* \*

"You see it?"

"Shoosh, I see it."

"You haven't always seen it."

"I *so* have."

"You totally haven't."

"Gah!"

I tore my gaze from Kenneth, who was cuddling his and Lena's brand-new daughter, Michelle, to his chest while sitting tucked up next to Lena in her hospital bed, and as was not unusual, the world had melted away for Kenneth.

The only people in it were him, his wife and his daughter.

"You think he's touched. I think he's got it goin' on. He only has space for what's important to him, what's interesting to him, what matters to him, and the rest fades away. It's genius," Darius whispered.

I couldn't argue.

I watched Mom try to get in there and get her hands on Michelle.

Kenneth ignored her, making googly eyes at his wife in turn with doing the same to his daughter, so into it, Mom had no choice but to back away.

"See?" Darius was still whispering. "Genius."

I gave him the side-eye.

He grinned at me when he caught it, then dipped down and

murmured in my ear, "I want one of those."

When he pulled away, I promised, "When the time comes, I'll do my best."

He smiled at me before he kissed me.

He kept his arm around me as we returned our attention to the newly expanded family.

Lena rested her head on Kenneth's shoulder and touched her daughter's cheek.

My cloud gave me a hug.

I sighed.

* * * *

*Not too long later...*

We didn't have near enough tickets for everybody in Liam's family.

Still, we managed to scrounge around and get Mom and Dad, Lena and Kenneth, Toni and Tony, Miss Dorothea, Gabby, Danni and Grandmoms Beverly in the stadium.

After Liam accepted his diploma and moved his tassel across his mortarboard, his steps determined, like he was already walking into the brilliant life he would lead, his honors stole flapping off to his sides, his gaze came direct to me.

I waved, hopping in my seat, and blew kisses.

His big smile got bigger, spreading across his face.

Then he stopped dead and sharply dropped his head, before he looked up at his father. Only after he did that did he pound his fist to his heart.

My throat closed.

Darius pounded his fist too.

Liam strode off.

I looked up to my man and I didn't have time to deal with the tears in my eyes.

I had to deal with the ones in his.

* * * *

It wasn't really a worry we couldn't get tickets for everybody.

When we went through the back gate after the graduation ceremony, I saw the RCHB had been busy. Our backyard was transformed. There were balloons and streamers and banners everywhere, tables groaning with food, more groaning with wrapped gifts, feet thick on the ground and booties resting in every lawn chair in the neighborhood and some brought in from other places besides.

The confetti floated dense in the air among whoops and hollers when Liam showed his face.

Lee was the first to grab him by the back of his neck, give him a manly shake, then pull him into a hug, beating his back so hard, I swear, Liam would have bruises.

Liam would never, not ever, complain.

He loved his Uncle Lee.

Eddie moved in next and did the same.

Liam wouldn't complain about that either, because he felt the same about his Uncle Eddie.

Daisy shouldered in next, reaching high, even if she was wearing Lucite, platform, stripper shoes that gave her at least an extra six inches (my boy was as tall as his daddy, and then some). She grabbed his face in both hands.

"Look at you, honey bunches of oats, makin' your momma and daddy proud. Headed off to Harvard!" She turned, bent double, and shouted, "*Harvard!*"

Everyone who had a glass raised it (which was most of them) and everyone who didn't (which was barely any) shouted, "*Harvard!*"

I laughed.

She turned back to Liam and smacked him gently twice on the cheek. "Proud of you, kid. Done good." Then she whipped around again and yelled, "Now, where's my margarita?"

"She's like a demented cheerleader," Liam muttered after she tottered away, but he was smiling, because she was, and he loved his Aunt Daisy.

It was Darius who grasped the back of his neck then, and he held on, walking his son forward, into the bosom of a whole bunch of people who loved him, saying, "That she is, son. That she is."

* * * *

*Not too long after that…*

He knew I was there.

Nothing got by my man.

But he didn't look up from his task.

"'And the baby elephant said to the bunny, "But why does the frog have to stay on his lily pad?"'"

He was rocking in the Jill bedroom.

Our daughter was on his chest, her big eyes drooping as her daddy's deep voice sounded around her and rumbled up into her as he read to her.

I left them to it.

I got all this goodness all to myself when I had Liam.

And I'd learned Darius would give me anything, but he was a baby hog.

I didn't mind.

Not even a little.

Instead of going downstairs to my chair and my book in the study, I went to the kitchen, because I'd had to give up wine for pregnancy and breastfeeding purposes, but now, I got it back.

I poured myself some then went to the turntable in the living room.

I put on the album.

And I curled on the couch and waited for him.

He showed not much later with a baby monitor in his hand.

His eyes came to me, but his body went to the kitchen.

He came out still with the baby monitor, but also with a glass of wine.

He set the monitor down on the side table then he curled his long body around mine from the back.

"Well?" he asked into my ear.

I knew what he was asking.

We had a big decision to make.

I rested against his wide chest.

"Life's an adventure, right?" I asked back.

"That's not an answer, baby."

I twisted my neck to look at him. "What do you want to do?"

No bullshit or prevarication, he said, "I wanna go."

"Lee and Eddie won't be there."

"Yeah, they will. They'll always be there. Maybe not as close, but they'll always be there."

He was correct.

"Mom's gonna retire soon. The weather is better there," he told me. "She's sick of snow and cold."

He was correct again.

"I'm sick of it too," he added.

"What'll we do with the house?" I asked.

"Rent it."

I made a face.

He smiled and said, "We can build a wine cellar anywhere, sweetheart."

I glanced around the space before saying to him, "It's not just that."

"We'll take the stuff with us," he said. "Or Danni and Gabby wouldn't turn down another job." He smiled again. "I'm outnumbered now. You and Antonia can make it what you want it to be."

"We want to be surrounded by you."

He closed his eyes and dropped his forehead to mine, and close up, I could see those long, curly lashes I fell in love with years ago in a row of books at a used bookstore resting against his cheeks.

When he opened them, I whispered, "Let's go to LA, baby."

He kissed me.

"So Long, Frank Lloyd Wright" ended and the arm of the turntable lifted up and whirred back in place.

Darius left me, flipped the album and set the needle.

He came back and curled around me.

And together, we listened to Darius's life in a song (for the most part), sitting close, sipping wine, our son across the country, preparing to take on the world, our daughter upstairs, sleeping and dreaming and carefree.

And Darius and me, on our couch, but riding a cloud.

# The End

\* \* \* \*

Also from 1001 Dark Nights and Kristen Ashley, discover After the Climb, Chasing Serenity, Taking the Leap, Making the Match, Fighting the Pull, Sharing the Miracle, Embracing the Change, Wild Wind, Dream Bites Cookbook, Wild Fire, Quiet Man, Rough Ride, and Rock Chick Reawakening.

Sign up for the 1001 Dark Nights Newsletter
and be entered to win a Tiffany Key necklace.

There's a contest every month!

Go to www.1001DarkNights.com to subscribe.

**As a bonus, all subscribers can download
FIVE FREE exclusive books!**

# Discover 1001 Dark Nights Collection Eleven

DRAGON KISS by Donna Grant
A Dragon Kings Novella

THE WILD CARD by Dylan Allen
A Rivers Wilde Novella

ROCK CHICK REMATCH by Kristen Ashley
A Rock Chick Novella

JUST ONE SUMMER by Carly Phillips
A Dirty Dare Series Novella

HAPPILY EVER MAYBE by Carrie Ann Ryan
A Montgomery Ink Legacy Novella

BLUE MOON by Skye Warren
A Cirque des Moroirs Novella

A VAMPIRE'S MATE by Rebecca Zanetti
A Dark Protectors/Rebels Novella

LOVE HAZARD by Rachel Van Dyken

BRODIE by Aurora Rose Reynolds
An Until Her Novella

THE BODYGUARD AND THE BOMBSHELL by Lexi Blake
A Masters and Mercenaries: New Recruits Novella

THE SUBSTITUTE by Kristen Proby
A Single in Seattle Novella

CRAVED BY YOU by J. Kenner
A Stark Security Novella

GRAVEYARD DOG by Darynda Jones
A Charley Davidson Novella

A CHRISTMAS AUCTION by Audrey Carlan
A Marriage Auction Novella

THE GHOST OF A CHANCE by Heather Graham
A Krewe of Hunters Novella

*Also from Blue Box Press:*

LEGACY OF TEMPTATION by Larissa Ione
A Demonica Birthright Novel

VISIONS OF FLESH AND BLOOD by Jennifer L. Armentrout and
Ravyn Salvador
A Blood & Ash and Flesh & Fire Compendium

FORGETTING TO REMEMBER by M.J. Rose

TOUCH ME by J. Kenner
A Stark International Novella

BORN OF BLOOD AND ASH by Jennifer L. Armentrout
A Flesh and Fire Novel

MY ROYAL SHOWMANCE by Lexi Blake
A Park Avenue Promise Novel

SAPPHIRE DAWN by Christopher Rice writing as C. Travis Rice
A Sapphire Cove Noveal

LEGACY OF PLEASURE by Larissa Ione
A Demonica Birthright Novel

EMBRACING THE CHANGE by Kristen Ashley
A River Rain Novel

# Discover More Kristen Ashley

### After the Climb: A River Rain Novel, Book 1

They were the Three Amigos: Duncan Holloway, Imogen Swan and Corey Szabo. Two young boys with difficult lives at home banding together with a cool girl who didn't mind mucking through the mud on their hikes.

They grew up to be Duncan Holloway, activist, CEO and face of the popular River Rain outdoor stores, Imogen Swan, award-winning actress and America's sweetheart, and Corey Szabo, ruthless tech billionaire.

Rich and very famous, they would learn the devastating knowledge of how the selfish acts of one would affect all their lives.

And the lives of those they loved.

Start the River Rain series with After the Climb, the story of Duncan and Imogen navigating their way back to each other, decades after a fierce betrayal.

And introduce yourself to their families, who will have their stories told when River Rain continues.

\* \* \* \*

### Chasing Serenity: A River Rain Novel, Book 2

From a very young age, Chloe Pierce was trained to look after the ones she loved.

And she was trained by the best.

But when the man who looked after her was no longer there, Chloe is cast adrift—just as the very foundation of her life crumbled to pieces.

Then she runs into tall, lanky, unpretentious Judge Oakley, her exact opposite. She shops. He hikes. She drinks pink ladies. He drinks beer. She's a city girl. He's a mountain guy.

Obviously, this means they have a blowout fight upon meeting. Their second encounter doesn't go a lot better.

Judge is loving the challenge. Chloe is everything he doesn't want in a woman, but he can't stop finding ways to spend time with her. He knows she's dealing with loss and change.

He just doesn't know how deep that goes. Or how ingrained it is for

Chloe to care for those who have a place in her heart, how hard it will be to trust anyone to look after her...

And how much harder it is when it's his turn.

\* \* \* \*

## Taking the Leap: A River Rain Novel, Book 3

Alexandra Sharp has been crushing on her co-worker, John "Rix" Hendrix for years. He's her perfect man, she knows it.

She's just not his perfect woman, and she knows that too.

Then Rix gives Alex a hint that maybe there's a spark between them that, if she takes the leap, she might be able to fan into a flame This leads to a crash and burn, and that's all shy Alex needs to catch the hint never to take the risk again.

However, with undeniable timing, Rix's ex, who broke his heart, and Alex's family, who spent her lifetime breaking hers, rear their heads, gearing up to offer more drama. With the help of some matchmaking friends, Rix and Alex decide to face the onslaught together...

As a fake couple.

\* \* \* \*

## Making the Match, A River Rain Novel, Book 4

Decades ago, tennis superstar Tom Pierce and "It Girl" Mika Stowe met at a party.

Mika fell in love. Tom was already in love with his wife. As badly as Tom wanted Mika as a friend, Mika knew it would hurt too much to be attracted to this amazing man and never be able to have him.

They parted ways for what they thought would be forever, only to reconnect just once, when unspeakable tragedy darkens Mika's life.

Years later, the impossible happens.

A time comes when they're both unattached.

But now Tom has made a terrible mistake. A mistake so damaging to the ones he loves, he feels he'll never be redeemed.

Mika has never forgotten how far and how fast she fell when she met him, but Tom's transgression is holding her distant from reaching out.

There are matchmakers in their midst, however.

And when the plot has been unleashed to make that match, Tom and

Mika are thrown into an international intrigue that pits them against a Goliath of the sports industry.

Now they face a massive battle at the same time they're navigating friendship, attraction, love, family, grief, redemption, two very different lives lived on two opposite sides of a continent and a box full of kittens.

\* \* \* \*

## Fighting the Pull, A River Rain Novel, Book 5

From *New York Times* bestselling author Kristen Ashley comes the new book in her River Rain Series, *Fighting the Pull*.

Hale Wheeler inherited billions from his father. He's decided to take those resources and change the world for the better. He's married to his mission, so he doesn't have time for love.

There's more lurking behind this decision. He hasn't faced the tragic loss of his father, or the bitterness of his parents' divorce. He doesn't intend to follow in his father's footsteps, breaking a woman's heart in a way it will never mend. So he vows he'll never marry.

But Hale is intrigued when he meets Elsa Cohen, the ambitious celebrity news journalist who has been reporting on his famous family. He warns her off, but she makes him a deal. She'll pull back in exchange for an exclusive interview.

Elsa Cohen is married to her career, but she wants love, marriage, children. She also wants the impossibly handsome, fiercely loyal, tenderhearted Hale Wheeler.

They go head-to-head, both denying why there are fireworks every time they meet. But once they understand their undeniable attraction, Elsa can't help but fall for the dynamic do-gooder.

As for Hale, he knows he needs to fight the pull of the beautiful, bold, loving Elsa Cohen, because breaking her would crush him.

\* \* \* \*

## Sharing the Miracle: A River Rain Novella

Elsa Cohen has everything she ever wanted.
A challenging career. A bicoastal lifestyle.

And an amazing man—the kind, loving and handsome Hale Wheeler—who adores her and has asked her to be his wife.

She isn't ready for the surprise news she's received.

And she doesn't know how to tell Hale.

Once Hale discovers that his future has taken a drastic turn, a fear he's never experienced takes hold.

He just doesn't understand why.

Family and friends rally around the couple as they adjust to their new reality, and along the way, more surprises hit the River Rain crew as love is tested and life goes on.

\* \* \* \*

## Embracing the Change: A River Rain Novel, Book 6
## Coming September 10, 2024

From *New York Times* bestselling author Kristen Ashley comes the new book in her River Rain Series, *Embracing the Change*.

\* \* \* \*

## Gossamer in the Darkness: A Fantasyland Novella

Their engagement was set when they were children. Loren Copeland, the rich and handsome Marquess of Remington, would marry Maxine Dawes, the stunning daughter of the Count of Derryman. It's a power match. The perfect alliance for each house.

However, the Count has been keeping secret a childhood injury that means Maxine can never marry. He's done this as he searches for a miracle so this marriage can take place. He needs the influence such an alliance would give him, and he'll stop at nothing to have it.

The time has come. There could be no more excuses. No more delays. The marriage has to happen, or the contract will be broken.

When all seems lost, the Count finds his miracle: There's a parallel universe where his daughter has a twin. He must find her, bring her to his world and force her to make the Marquess fall in love with her.

And this, he does.

\* \* \* \*

## Wild Wind: A Chaos Novella
### By Kristen Ashley

When he was sixteen years old, Jagger Black laid eyes on the girl who was his. At a cemetery. During her mother's funeral.

For years, their lives cross, they feel the pull of their connection, but then they go their separate ways.

But when Jagger sees that girl chasing someone down the street, he doesn't think twice before he wades right in. And when he gets a full-on dose of the woman she's become, he knows he finally has to decide if he's all in or if it's time to cut her loose.

She's ready to be cut loose.

But Jagger is all in.

\* \* \* \*

## Dream Bites Cookbook: Cooking with the Commandos
### Short Stories by Kristen Ashley
### Recipes by Suzanne M. Johnson

From *New York Times* bestseller Kristen Ashley and *USA Today* bestseller Suzanne M. Johnson…

See what's cooking!

You're invited to Denver and into the kitchens of Hawk Delgado's commandos: Daniel "Mag" Magnusson, Boone Sadler, Axl Pantera and Augustus "Auggie" Hero as they share with you some of the goodness they whip up for their women.

Not only will you get to spend time with the commandos, the Dream Team makes an appearance with their men, and there are a number of special guest stars. It doesn't end there, you'll also find some bonus recipes from a surprise source who doesn't like to be left out.

So strap in for a trip to Denver, a few short stories, some reminiscing and a lot of great food.

(Half of the proceeds of this cookbook go to the Rock Chick Nation Charities)

Welcome to Dream Bites, Cooking with the Commandos!

* * * *

## Wild Fire: A Chaos Novella
### By Kristen Ashley

**"You know you can't keep a good brother down."**

The Chaos Motorcycle Club has won its war. But not every brother rode into the sunset with his woman on the back of his bike.

Chaos returns with the story of Dutch Black, a man whose father was the moral compass of the Club, until he was murdered. And the man who raised Dutch protected the Club at all costs. That combination is the man Dutch is intent on becoming.

It's also the man that Dutch is going to go all out to give to his woman.

* * * *

## Quiet Man: A Dream Man Novella
### By Kristen Ashley

Charlotte "Lottie" McAlister is in the zone. She's ready to take on the next chapter of her life, and since she doesn't have a man, she'll do what she's done all along. She'll take care of business on her own. Even if that business means starting a family.

The problem is, Lottie has a stalker. The really bad kind. The kind that means she needs a bodyguard.

Enter Mo Morrison.

Enormous. Scary.

Quiet.

Mo doesn't say much, and Lottie's used to getting attention. And she wants Mo's attention. Badly.

But Mo has a strict rule. If he's guarding your body, that's all he's doing with it.

However, the longer Mo has to keep Lottie safe, the faster he falls for the beautiful blonde who has it so together, she might even be able to tackle the demons he's got in his head that just won't die.

But in the end, Lottie and Mo don't only have to find some way to keep hands off until the threat is over, they have to negotiate the overprotective Hot Bunch, Lottie's crazy stepdad, Tex, Mo's crew of frat-boy commandos, not to mention his nutty sisters.

All before Lottie finally gets her Dream Man.

And Mo can lay claim to his Dream Girl.

\* \* \* \*

### Rough Ride: A Chaos Novella
By Kristen Ashley

Rosalie Holloway put it all on the line for the Chaos Motorcycle Club.

Informing to Chaos on their rival club—her man's club, Bounty—Rosalie knows the stakes. And she pays them when her man, who she was hoping to scare straight, finds out she's betrayed him and he delivers her to his brothers to mete out their form of justice.

But really, Rosie has long been denying that, as she drifted away from her Bounty, she's been falling in love with Everett "Snapper" Kavanagh, a Chaos brother. Snap is the biker-boy-next door with the snowy blue eyes, quiet confidence and sweet disposition who was supposed to keep her safe…and fell down on that job.

For Snapper, it's always been Rosalie, from the first time he saw her at the Chaos Compound. He's just been waiting for a clear shot. But he didn't want to get it after his Rosie was left bleeding, beat down and broken by Bounty on a cement warehouse floor.

With Rosalie a casualty of an ongoing war, Snapper has to guide her to trust him, take a shot with him, build a them…

And fold his woman firmly in the family that is Chaos.

\* \* \* \*

### Rock Chick Reawakening: A Rock Chick Novella
By Kristen Ashley

From *New York Times* bestselling author, Kristen Ashley, comes the long-awaited story of Daisy and Marcus, *Rock Chick Reawakening*. A prequel to Kristen's *Rock Chick* series, *Rock Chick Reawakening* shares the tale of the devastating event that nearly broke Daisy, an event that set Marcus Sloane—one of Denver's most respected businessmen and one of the Denver underground's most feared crime bosses—into finally making his move to win the heart of the woman who stole his.

# Avenging Angel
By Kristen Ashley
Coming April 2, 2024

Rachel Armstrong has a burning need to right the world's wrongs. Thus, she becomes the Avenging Angel.

And maybe she's a bit too cocky about it.

While riding a hunch about the identity of a kidnapper, she runs into Julien "Cap" Jackson, who was trained by the team at Nightingale Investigations in Denver. Now he's a full-fledged member at their newly opened Phoenix branch.

It takes Cap a beat to realize Raye's the woman for him. It takes Raye a little longer (but just a little) to figure out how she feels about Cap.

As Raye introduces Cap to her crazy posse of found family and his new home in the Valley of the Sun, Cap struggles with his protective streak. Because Raye has no intention to stop doing what she can to save the world.

But there's a mysterious entity out there who has discovered what Raye is up to, and they've become very interested.

Not to mention, women are going missing in Phoenix, and it seems like the police aren't taking it seriously.

Raye believes someone should.

So she recruits her best friend Luna, and between making coffees, mixing cocktails, planning parties and enduring family interventions (along with reunions), the Avenging Angels unite to ride to the rescue.

\* \* \* \*

## Chapter One
### *Natural Badassery*

"I'm gonna go in."

"Are you *insane*? You can't go in!"

"I'm just gonna have a look around."

"What if you're right? What if this guy is the actual guy?"

"Then I'll call the police."

"What if he sees you?"

I sighed. "Luna, this isn't my first rodeo."

"Exactly!" she cried in a "Eureka!" tone. "So, yeah, let's talk about that, Raye."

Sitting in my car, talking to my bestie on the phone and casing the house in question, I cut her off quickly, before she could start in—*again*—about how she felt about what I'd been up to lately.

"I'm just going to wander across the front of his house and look in the windows. No biggie."

Truthfully, I was hoping to do more than that, but my best friend of all time, Luna, didn't need to know that.

We'd had chats about what she called my unhinged shenanigans, or my lunatic tomfooleries, then there were also my deranged mischiefs (Luna read a lot and her vocabulary showed it).

But I did what I did because, well…

I had to.

Luna spoke into my thoughts. "Okay, so if *I* kidnapped a little girl from my church. And *I* was holding her for things I won't even contemplate why someone might do that. And some woman I'd never seen in my neighborhood casually strolled in front of my house and looked in my windows, what do you think *I* would do?"

"Sic Jacques on them, whereupon he'd lick them and dance around them and race away only to race back, bringing his toys so they'd play?"

Jacques was Luna's French bulldog. He was gray, had a little white patch on his chest, and I considered myself for sainthood that I hadn't dognapped him yet. I was pretty sure I loved him more than Luna did, and the Tiffany's dog collar I'd splurged and bought him (that she refused to let him wear because she said it was too "bougie," like that was a bad thing) rested my case on that.

"This isn't funny, Raye," Luna said softly.

That got to me, her talking softly.

She was Yin to my Yang. Ethel to my Lucy. Shirley to my Laverne. Louise to my Thelma. Dorothy to my Rose/Sophia/Blanche (and yes, I could be all three, dingy, slutty and sarcastic, sometimes all at the same time, I considered it my superpower).

You get the picture.

We were opposites, but she loved me.

And I loved her.

"I promise to be careful. It's gone okay so far, hasn't it?" I asked.

"Luck has a way of running out."

Hmm.

I struggled for a moment with the use of the word "luck,"

considering I thought I was pretty kickass, but I let it go.

There was a little girl missing.

And I had a feeling I knew where she was.

"I need to do this, Luna."

It was her turn to sigh, long and loud.

She knew I did.

"Call me the instant you get back to your car," she ordered.

"Roger wilco," I replied.

"You don't even know what that means," she muttered.

"It means I heard you."

"Yes, it also means *you will comply with my orders*, short for *wilco*."

See?

She totally read a lot.

"Okay, so, samesies, yeah? I heard you, and I'll call."

Another sigh before she said, "You won't call because either a, you'll be tied up in some villain's basement, and I'll then be forced to put up fliers and hold candlelight vigils and harass the police to follow leads. This will end with me being interviewed, weeping copiously, naturally, telling people you lit up a room for a Netflix docuseries on solved cold case files once some hikers find what's left of your body at the bottom of a ravine in fifteen years. Or b, you won't get anything from the guy, so you'll start devising some other way of figuring out if it's him or not. You'll then immediately begin scheming to implement plans to do that at the same time you'll remember you forgot to buy tampons for your upcoming cycle, and you need to pop into CVS, after which you'll realize you're hungry and you'll stop by Lenny's for a cowboy burger and a malt."

She was hitting close to home with that first bit, but she knew that and did it on purpose due to the fact that, overall, she knew me too well.

Including when my period was coming, something she always reminded me to prepare for because I always forgot, and as such, was constantly bumming tampons from her. Though, her remembering this wasn't a feat, since we were together so often, including working together, so we were moon sisters.

"I will totally call," I promised.

"If you don't, I'm uninviting you to my birthday party."

I gasped.

"You wouldn't," I whispered in horror.

Yes, you guessed it. Luna threw great parties, especially when she was celebrating herself.

"Try me."

# About Kristen Ashley

Kristen Ashley is the *New York Times* bestselling author of over ninety romance novels including the *Rock Chick*, *Colorado Mountain*, *Dream Man*, *Chaos*, *Unfinished Heroes*, *The 'Burg*, *Magdalene*, *Fantasyland*, *The Three*, *Ghost and Reincarnation*, *Moonlight and Motor Oil*, *Dream Team*, *River Rain* and *Honey* series along with several standalone novels. She's a hybrid author, publishing titles both independently and traditionally, her books have been translated in fourteen languages and she's sold over five million books.

Kristen's novel, *Law Man*, won the *RT Book Reviews* Reviewer's Choice Award for best Romantic Suspense. Her independently published title *Hold On* was nominated for *RT Book Reviews* best Independent Contemporary Romance and her traditionally published title *Breathe* was nominated for best Contemporary Romance. Kristen's titles *Motorcycle Man*, *The Will*, *Ride Steady* (which won the Reader's Choice award from *Romance Reviews*) and *The Hookup* all made the final rounds for Goodreads Choice Awards in the Romance category.

Kristen, born in Gary and raised in Brownsburg, Indiana, was a fourth-generation graduate of Purdue University. Since, she has lived in Denver, the West Country of England, and now she resides in Phoenix. She worked as a charity executive for eighteen years prior to beginning her independent publishing career. She currently writes full-time.

Although romance is her genre, the prevailing themes running through all of Kristen's novels are friendship, family and a strong sisterhood. To this end, and as a way to thank her readers for their support, Kristen has created the Rock Chick Nation, a series of programs that are designed to give back to her readers and promote a strong female community.

The mission of the Rock Chick Nation is to live your best life, be true to your true self, recognize your beauty and take your sister's back whether they're friends and family or if they're thousands of miles away and you don't know who they are. The programs of the RC Nation include: Rock Chick Rendezvous, weekends Kristen organizes full of parties and get-togethers to bring the sisterhood together; Rock Chick Recharges, evenings Kristen arranges for women who have been nominated to receive a special night; and Rock Chick Rewards, an ongoing program that raises funds for nonprofit women's organizations

Kristen's readers nominate. Kristen's Rock Chick Rewards have donated over $180,000 to charity and this number continues to rise.

You can read more about Kristen, her titles and the Rock Chick Nation at KristenAshley.net.

# On Behalf of 1001 Dark Nights,

Liz Berry, M.J. Rose, and Jillian Stein would like to thank ~

Steve Berry
Doug Scofield
Benjamin Stein
Donna Perry
Kim Guidroz
Chelle Olson
Tanaka Kangara
Asha Hossain
Chris Graham
Jessica Saunders
Stacey Tardif
Dylan Stockton
Kate Boggs
Richard Blake
and Simon Lipskar

Printed in Great Britain
by Amazon

37148907R00138